THE HIGHLANDER &
THE COUNTERFEIT QUEEN

The Queen's Highlanders
Book 3

Heather McCollum

© Copyright 2023 by Heather McCollum
Text by Heather McCollum
Cover by Dar Albert

Dragonblade Publishing, Inc. is an imprint of Kathryn Le Veque Novels, Inc.
P.O. Box 23
Moreno Valley, CA 92556
ceo@dragonbladepublishing.com

Produced in the United States of America

First Edition May 2023
Trade Paperback Edition

Reproduction of any kind except where it pertains to short quotes in relation to advertising or promotion is strictly prohibited.

All Rights Reserved.

The characters and events portrayed in this book are fictitious. Any similarity to real persons, living or dead, is purely coincidental and not intended by the author.

ARE YOU SIGNED UP FOR DRAGONBLADE'S BLOG?

You'll get the latest news and information on exclusive giveaways, exclusive excerpts, coming releases, sales, free books, cover reveals and more.

Check out our complete list of authors, too!

No spam, no junk. That's a promise!

Sign Up Here

www.dragonbladepublishing.com

Dearest Reader;

Thank you for your support of a small press. At Dragonblade Publishing, we strive to bring you the highest quality Historical Romance from some of the best authors in the business. Without your support, there is no 'us', so we sincerely hope you adore these stories and find some new favorite authors along the way.

Happy Reading!

CEO, Dragonblade Publishing

Additional Dragonblade books by Author Heather McCollum

The Queen's Highlanders Series
The Highlander & The Queen's Sacrifice (Book 1)
The Highlander & The Lady of Misrule (Book 2)
The Highlander & the Counterfeit Queen (Book 3)

Also from Heather McCollum
Rohaise the Red

Dedication

For Johanna, my dragonfly sister.

Your support over the years means the world to me. I still remember you talking me into continuing to follow my dream of writing when I was at my lowest. Without you this book might never have existed. Thank you for believing in me. I believe in you too.

Scots-Gaelic and French Words Used

An aithne dhut mo chridhe? (SG) – Do you know my heart?

arrêt (F) – stop

daingead (SG) – damnit

heigh, my heart – (Elizabethan English) encouraging exclamation

Je peux t'apprendre (F) – I can teach you

mattucashlass (SG) – dagger sharpened on both sides of the blade

mo chreach (SG) – my rage

mo Dia (SG) – my God

sacrebleu (F) – damn it

sgian dubh (SG) – black handled dagger with only one side of the blade sharpened

tais-toi (F) – shut your mouth

Votre Majesté (F) – Your Majesty

CHAPTER ONE

"To be a king and wear a crown is a thing more glorious
to them that see it than it is pleasant to them that bear it."
Queen Elizabeth I of England and Ireland

10 February 1574 AD
At an inn north of London

"WE WILL GO our separate ways, and no one will know," Her Royal Majesty, Queen Elizabeth I, said, her voice soft in the light cast by the lantern that her lady held.

Cordelia Cranfield stood in her traveling costume before the queen and Elizabeth's Spy Master, Sir Francis Walsingham. She'd just arrived, draped and hidden as requested. Her heart galloped like her borrowed horse had been doing for hours as she rode beside two trusted Whitehall guards. It was one thing to talk about this daring plan and quite another to enact it.

"And only Lady Anne Bixby knows 'tis I who continues on to Haddon Hall?" Cordelia asked, glancing at the tall, frowning woman who had accompanied the queen from Whitehall. If she pursed her lips any tighter, she'd suck her cheeks in and look like a puckered fish.

"As long as the lady doesn't reveal through tone or words that you aren't truly the queen," Walsingham said, staring at the obviously disapproving lady of the queen's bedchamber.

Elizabeth slapped her beringed hand down on his arm. "She

will behave. Won't you, Lady Anne?"

Anne dipped into a curtsey before the queen, her back as straight as if she wore a broomstick laced in her stays. "Of course, Your Majesty."

"For you know my wrath would be fierce if people were to find out about my secret mission."

Anne bowed her head again, and the queen turned to Cordelia, smiling without revealing her browning teeth. "I will be back before I'm missed, two days and two nights at Chatsworth House is all I need to speak to my foolish cousin, Mary. But no one must know. I would give none of my advisors heart failure with the knowledge that I undertake such risks."

"My heart is nearly beyond repair as it is," Walsingham mumbled. "There are Catholics who would comb the forests for you if they knew you were out from behind the walls of Whitehall."

"Tut, tut," Elizabeth said. "'Tis why no one even knows we left Whitehall except those in this small party. And of those in this small party, only four of us know that I travel on to see Mary Stewart, my cousin and Queen of the Scots. I will be back behind your walls within a week, Sir Francis."

She looked at Cordelia. "No one even knows you have arrived at the inn, following us. The two who brought you will accompany me to Chatsworth House and then go on to deliver a few royal packages up here in the north before heading back to Whitehall. They will be sent to the Tower if they speak of this journey to anyone."

Walsingham rubbed a hand down his pointy beard and looked at Cordelia. "Your red hair is close to Her Majesty's shade." Everyone knew Elizabeth wore wigs, but Cordelia had the natural color Elizabeth enjoyed in her youth and continued to present in her hair pieces.

"Just stay draped and flash my ring about," the queen said.

Cordelia held up her hand where the queen's gem-encrusted locket ring sat on her third finger. It had rubies around the band

and two miniature portraits inside the locket: one of a young Elizabeth and one of her mother, Anne Boleyn. Cordelia wore some of the queen's other rings as well, but the locket ring was personal. It was a ring that the queen would never take off, let alone give to one of her ladies to wear.

"Guard it with your life," Elizabeth said, her voice full of majestic power.

Cordelia bobbed a curtsey. "Certainly, Your Majesty."

"And now," Elizabeth said, "take upon the heavy mantle of queen for two days, Lady Cordelia, and you'll earn my unwavering trust and enough gold to move to Scotland with your sister, Lucy. Where you won't be around to let it slip about this ill-advised visit with my cousin who is said to bewitch her visitors." Elizabeth huffed a dark laugh and looked at Walsingham. "Perhaps I will bewitch my cousin into quitting her treasonous leanings."

This task, successfully pulled off, would also cleanse the taint of traitor from the Cranfield name. 'Twas why Cordelia had agreed despite the discomfort and possible danger.

"Thank you, Your Majesty," Cordelia said, curtseying once more.

Walsingham took Elizabeth's arm. "'Tis soon to be night. We must ride, Your Majesty, before the wolves begin to roam about."

"Then we are off on this wild adventure," Elizabeth said, raising one hand as if to bid them farewell. She laughed and her eyes were wide like when she danced the Volta.

"God help us," Walsingham said.

Cordelia would continue the queen's journey to take the cold winter air at Haddon Hall to calm her nerves. Which everyone would agree, always needed calming, and no one would know the most important woman in all of England was secretly riding away with only two soldiers and her Security Advisor to guard her.

Elizabeth and Walsingham left the room silently. Their horses and the two men who'd brought Cordelia from London waited behind the inn. Anne looked at Cordelia, a terse rigidity to her smooth, young features. "I'll come back before dawn to do your hair and help you dress." Anne wasn't a friend to the Cranfield sisters, but she knew better than to go against the greatest queen in Christendom. She could put up with Cordelia being her sovereign for two days.

And then I'll be free. Cordelia longed for it, the freedom from the Cranfield name, the name of her traitorous mother. Her sister, Lucy, had escaped London on the arm of a handsome Highlander, and Cordelia wanted nothing more than to follow her up to where people didn't question her every movement. Freeing herself from court service and the damning looks of everyone there was worth the risk of playing the queen of England and Ireland for two days.

CORDELIA SAT IN the chair before the mirror. Anne Bixby had already teased and pinned her hair into a wide, braided bun around the back of her head, encouraging the curls that Elizabeth favored to fall around her face. The queen's stays were tight across Cordelia's breasts since the queen liked the swell they provided above the edge. Otherwise, the clothes fit Cordelia's form well.

"They should already be at Chatsworth House," Anne said as she stuck another pearl-topped pin into the piled hair. Cordelia grimaced as the woman scraped her scalp yet again. Surely she didn't bloody the queen when she secured her wig to her head.

"We can forgo the layers of makeup," Cordelia said. "Since I'll be under a veil."

Elizabeth was over two score years now while Cordelia was twenty-five. Even though the majestic woman was still quite comely, she raged against every wrinkle that dared to cut into her face. Time was her mortal enemy, and she battled it and the scars from her battle with smallpox by applying Venetian ceruse, a heavy white makeup.

"I hope no one insists on seeing me."

"Just keep under the veil," Anne said, handing her a white piece of silk. It was edged with tiny pearls to weigh it down around Cordelia's shoulders. "And don't talk. I will say you have a pained throat and wish to be left alone."

Cordelia sighed. "How did you get stuck with this ruse?"

Anne glanced at her and gave a weak smile. "Same as you, I suppose. She wishes to know if she can trust her ladies. You because your mother was a traitor who tried to kill her, and me…" She shrugged her shoulders. "Because she thinks I am trying to entice her Sweet Robin to my bed."

"Are you?" Robert Dudley, the Earl of Leister was a handsome, powerful man at court, but everyone knew he belonged to the queen.

"No," Anne said and rolled her eyes. "She should look to Lettice if she wants to be jealous over one of her ladies."

Cordelia stood, feeling the heaviness of Elizabeth's gown. Court ensembles weighed somewhere under twenty pounds, but the queen's gowns had a vast number of jewels sewn on it, making it even more cumbersome. Not only did Elizabeth Tudor have the weight of her country on her soul, but also the weight of her courtly encumbrance on her thin body.

"Why do I feel like I am now wearing a target before a world of archers?" Cordelia said.

Anne chuckled. "And the queen feels that every day. I say, if she is successful at this duplicity, I foresee many of us ladies portraying the queen in the years to come. Perhaps you should get shot during this masquerade to save the rest of us. That way too, your family name will be cleansed."

"I prefer to cleanse the Cranfield name without dying, thank you."

Anne smirked. "Do you really think anything will accomplish that, Cordelia? Your mother has marred the Cranfield name forever. You would do well to get rid of it."

Her bitter words added more weight to Cordelia. She and her sister, Lucy, had been esteemed members of Elizabeth's court. At one time, she could hold her head high and know that any whispers about her likely included what rich courtier she was enticing with her beauty, charms, and family riches. Now everyone whispered about her mother and how tainted the Cranfield sisters were by the woman's fanatical actions.

"Dying or living, either way, eat your breakfast," Anne said with a flutter of her fingers toward the tray she'd brought. "'Twill be some time before we make it to Haddon Hall this afternoon, and I can't have you fainting and revealing your face."

Cordelia inhaled fully and forced herself to eat the eggs and ham brought for the queen even though her stomach felt rocked by nervousness like the ocean under a boat. No one knew she was even there, so no one would guess her to be anyone other than the queen. *And then I'll be free.*

MARCUS EXHALED A puff of white and looked upward at the heavily laden trees. *More damn snow.* For weeks it had stormed and snowed like God was trying to encase the world in frigid crystals. Marcus sat on his horse, Elspeth, her white coat blending in with the winter landscape.

With white fur bound over his boots to keep his legs warm, and his pale-colored plaid, Marcus and Elspeth blended into the woods where they waited. The woolen cloak draped over Marcus, and the horse's body heat kept him warm enough despite the increasing breeze.

Elspeth's ears twitched, and Marcus listened. The French commander of the small group of Catholic warriors under Catherine de' Medici's orders, would be arriving at the ambush point ahead very soon. But Marcus was already there, had been for the last hour. In order to protect their target, Elizabeth Tudor, Queen of England and Ireland, he needed to reach her first.

His mission was highly secret, convoluted, and the riskiest he'd ever taken on before. When word had reached Lord Douglas, 4th Earl of Morton that Queen Elizabeth was making a secret sojourn to Haddon Hall, Morton had dispatched Marcus immediately. Which was a critically good move in this game of Protestants versus Catholics, because Catherine de' Medici, the Catholic Dowager Queen of France, had received the same information.

Catherine, who called herself the Queen Mother since her younger son took the French throne, had raised Mary Stewart until the widowed girl left France to return to Scotland. Even though Catherine had never shown much kindness to Mary, the exiled Scottish queen was Catholic and Catherine de' Medici would do anything to further Catholicism, which meant getting Mary on the English throne. Publicly, Catherine pushed for Queen Elizabeth to marry a French noble who would then protect them from the constant threat of Spanish interference. Either way, Catherine de' Medici desired Elizabeth to come to France, and this secret journey of Elizabeth's was the perfect chance to see it done.

Wind blew the falling snow sideways. Maybe the English queen would remain at the inn for the day due to the weather. Either way, Marcus was stuck in this near blizzard just in case. The weather would not stop the ambush planned by Captain Noire.

Elspeth shook her mane, which was dotted with snow. Her ears flicked again, and she shifted.

Marcus leaned over her neck, patting her. "What is it?"

A flash of red caught his gaze far off between the trees. Remaining still, he watched four riders emerge along the path leading north. A horse-drawn coach followed them on large, creaky wheels, and four more riders brought up the rear, several of them being ladies.

So the hearty queen of England had risked traveling in this snow. Her need to escape London for a short respite must be imperative. When her ministers learned of it, which they would whether or not she was captured by the French, they would rage. The trip made little sense and would never have been approved. The secret of her outing would have kept her safe if not for the traitor in her inner circle.

Marcus turned his horse to ride alongside and somewhat ahead of the entourage, far enough over so as not to be readily seen in the blinding snow shower. The guards wore swords, but that didn't rule out the possibility that they also carried pistols, which were becoming more commonplace.

I could warn them now. The thought sliced through his head. But that was not his mission. Morton's instructions were clear.

Let the queen nearly be captured and rescue her in the name of King James. Bring the queen to Canonbie Parish on the English-Scottish border where I and my army will meet them to escort the queen back to London. Let her be so thankful that she names James her heir.

Lord Morton had made it sound simple in Edinburgh Castle before a warm fire. Out here in near-blizzard conditions with the French soldiers hiding somewhere, the plan seemed questionable at best.

His gaze slid along the English queen's attendants. Two ladies rode outside the small carriage. The carriage was draped by white curtains that likely did not keep out the wind. He saw a hand resting on the sill of one of the large windows. *Elizabeth.*

They rode along the well-traveled route toward Haddon Hall, the manor house owned by John and Dorothy Manners, known Protestants. Movement way ahead at an outcropping of boulders alerted one of Elizabeth's guards.

"Make way," the queen's guard called, pulling his sword, even though they were a good distance away.

Marcus slapped on the French blue cap he'd been given by his French contact and leaned over Elspeth, guiding her toward the English group from behind as the French appeared ahead of them. Everything happened quickly as if it were rehearsed or at least anticipated. A shot broke the muted quiet of the snowy forest, causing at least one of the ladies to scream. The coach had stopped, and a veiled woman jumped out.

As Marcus raced toward her, one of the guards lifted her onto his horse, slapping the beast's hindquarters. "Go!" the soldier yelled. "Back to the inn."

"Arrêt! Halt!" one of the French soldiers yelled. A dozen of them rode around the boulders that they'd chosen for an ambush. Marcus left them behind as he charged after the queen.

Cordelia's breath coursed back and forth with her gusty inhales and exhales, the cold air making her throat ache. Her view of the ambush had been hazy through the thin veil, men running out from behind boulders ahead, blue caps sitting on their heads. Were they border raiders happening upon a rich retinue? But they were in Derbyshire, which wasn't near the border to Scotland.

"Take my horse to escape, Your Majesty," one of the gentlemen, Lord Oliver Gupton, had said, dismounting. His large hands grabbed her around the waist, and he'd practically thrown her onto the tall bay. "We will hold them off."

Elizabeth was an experienced horsewoman and would not have a problem with this. Cordelia had ridden horses before, but it had been a long time since she and her sister had owned one to ride each day. But she'd taken the offered reins and pressed firmly into the sides of the horse, her gaze frantic to see the carriage wheel tracks that would lead her back to the inn.

She galloped away, abandoning Anne and the other ladies in the retinue. Fear for them almost made her turn around, but there was no time to feel guilt, and she must act like the queen.

Snow flew in her face, and the veil covering her pressed against her open lips. The queen's heavy skirts rose nearly to her knees, exposing her stockinged legs to the cold. Without being able to reach the stirrups, which flapped alongside the horse, Cordelia used her knees and hands to hold herself as best she could on the horse's back. This was no side saddle, but a wide saddle made for a large man. How would she ever stay seated?

They'd ridden over an hour toward Haddon Hall. Could she run all the way back to the inn without being caught? Would Elizabeth's guards survive? Would Elizabeth's ladies? Anne had been the only one allowed to ride in the carriage with her, saying that the queen was unwell. The two other ladies should ride back to the inn with her. Perhaps they were behind her now.

Cordelia glanced over her shoulder, and her stomach clenched. Her ladies didn't follow, but a large man did. Someone had yelled a French word. Was the man French? His white mount gave him an eerie look of flying through the forest trees on his own as the snow swirled around him in growing fury, masking his horse.

The storm made it harder for her to see, and she yanked off the concealing veil, dropping it to float away. The pretense was over anyway. If the English soldiers managed to rout the attackers, they would insist on seeing Elizabeth well. They'd discover that the queen was gone, and they'd be relieved she wasn't in the attack. But if any of them died while protecting her, as if she were the true queen, the survivors would despise Cordelia even more.

Did the blue-capped rider think she was Elizabeth? Would he leave off if he knew she wasn't the queen? She wasn't about to turn around and tell him she wasn't. If he was a raider, he might not care who she was or wasn't. For surely this wasn't a planned attack on the queen. The trip to Haddon Hall was a closely-guarded secret.

The snow pocked her face, stinging her freezing skin. She squinted, trying to see the tracks from the carriage. *Damn snow!* It was covering the path. She tried to stay along what looked like a wide parting between the trees where the road must continue, but Cordelia quickly found herself amongst trees. The horse luckily seemed trained to maneuver through battle and dodged trees while Cordelia held on. Her thighs ached to hold herself on the horse. Her arms strained to keep her from slipping off the well-worn saddle, and she struggled to hold onto the reins with her numb fingers. Elizabeth rarely wore gloves so Cordelia had foregone them to let her ladies and guards see her rings as she gripped the carriage window ledge.

Another glance showed the man closing in, and Cordelia pressed harder into the horse's sides. The well-muscled steed took off like an arrow from a longbow, its breath huffing out of its nostrils. "Good Lord," she whispered as she slipped again, clinging with both hands to the pommel, the reins underneath.

"Your Majesty, stop!" the man called. "Slow down!"

Your Majesty? The raiders knew they were a royal entourage.

Cordelia frantically sped onward toward a clearing through the trees. She could go faster across it than inside the forest. *But so can he.*

There was no time to think as they barreled onward, the clearing in sight. The horse whinnied in a high-pitched alarm and suddenly turned, skidding to a halt. The force of the halt threw Cordelia off the side of the saddle. *Holy God, no!*

She screamed and hit a drift of snow, her whole body jarring at the impact. The snow gave way instantly, and she rolled down a steep slope. Cordelia covered her head with her arms because there was nothing to grasp onto, the cold snow washing her face and filling her mouth and nose. She blinked and sputtered, trying to halt her fall, but she kept tumbling, over and over again. All she could see was white until pain erupted in her head, and she squeezed her eyes shut.

Chapter Two

"Jesu! Doth not your mistress see plainly that she will always be in danger till she marry? If she marry into some good house, who shall dare attempt aught against her?"
Catherine de' Medici to English courtier, Sir Thomas Smith, about the necessity for Elizabeth to marry into French royalty.

MARCUS LEAPED OFF his horse, his gaze following the queen as she rolled down the snowy hill into the gully. "Bloody hell," he cursed and ran down the slope, his boots churning through the snow as he tried to stay upright, his hands grabbing at limbs. Luckily the queen's horse had stopped or the two would have tumbled, killing them both. Catherine de' Medici and the Catholics would be happy, but Marcus would probably be executed for allowing her death.

With each step he sunk deeper, the snow from the last month having piled up down the ravine that led to a narrow river cutting through the English landscape. It was frozen over, and Elizabeth lay unmoving along the bank.

Breath coming in gusts, he fell to his knees beside her, the icy snow prickling the skin above his fur wrapped knees under his woolen wrap. Her red hair lay in brilliant contrast against the white snow, splayed out from her head. Her almond-shaped eyes were closed, her red lips parted. He'd never seen the queen of England before, only glancing at one miniature portrait that Lord Morton had shown him before he left Edinburgh. Red hair, pale face, ruby lips, and brown eyes. The woman's eyes were closed, but everything else fit the queen's description. Except she didn't look to be over two score in years. Nay. She looked a score years younger.

He bent over her, his fingers before her parted lips. "Are ye alive?" he murmured.

"No," she whispered back.

He dropped his head in relief and then looked closer. "Are ye Elizabeth, the Queen of England and Ireland?" he asked against the blowing wind. She must be. The woman had come from the carriage that was headed to Haddon Hall, and the guard had given up his mount to send her flying. Who else would have been important enough to make a warrior give away his trusted steed?

"Dead queens in excruciating pain do not talk," she said, her words slightly slurred as if they took too much effort to speak.

"I am going to check to see if ye are broken anywhere," he said.

"Molest a queen, and you will end up swinging from Tower Bridge."

"For someone who is dead, ye talk a lot, Your Majesty."

Despite the cold wind, Marcus took his time inspecting the queen's body, feeling the bones in her shins and knee, but not daring to go higher up her thighs or be accused of taking liberties. His fingers probed her arms, sliding down to her bare hands. He paused on one of her rings, sitting askew on her thin finger. He righted it and inspected the rubies and a small locket. The queen curled her fingers inward so he couldn't take it off.

"Don't worry," he said. "I'm no thief."

"Just an assassin."

"I'm here to help ye," he whispered close to her ear. "But first we must get ye out of this ravine and storm." He needed to transport her to one of the hunting shacks he'd found south of Haddon Hall. With luck, he'd avoid the Frenchmen who were probably combing the woods for her now.

"Daingead. We must go now, Your Majesty." Marcus lifted

under her and noticed the blood where her head had rested. "Foking hell," he murmured and set her back down to whip out a sash.

"Excruciating pain," she mumbled, but didn't try to touch her head or move.

Turning her to the side, he used fresh snow to wipe the wound at the back of her head and then tied the linen around her head, the ends flapping in her face. It wouldn't do to have her die of fever either.

"See," she said. "You have killed me."

Lifting her again, Marcus held her against his chest and carefully trudged up the slope. He slipped twice on the frozen ground, but she didn't gasp or move. It was as if she'd truly lost consciousness. God help him. Unlike her father, Elizabeth Tudor was a slight figure, delicate in her features, and yet this proud woman ruled all of England and Ireland. It was a position that Lord Morton craved for his young majesty, James, King of Scotland. But without Elizabeth's blessing, war would roar across all of Britain as Lord Morton pushed King James upon her throne. And it would be Marcus's fault for letting her die.

CORDELIA FOUGHT AGAINST the heaviness of sleep. *Thirsty. So thirsty.*

As if she'd spoken the thought out loud, the cool edge of a cup touched her lips and cold water wet her tongue. She didn't even question it but drank as much of the clean water as she could until the cup seemed empty.

She was lowered flat on her back. Her head hurt, as well as the arch in her back, and her left hip felt bruised. Cordelia shifted, trying to stretch or turn, and her muscles and bones screamed at her. A small moan came from her lips. The sound brought footsteps. Where was she? *Frenchmen in blue caps. Galloping through the snow. The fall and rolling. Pain. A Scottish brogue. Strong, gentle hands.*

Am I dead? Surely, she wouldn't feel so battered in Heaven, judging her guilty of lying. Surely God knew the queen had asked her to pretend to be royal.

"Your Majesty? Are ye awake?" The familiar voice caused her to still. It held the low burbling accent of the people to the north, the Scots. At least it wasn't French.

"No," she whispered.

"Drink some more," he said, apparently not believing her. In truth she really wasn't awake, at least not in any condition to act awake. An arm helped her sit up, and once again a cool edge touched her bottom lip.

Over the rim of the cup, Cordelia opened her eyes, taking a sip as she saw the man up close. His face wasn't the vicious one she'd imagined as he chased her through the snowy woods before her fall. Dark brows gathered over dark, expressive eyes. His strong jaw held full lips and a closely clipped beard.

"Ye're awake, Yer Majesty," he said with a smile that showed straight white teeth. She choked on a bit of the water. Her surprise was from the title, not the handsome face of her tormentor. He pulled the water away. "Easy now," he said. "Ye took a tumble."

She coughed into her fist and then narrowed her eyes at him. "Because you were chasing me."

He inhaled, his smile fading. "Aye. I am sorry for that, but 'twas necessary."

"Who are you? And why did you attack our caravan?"

"I did not attack your caravan," he said, and she watched him walk over to a small cold hearth where he had several cups set out. Two lanterns sat on the floor there and one near her. The cottage was bare of all but the bed she was lying upon, and a stout little table and two chairs. From the sound of the wind beating against the walls, the storm was still raging.

"You wore the same blue tam the others wore," she said. "They sounded French, but you are Scottish. Are you working with the French?"

"Aye to all three," he said, bringing a plate of cold oatcakes over to her. His head nearly grazed the ceiling. He was broad through the shoulders and narrow through the waist. The wrap around his hips hung so that only a small part of his leg was revealed, showing boots laced up with furs. He looked nothing like the dandies prancing around court in their hose and wide breeches, ruffs about their thin necks. "Are ye hungry?" he asked.

She was starving. From the darkness in the one room, it was night, and she hadn't eaten since that morning.

She looked up into his face and frowned. "They could be poisoned."

"If I wanted ye dead, I would have left ye to freeze at the bottom of the ravine." His thick northern accent rolled off his tongue. He held the plate out to her. "Yer Majesty."

She took a bite, and the honey-sweetened cake instantly loosened the tight ball of hunger in her stomach. After devouring the two cakes he offered, she pushed up to lean against the logs making up the walls of the cabin. She held her hand before the chinking and felt the cold wind blow through.

"Your name," she said.

"Marcus…Marcus Blythe of Edinburgh. I aid King James's regent, the Earl of Morton."

"But you're working with the French to capture the queen of England," she said, her words snapping and her eyes narrowed.

"That's precisely what I want the French to think." He lowered his large frame into the chair he'd moved beside the bed. He looked uncomfortable in the small room, a falcon in a cage wishing to fly. "Without them thinking I was there to help, they wouldn't have used me as a guide to this area, and I wouldn't have known where ye'd be to save."

"Save? You nearly killed me."

He exhaled. "It would be best if ye moved past that to me saving ye from Catherine de' Medici's group of elite soldiers."

"Catherine de' Medici knows the… that I was headed to

Haddon Hall? How?" Walsingham had selected Elizabeth's closest ladies and men who knew her personally.

"There's a Catholic spy within your circle of intimates. Word got out that ye were traveling this way with a dangerously small defense, and the French acted immediately to send men across the channel." He shook his head, crossing his arms over a broad chest. He caught his hands in his armpits as if he were casually watching a tournament. "Ye don't leave the safety of London except on progress in the summer, surrounded by three hundred people. A group of eight to protect ye was too good an opportunity for the Queen Mother to ignore."

A traitor amongst Elizabeth's inner circle? Who was it? Cordelia had heard about the plan before her sister left a month ago, but the rest of the queen's escort hadn't been told until two weeks before the trip. That was hardly time to send word and dispatch soldiers. Did the blasted woman have courier pigeons flying to and from Whitehall?

Cordelia closed her eyes. This was a bloody disaster. *God's teeth!* Everyone would think it was she who'd sent word to the Catholics because she was a Cranfield. Would Elizabeth think that too? That Cordelia had sent a message abroad to the Catholic powers in France as soon as she'd been told she'd have to play along with this subterfuge?

Holy hell. She'd end up in the Tower of London, especially if the bandits continued their chase, following Elizabeth to Chatsworth House where Francis Walsingham alone protected her. Some said that Lord Shrewsbury and his wife favored their captive, Mary Stewart, the Catholic queen of Scotland who was forced to abdicate, giving the rule of Scotland to her Protestant son. Would Shrewsbury and his soldiers turn against Elizabeth if the French soldiers caught up to them?

Cordelia shivered at the horrible thought. She must convince her captors that she was Elizabeth until the queen had a chance to ride back to the safety of London. Otherwise, they would hunt her down.

"Is it so hard to believe that someone would turn against ye?" the Highland warrior asked.

She opened her eyes and turned her face to him. "Yes. Those who attend…me are inspected with care."

"Didn't a family of nobles nearly kill you a couple years ago?"

Good bloody Lord! Did everyone know of her family's shame?

"Only the mother," she answered. "The rest of the family, especially the two daughters, would give their lives for me."

Was that true? Would she give her life for the queen? Right now, Cordelia was certainly playing the loyal lady by making this huge and obvious lethal man think she was the queen. At least until she was certain he wouldn't run to tell his French partners that Elizabeth was visiting Mary at Chatsworth House.

"Are any of the traitor's family members part of yer inner circle?" he asked.

She frowned. Elizabeth Tudor wouldn't allow anyone to question her with the tone the Highlander was using. "No," she snapped. "One has married and moved to your country and the other is back in Whitehall." She crossed her arms over her chest, which felt rather numb in the tight stays of Elizabeth's traveling costume. Inside she shook, whether from cold or fear or recovery from the fall. But on the outside, she kept her face smooth in an unemotional reprimand. "And you may call me Your Majesty, Your Grace, Your Highness, or My Queen."

He bowed his head briefly, but then met her gaze. "But ye aren't *my* queen."

"I think you have a king. No queen. Or is Mary your queen, one you also wish to see seated on my throne in London?" That sounded more like Elizabeth.

"I am loyal to King James VI of Scotland. Since he's only seven years old, I follow the orders of his regent, James Douglas, 4th Earl of Morton. And those orders are to keep ye alive." He paused. "Yer Majesty."

"So nice of Lord Morton to send *one* man to do that," she said, finding it rather easy to act with queenly annoyance.

Cordelia didn't have to guard her tongue as much as a queen.

He frowned. "A battalion wouldn't have allowed me to lure the French soldiers into the English interior for your guards to apprehend." He ran his hand through his dark hair. It looked damp from the snow and was drying in thick waves. "Although I thought ye'd have brought more with ye." He shook his head. "Captain Noire and his soldiers may have slaughtered them. Especially when they found ye gone."

Cordelia closed her eyes. *Please Lord, protect Anne, her sister, Margaret, and Mary Hall. Protect the guards and, of course, the queen.* Poor Lord Oliver Gupton and Master Geoffrey Winslow along with the other two guards who'd ridden with them. Oliver had survived numerous attempts on Elizabeth's life. Would this be the one that saw him dead? Also Anne Bixby. She was the only one who knew Elizabeth had ridden west with Walsingham. Would she tell the Frenchmen the truth if questioned? Would they torture her? Anne's sister, Margaret, rode behind the carriage along with Mary Hall. Were they slain? The thought stuck in Cordelia's throat.

"I must get back to London," she said, tipping her gaze to the ceiling in case the ache of tears released one. The queen might rage and sob behind doors, but she would never cry before a criminal.

Marcus leaned back in his chair, his gaze shifting to the door. "Right now, neither of us is going anywhere. Not with that banshee of a storm screaming out there and ye with a nasty bump on the head."

Cordelia parted her hair in the back and grimaced as her fingers found the large lump. "Are those stitches?" she asked, her eyes widening.

"I thought it best to sew your flesh while ye were unconscious."

This Highland soldier had stitched her skin? "Did you wash it first and use a clean needle and thread?"

"Aye," he said, the word coming out with a bit of contempt.

"Yer Majesty."

"Good. I'd hate to die of something as bland as fever from a cut."

Marcus tipped his chair, balancing on the back two legs. It was a wonder the rickety wood legs didn't buckle under the man's weight. He resembled the mountains of the Scottish landscape, hard and rugged, meant only for the truly adventurous to climb. Climb? She flushed red at the thought that swiftly turned to another type of climbing with a man. Many ladies at court would forgo caution to bed a man as brawny and handsome as Marcus Blythe. But not right after he'd abducted them.

"I was schooled on how to care for ye, Your Majesty," the Highlander said. "Lord Morton insists that keeping ye safe is extremely important." He rose out of his chair to stride to a large bundle by the door. "He even sent ye warm clothes to wear that will help ye blend in with the common folk while I get ye to safety."

Unbuckling the thick bag, Marcus pulled out a set of women's clothes in blue wool. The petticoat, bodice, and jacket looked warm and sturdy, something suitable to a common housewife. There was even a long shawl for her head.

"Lord Morton thought of everything," she murmured tersely, suddenly feeling the need to get out of the confining clothes that trussed her up like a partridge to be roasted over the fire. "Everything except to send more men."

Marcus dropped the clothes in the chair he'd vacated. "I have a certain set of skills. He trusts me to see ye safe, Your Majesty."

She blinked, her brow rising as she'd seen the queen do often. "Skills? Protection skills?"

"Aye. And I speak French and am most congenial."

She snorted and grimaced at the pain it caused, her hand going back to her head. "Well you don't have skills to keep me from falling down a ravine to my death," she said.

"'Twas an unexpected turn."

She pushed her sore legs over the edge of the bed. Lord, even her wet boots were still on. A small groan came out with her exhale as her muscles protested the movement. The press of her bladder was making it imperative that she get up, and she needed to loosen the pinching stays.

"There's no privacy screen," she said, looking around the small room. "Wait outside while I dress."

In answer, the wind lashed the cabin, making it shake. "I will turn my back," he said.

"Are the horses out in this?" she asked, shrugging out of her riding jacket. The removal of the fur ruff allowed the chill to funnel down her bodice. It couldn't be helped. She needed to get out of this painfully binding costume.

"There's a barn out back. The two of them are covered with blankets and have food and water. 'Tis sturdy enough to withstand the storm. Or at least as sturdy as this cabin."

Cordelia tried to reach the ties behind her back while watching the walls of the structure that might collapse on them at any moment. What the hell had she gotten herself into?

Hmph. "I can't untie the stays at my back. Can you reach them?"

"Ye want me to undress ye?" Marcus asked, his brow raising.

Cordelia spun around to present her back. "A queen's costume is not made to be put on or removed by oneself. I usually have four ladies assisting me. But one of you will have to do."

He walked over. "I can't say I've been taught to be a lady's maid, although I have some experience with getting a lass out of her clothes." His teasing tone sent heat up her neck and into her cheeks. Cordelia was well accustomed to innuendos at court, but this was a completely different situation. She was alone with this Highlander, a brawny Highlander with "a certain set of skills." She'd always envied her sister, Lucy, and their friend, Maggie, for the pulse-escalating, well-muscled Highlanders who'd saved them. Surely that's why his words brought heat to her body with prickles of awareness.

"Just remember that I am the Queen of England and Ireland,

someone you were sent to protect, not molest. To touch a queen inappropriately would see you castrated for certain."

"Don't fear, Your Majesty. One thing I have in heaps is honor and integrity."

"So says the man who chased me off a cliff."

"Again, not my fault." His fingers brushed against her hair that had fallen about her shoulders with pins poking out like iron toothpicks. "Flying through the air to catch ye is not one of my special skills."

Cordelia exhaled slowly as he slid his fingers along her back, down the breach in her stays, his gentle tugs releasing the tight binding. She sighed at the release. "What *are* your special skills?" she asked, her voice sounding husky to her ears. His fingers stopped at the bottom on the swell over her hips.

She cleared her throat and took several steps away. "I mean, to protect a queen." She turned, her hand holding her loosened stays over her breasts.

He blinked, his gaze going quickly to her face. With her hair down, and her stays loosened, no doubt she looked ravished. "You said you would turn around." Her words came out like a whisper with the wind howling.

Marcus slowly turned. "I can shoot any weapon well," he said, reminding her which question she'd asked. "I am usually able to talk most people into agreeing with me. I speak French, and I can drink a high amount of alcohol without feeling its effects."

"Most men think they possess that last skill," she said, quickly sliding the stays and petticoat down.

He chuckled. "I suppose they do."

Her smock was not the cleanest either with her frantic fleeing, so she used the one he'd set on the chair with the rest. Warm linen, edged in lace, was welcome after the few seconds of standing naked in the cold room, depending on the honor of a near stranger with connections to the French.

She watched his back while she dressed, making sure he

didn't turn around. He was broad through the shoulders and back, which tapered down to a narrower waist. Her gaze rested momentarily on his arse, but the pleats of his plaid hid it well. Did he wear anything underneath? It was terribly cold to go without, although ladies certainly did. She closed her eyes and frowned, turning away. A queen certainly wouldn't ogle a Highland soldier.

The wool petticoat of gray and blue plaid went on easily over her head and floated down to cover the bottom of the smock. She shrugged into the simple gray bodice tightened with built-in stays across the top of her body. A thick shawl in pale blue finished the outfit, and she turned back, plucking the loose pins from her curls.

"You can turn around now," she said.

"Are ye certain?" he asked. "I wouldn't want to be accused of peeping at the undone queen."

She huffed at his teasing. "Stare at the door all night for all I care."

He turned around, nodding at her. "More comfortable?"

"Yes. Lord Morton was good to have sent it." Cordelia wrapped the shawl tighter around her arms and placed the cap on her unruly hair. She left it down to help protect her neck against the cold, which moved on unseen currents through the room.

He motioned to the hearth. "I didn't want to draw anyone to our cabin with the smell of a fire, but with that storm raging outside, no one can see, hear, or smell anything." He crouched before the blackened hearth and arranged some dry wood and some hay that he'd braided. "A fire and then to fortify the cabin."

"Fortify? Are you going to build walls around us here?" she asked. "Wouldn't it be easier to take me back to London?"

"Not in this storm," he said and grasped her hands. "By the devil, they are white blocks of ice." They were indeed numb.

Marcus clasped them, careful not to yank her rings, and rubbed, warming them with his own body heat. She didn't know if she should pull them away. After all, 'twas a most intimate gesture, but the warmth of his hands was too needed.

"Hold them over the lantern while I start the fire," he said and released her, striding to the blackened hearth. Hopefully nothing was lodged in the chimney that would cause the smoke to back up inside.

"What are *your* special talents?" he asked as he worked.

"Pardon?" Cordelia curled her fingers together over the lantern, but the heat wasn't as thawing as Marcus's rubbing.

"Ye asked me mine. So what are yours? Besides ruling countries, avoiding marriage, and…?" He tilted his head to the side, studying her in the low light. "Looking fifteen years younger than your forty-one years of age."

She frowned at him. "You really do *not* know how to comport yourself in the presence of royalty, do you?"

He scratched his neck under his ear where his hair curled. "I suppose I don't. The only royalty I've encountered is King James, and he's still a lad who likes to chase the pups I bring him in the bailey."

He stared at her, waiting. Did he expect her to answer his ridiculous question? Cordelia crossed her arms under her bosom and pushed back onto the bed to lean against the wall. "I use makeup to hide my age."

He glanced at her over one shoulder. "Ye aren't wearing any makeup that I can see."

She waved her hand as if negating his observation. "'Tis a skin regimen that I use that keeps the skin youthful. And then, when my ladies are with me, they apply my makeup."

"So ye are forty-one years old?" he asked.

Panic flickered in her chest. "A lady does not discuss her age, and a man with honor does not hound her about it."

He leaned back. "I think ye should have your portrait redone to convey your beauty. Ye would have princes lining up to wed ye."

She pushed off the bed, ignoring the ache in her head. "They *are* lining up to wed me. I choose not to wed *them*." She looked around the room. "Where is the privy in this place?"

He hooked his thumb toward a chamber pot beside a small table with a water pitcher and basin made from cracked pottery. "Either there or outdoors around the corner of the cabin."

Cordelia looked at him and then the door and then at him again. "You jest? There isn't even a privacy screen."

The wind howled and buffeted the house again, as if the storm laughed and dared one to step even one foot outdoors.

He lifted a lit braid of hay into the chimney to warm it so the smoke would draw upwards. "I do jest often." Keeping the torch in the hearth, he indicated the room with his free hand. "But not about the privy, as ye can see."

Cordelia looked at the door. *We can't be still traveling after dark. Hungry wolves roam the woods in the winter.* Anne's warning to the group as they left the inn later than expected that morning echoed in Cordelia's mind. "I am not going outdoors to… refresh myself. You can go to the barn, and I will refresh myself here alone." Twice she almost said "please," but Elizabeth surely wouldn't. She'd demand royal treatment. 'Twas not as easy as Cordelia had thought it would be.

She cleared her throat and stood up tall from the bed. "You will leave me to ready myself for the night. You may sleep in the barn or return here to sleep before the hearth." In truth, she didn't like the idea of sleeping in the rickety cabin alone. Wolves, Frenchmen, and the storm could all bring disaster. And if he hadn't attacked her while unlacing her stays, she was fairly confident Marcus Blythe would keep his distance.

"That's so gracious of ye, Your Majesty," Marcus said, the edge of sarcasm making Cordelia bristle.

"It is," she said and pointed toward the door like she'd seen the queen do whenever she wanted her ladies to exit her room. It was usually when her dearest Robin, Lord Robert Dudley, came to visit.

Marcus threw a blanket over his head and shoulders. "I need to check on Elspeth anyway."

"Elspeth?" she asked.

"My horse."

"Odd name for a horse."

"'Tis my sister's horse. She named the filly and I had need to borrow her."

"Oh," she said. "'Tis good you have a sister kind enough to lend you such a prize."

He looked at her. "Your sister tried to have ye killed."

For a moment, Cordelia thought to protest. Lucy had never done such a thing. Luckily she remembered that she wasn't Cordelia but Elizabeth.

"But she did not," Cordelia said, her nose in the air.

"I'll take care of your horse too, since ye probably have no clue how to do so," he said.

"You brought the horse? From the top of the ravine?"

"Leaving him would have signaled that ye didn't escape alone. And we'll need him when we leave our little castle here," he said, indicating the beams overhead.

"Quite right."

Cordelia waited until he left the cabin and then hurried to roll a log against the door. She didn't need to worry about him peeking in windows since the only two there were covered with hides that barely kept the cold out. How long would it take him to feed and water the horses? She used the chamber pot and the moss left there for such a process. Good Lord! This was a far cry from the modern conveniences of Whitehall.

She then poured water sitting near the fire into the separate washing basin, splashing warmed water from the melted snow onto her face, neck, and arms. The bundle that Lord Morton had prepared also had twigs, mint, and rosemary, so Cordelia cleaned her teeth. She used a brush that she found with the implements to comb through the mess of hair down her back, and a few pins jumped out to plink dully on the boards that made up the floor. She grimaced as she grazed the lump on the back of her head where the prickly stitches were tied.

"There," she murmured. "As clean as I can be in this primitive place." Cordelia glanced at the chamber pot and water basin. "He won't empty them," she murmured. Neither would the queen, but Marcus was still in the barn. She could empty them, and he'd think she just didn't need to make water. She'd crawl into the bed and pretend to be asleep when he returned.

Walking across the floor, Cordelia noticed a creak. In Elizabeth's chamber at Whitehall, she'd mapped out all the squeaks and creaks across the queen's floor, alerting the other ladies in case any of them had to leave during the night. No one wanted to wake the queen, and Elizabeth refused to sleep alone. She said it was so none could question her virginity, but Cordelia had seen panic pinch Elizabeth's face when she found herself in the dark. After the queen had suffered in the dark Tower of London, there was no doubt she had a dislike of the shadows.

Cordelia shoved the log away from the door and lifted the latch. The wind blew the door into her, making her gasp. "God's teeth," she murmured, letting the door remain open so she could lift the chamber pot. She took two steps out into the swirling snow and poured her urine onto the ground, scooped some snow that would melt to wash it, and hurried back inside. Setting it down, she grabbed the basin of wash water. She stepped out where the wind blew her hair forward, blinding her with her own tresses, and she threw the contents.

"Foking hell!" Marcus yelled, making her jump and drop the basin. Cordelia brushed her hair from her eyes to see that the water had doused his face.

Chapter Three

The queen "had bathrooms with piped water in at least four of her palaces, as well as a portable bath that she took with her from palace to palace and used twice a year for medicinal purposes…She cleaned her teeth with toothpicks of gold and enamel, and then buffed them to a shine with a tooth-cloth. In old age, she chewed constantly on sweets in the mistaken belief that they would sweeten her breath."

Allison Weir, The Life of Elizabeth I

Marcus shook his head, but the swirling snow and wind froze the liquid to his face. "Ye threw piss on me?"

"No," the queen yelled, the storm trying to snatch her word away. "'Tis wash-water."

He scooped up a handful of snow and scrubbed it over his face. He'd just washed with the icy crystals in the barn, and he would again if she'd soaked him in piss. "Ye're sure it was wash-water and not piss."

The wind threw her red hair all out around her shoulders as if she were a vengeful wood fairy directing the storm to rage at him. "A queen does not piss," she said, the word hissing out between her teeth.

He stared at her, mouth open, for a moment. "Of course, a queen pisses."

"She makes water, royal water," she called over the wind,

although her hands held her cheeks as if she were upset that she'd hit him.

"A queen's waters is still piss," he yelled back and scrubbed more snow over his face.

"Fine," she said, throwing her arm out behind her. "I emptied the piss over there. That was wash-water."

He stomped toward her, and she grabbed up the basin, striding into the cabin. Wind swirled around them both as he followed her inside. One look at her without the storm whipping her hair across her face, and he could see the humor in her eyes. He narrowed his gaze. "'Tis not comical."

She pursed her lips as if to squash a smile. "Of course not." She carried the basin back to the small table near the chamber pot in the corner. "See," she said, indicating the chamber pot and then the pitcher and basin. "Wash water. In fact, I might have made you cleaner."

"Bloody hell that," he grumbled. "I washed head to toe in freezing snow out there."

"Oh."

He spotted the sharpened twig and rosemary from Lord Morton's supplies, his gaze shifting abruptly to her. "Your Majesty brushes her teeth? And ye have washed your face for bed?"

"Of course," the queen said, moving directly to the small bed. Her grace was that of royalty so that she seemed to float across the weathered wooden floor. She lifted the covers, checking for vermin, shaking them before sitting on the bed.

Marcus walked over to her. "Yer skin is flawless. Smooth with a bit of freckles." He reached out for her chin, catching it to pull her bottom lip down slightly. Astonishment made her freeze for a moment, her beautiful almond-shaped eyes opening wide. "Yer teeth are white and straight."

She smacked his arm with both of her hands in a flapping manner, and he released her chin. Impotent dread filled his chest, making it feel leaden. "Ye are not Elizabeth Tudor, Queen of

England and Ireland."

"Of course, I am, you slack-minded fool." She flopped down in the bed, her glorious red hair spilled across the flat pillow, upon which she'd spread one of Lord Morton's handkerchiefs. She grimaced slightly and touched the back of her head where he'd stitched.

Marcus straightened, staring down at the woman. "Queen Elizabeth is forty-one years of age. A decade ago, she contracted smallpox, and everyone feared she would die. She didn't, but the illness left her face scarred, which is why she wears heavy cream on her skin. She is also known to have brownish teeth, some of them loose from disease."

"Lies made up by my enemies and those who wished I *had* died from smallpox," she said, but presented her back to him. She wore the full costume that Lord Morton had sent, either for warmth or modesty or both.

Marcus stared at her, his mind spinning. He'd been sent to protect the queen of England. This woman had been in the queen's coach with her guards around her and her ladies. Could the reports of Elizabeth's appearance be false? Could she really be the beauty lying stubbornly before him? If she wasn't, where was the real queen, and how could he complete his mission?

He turned away, his hand grabbing the back of his neck where the dampness of his hair felt icy. With the wind howling outside, trapping them in this snow-covered hovel, there was nothing he could do except get some much-needed sleep. He settled on the floor before the hearth, a folded blanket under him. He turned over to stare at the woman on the bed. Was she someone else from the court, a decoy? A beauty not wed to anyone or England? The idea caused both a warming inside him and a chilling panic. They collided, making his stomach churn around the oatcakes he'd eaten.

Bloody hell. She must be the queen. Else he was a fool, and Lord Morton would take away his position at court, or perhaps his head.

Cordelia shivered as she walked along the stone corridor, the sound of dripping water echoing with her footsteps. Iron bars flanked her on both sides, and the cold seemed to grip her, making it hard to breathe.

"Traitor," someone called from the shadows in a cell.

Cordelia turned her face to peer through the bars but couldn't make out who had spoken. "I am no traitor," she said.

"Traitor! Traitor!"

Cordelia turned to the other side to see long thin arms reaching for her from behind the bars. She backed away.

"Keep moving," came a man's voice from behind. Francis Walsingham appeared out of the gloom, and he pointed for her to walk forward past the hands and toward the door at the end. With only a few steps, she reached the end and stepped through into a blinding snow. The wind kept whipping her hair in front of her eyes. She shoved the strands away and stared before her at a scaffold.

"Climb up," Walsingham ordered.

She clutched her hands before her and squeezed her eyes shut. "I am asleep."

The queen's spy master grabbed her shoulder, shaking her slightly, and she looked at him. "Cordelia Cranfield, you are a traitor like your mother." He pointed upward. "Climb."

Cordelia was numb from the wind and snow, but it was nothing compared to the numbness of fear that overtook her as she raised her gaze to the executioner at the top of the platform. He wore a hood and leaned on an ax.

Cordelia turned back to Walsingham. "I did my best."

Walsingham shook his head. His lips pursed in disappointment, and suddenly his face turned into that of her father. "Papa?" she said.

"You didn't stop your mother, and you didn't stop the French from killing the queen." He pointed to the steps. "Climb, Cordy," he ordered with the name he'd used for her.

Obeying the man she'd always tried to impress, she took the steps. Her heels clicked on the boards above the muted silence even though the wind blew viciously around her. She walked up to the executioner. "I tried my best."

"Yer teeth are white," the executioner said, his brogue thick. A flicker of warmth came from him, and she stepped closer as if he were the flame of a candle. He pulled off his hood, and Marcus Blythe stared back at her. He clutched her chin to look at her teeth. "Polished and white." But instead of being a reprimand, he grinned, and slowly his mouth lowered to hers.

The kiss changed everything. They were suddenly alone in a small cottage. Warmth slid over her, negating the wind and cold, and her heart started to thump harder like a bird frantic to escape a cage. His arms encircled her, pulling her into him. He smelled clean, and she ran her hands over his chest, basking in the warmth he gave off.

"Marcus," she whispered against his lips. "Marcus." The kiss consumed her, and the fire he'd sparked inside flooded her with heat and achiness, making her shift, pressing her pelvis into him. His fingers lifted her skirt and smock, finding the secret heat between her legs. He played there until she felt her pleasure building to wild heights. "Yes," she said, thrusting against his hand. His fingers moved inside and outside her body, faster and faster, making her groan, and she fell over the edge of bliss.

Cordelia jerked awake, immediately feeling the heat between her legs. Under the blankets, she rubbed against the delicious ache with her fingers and swallowed her moan. For a moment she couldn't remember where she was, and she twisted, turning in the little cave of warmth surrounding her body made by the blankets. Across the room was a dimly lit hearth, a man laying before it. *Marcus.* And his eyes were open. Her breath caught as the heated ache tortured her with another tightening.

"Are ye well?" he asked as he stared at her.

As if he might be able to see under her blankets, she curled her fingers away from the crux of her legs. "Yes."

"Ye seemed cold, so I put another blanket on ye."

Cordelia realized then that another blanket was spread over her, one that smelled clean with a hint of leather and a gentle musk.

"Were ye having a nightmare?" he asked, pushing up on his elbow. "Ye were thrashing a bit." The neckline of his tunic gaped open, showing a shadowed patch of skin.

The dream had certainly started as a nightmare, but then it had taken a carnal turn that had left her as achy as when she'd had that brief, unfortunate affair with Johnathan Whitt before she realized he was a traitor. She'd foolishly given her virginity away to a man whose rotted head still stood on a pike lining Tower Bridge in London.

"I… Yes, 'twas a nightmare," she said, forcing her gaze away from his strong neck. "I fear the fall has affected my brain after all." She swallowed. Surely it was the fall, along with the warm blanket that smelled of the Highlander, that had made her dream turn so scandalous. "I didn't mean to wake you."

"Nay worries, lass," he murmured. "Try to get some more sleep before dawn."

He turned over, and Cordelia watched his broad back. She could see the slight swell and fall of his breaths, and they eventually evened out into the long, deep breaths of sleep. Her fingers slid back between her legs, pressing to rid herself of the ache that persisted. What would it be like to lay with a man like Marcus Blythe? He was much larger than Johnathan. Would his yard be larger too?

She rolled her eyes in the dark. Thoughts like that would only make her more uncomfortable. Lord help her! Even though her wanton body cooled, her creative mind wandered through the nightmare that had started the dream. The reaching hands from iron bars. Sir Francis Walsingham calling her a traitor and walking her to the scaffold.

Her eyes squeezed tight at the panic. *God's teeth!* When Walsingham found out that she'd disappeared after the ambush, he would assume she was part of the French plot to capture Elizabeth. That she'd alerted Catherine de' Medici to Elizabeth's secret visit to Haddon Hall. Walsingham hadn't told Cordelia exactly where Mary Stewart was being held until the night before

Cordelia was to assume the role as queen. There would have been no time to give the real location to French contacts.

Cordelia rubbed her face. If she didn't get away and try to show her allegiance to the queen, she might very well find herself on the scaffold in her dreams. *Oh Lucy, what do I do?* Her sister was waiting for her to come to her north of Edinburgh where she'd moved with her new husband, Greer. What would she think if she received a report of execution instead?

With absolute silence, learned from a lifetime of sneaking around court, Cordelia gently rolled back the covers. The sore muscles from her fall made her stretch a bit before rising, all the while watching Marcus for movement. But he continued to breathe easily as if in deep sleep.

The wind outdoors had died away. If it was almost dawn, she could climb on Oliver Gupton's horse and ride south. She prided herself on a keen sense of direction and endurance. If she could get back to the inn, she could find out who survived the ambush and reveal the true danger to Elizabeth. No one could call her a traitor then.

She'd left her boots on even as she slept and carefully bundled up the blanket that Marcus had lain over her. Clutching it to her chest, she moved across the room without a sound. Heel to toe. Heel to toe. Her footsteps were silent, and she stepped around the one creaky board she'd discovered earlier in the night.

Lifting the bar on the door required her to put the bundle on the floor, but she managed to do all of that, including setting the wooden slab on the floor, with barely a whisper. A quick glance at Marcus showed him still breathing slowly, his back to her. She exhaled in relief, stopping the sound by snapping her lips shut, and slipped out the door.

She glanced once more at him lying there. Would she ever see Marcus Blythe again? Would she discover that he too was a traitor, bent on capturing Elizabeth, like Johnathan Whitt had been? Hopefully his head wouldn't sit rotting on a pike. It was a most handsome head. *Fool*, she chided herself, and lowered the latch with the utmost care. Turning around, she paused.

White crystals coated the world in sparkling splendor. The sun breeched the horizon through the trees, casting gold over the snow and ice that clung to the logs of the cabin and barn. Every tree limb, from the thickest to the thinnest, was encased in icy sleeves. Everything sparkled. The morning was silent, all noises muted by the heavy snowfall. The magnificence of it all caught her breath. She would stay there mesmerized by nature's glorious beauty if she didn't have to warn the queen and save her own head.

Cordelia stepped off the porch and cringed at the crunch of her boot. The snow had a layer of ice on top, giving the hills a smooth coating like sugared paste over cakes. The crunching noise couldn't be helped, and she was losing time. Cordelia lifted her skirts, thankful once again for Lord Morton sending woolen clothing, including woolen hose, and ran across the field to the barn.

Looking straight ahead, Cordelia didn't see the white line tied across the yard until it hit her shins. She lost her balance. With arms flying out, she fell over the cord into the snow, the blanket tumbling out of her hold. Frozen, sharp snow hit her face and filled her mouth, eyes, and nose. Behind her, the sound of pots hitting the floor inside the cabin made her push up and flop over onto her back. She spit snow out of her mouth and wiped her hands over her ice-washed face, pinching her nose, as the cabin door banged open.

"God's teeth," she whispered as foot falls thudded toward her. There was no way to beat Marcus to the stables, so she lay there, arms and legs spread wide in helpless impotence and guilt.

Her breath puffed up from her lips in little white clouds to disappear against the lightening sky. She continued to watch it grow bluer by the second with the dawn. The glorious morning view was broken by Marcus's face stopping to stare down at her. His wavy hair was ruffled, having dried in odd curls, and his eyes were wide with incredulity. They were a warm brown color, like rich soil.

"What the bloody hell are ye doing?" he asked.

She huffed and took a moment to inhale. "'Twas so beautiful I thought I'd…make angels in the snow." She moved her arms up and down, pushing the thick, brittle snow to make a pattern of wings like she and Lucy used to do as children in the yard behind Cranfield House.

Marcus crossed his arms over his chest that was only covered by the tunic he'd worn to sleep. He hadn't bothered with the wrap around his hips, but the tunic kept his modesty. The breeze teased the edge as if it might blow upward. He must have slept with his stockings and boots on but had removed the furs. Lord help her, he was brawny. The dream she'd had was still heating her blood, even though she laid in the frozen snow. "Aren't you cold?" she asked from her position, her arms stilling out to her sides.

"I think ye were trying to leave on your own," he said and reached a hand down to help her up.

Without dislodging him the slightest with her weight, he lifted her easily out of the snow. Brawny and strong. He was probably radiating heat too. His hand wiped at the snow coating her back and front, grazing her arse. Moving away before she did something insane like lean into him, she threw her arm out to the pattern. "See, an angel in the snow."

"Yer Majesty," he said with a frown. "Were ye trying to leave on yer own?"

Cordelia planted hands on her hips. "Of course, I was trying to leave, you foolish knave." Elizabeth liked to call people knaves, and Cordelia made her tone very condescending.

"On your own, ye'll be captured by the French or eaten by wolves," Marcus said. "So if anyone is acting the fool this morn, 'tis ye, Yer Majesty."

Cordelia's stomach growled, and she pointed a finger at it. "My royal belly is also empty, so unless you have more food stashed away somewhere, we need to find some in a village." She crossed her arms to mimic his battle stance. "The good people of England will feed me."

Marcus ran his hand through his full head of hair. Was it as soft as it looked? "Finding food is my plan for the day, but ye cannot go alone and we must disguise ye."

"Did Lord Morton send a disguise too?" she asked and started to trudge back to the cabin. She spied the low rope this time and made a point to step over it. "You set this last night?" she asked.

"A number of them surrounding the cabin to wake me if anyone was walking close."

The man was more than magnificently built. He was clever too.

"Is that one of those special skills you mentioned?"

"Aye," he said. "As far as a disguise…" He indicated what she was wearing. "And I have a black wig. Your flaming hair would give ye away."

Perhaps he'd heard that Elizabeth kept her hair sheared very short and only wore wigs now. But he didn't ask, just picked up the fallen blanket, shaking the snow from it.

"I'm not certain it will fit over my hair, and I forbid you to cut it," she said.

"We will find a way."

She turned in the wide-open doorway. "I haven't freshened up yet. I need some privacy."

He exhaled in a huff. "Throw me my wrap."

Cordelia hurried to the folded length of plaid. It was heavy. "Here," she said, handing it to him. His hand grazed hers. It was warm, at least warmer than her frozen fingers.

"And the belt."

She pulled away and fetched the thick leather belt. When she handed it to him, he turned around to traipse back to the barn. "I'll get the horses ready."

"Thank you," she said and then clamped her mouth shut. It had rolled off her tongue like she'd been taught by her well-mannered mother, well-mannered until she tried to kill the queen that is.

He didn't turn around. Perhaps it didn't even register in his irritation that a queen never said those words, expecting everyone to wait on her without warranting gratitude. Cordelia strode inside and placed the log before the door again. She must act more like a queen if she was to convince Marcus that she was Elizabeth.

Perhaps I should tell him. "And perhaps he'll kill me." She whispered the words, but her gut told her they weren't true. He could simply abandon her, taking her horse. She didn't know anything about Marcus Blythe. And despite his promise to her that he was protecting her from the French, he very well could be working with the deposed Scottish queen, Mary, who the real Elizabeth was visiting.

No. Cordelia must remain the queen until Elizabeth took her duty back. And a queen didn't give into carnal urges from unwanted dreams.

⋙⋘

Thank you? What queen thanked a knave or anyone for that matter?

Marcus clicked his tongue to get both horses moving into the forest outside the cabin. He let the woman hold her own reins. "Don't try to race off," he said. "Last time didn't work out too well for ye."

She snorted regally and tipped her nose upward.

Their tracks would be seen, but there was nothing he could do but pray the sun melted the snow or another squall blew across them. The horses shook their manes in the chilled air, their breath puffing from their nostrils. Elspeth snorted and shied away from the large bay horse that carried Elizabeth. If she *was* Elizabeth Tudor.

Her teeth were white and straight. Her face was smooth from

pox. She had her own hair and looked at least fifteen years younger than she was supposed to look. *But that one ring.* It was covered in rubies and diamonds set to form the letter E. It truly looked like the ring that Elizabeth was purported never to remove. *And she's arrogant and domineering.* Although she seemed to downplay her beauty, which was not queenlike at all. Especially not like Elizabeth Tudor who was said to flaunt her still youthful body and make certain that her ladies were dressed drably so as not to draw attention away from her. This Elizabeth had lush, long hair without a hint of white or gray. They'd given up putting the wig on her head and instead she'd braided it, pinning it under a shawl.

"What is the name of your horse?" he asked, watching the graceful way her body moved with the beast under her. It was obvious she knew how to ride. That at least was true of the English queen.

"'Tis not mine. One of my guards gave me his." She looked at him. "I do not know the names of all the men in my armies, and therefore can't possibly know the names of their horses. But he's fast so I shall call him Racer."

The horse's ears didn't even flick. "He won't respond to it," Marcus said.

They walked around a snow-covered bramble bush and over some fallen trees. Elspeth was agile and so was Gupton's horse.

"How far to the town?" she asked when they once again drew side by side. "We were about an hour from the inn when the bandits attacked."

"We aren't riding back to the inn," he said. The French commander, a seasoned warrior named Jacque Noire, would have ridden directly there to see if the queen had returned.

She frowned at him. "I do believe I'm a prisoner." With the shawl covering her hair like a common housewife, her lovely features looked softer somehow. With lips perfect for kissing, 'twas a shame she hadn't found someone to her liking. She'd rejected all the princes in Christendom, remaining the virgin queen.

He looked forward, watching the trees ahead for signs of danger. "I will do what I must to keep ye alive on English or Scottish soil, Yer Majesty."

"If you speak the truth, then we have the same mission," she said.

Aye, but his mission extended much further than keeping the English queen simply alive.

Chapter Four

Description of a Frost Fair – "Coaches plied from Westminster to the Temple, and from several other staires to and fro, as in the streetes, sliding with skeetes, a bull-baiting, horse and coach races, puppet plays and interludes, cookes, tipling and other lewd places, so that it seemed a bacchanalian triumph or carnival on the water…"
The Blanket Fair on the River Thames in 1683 described *by diarist, John Evelyn*

THE SMALL HAMLET of Bradwell was crowded with festival goers enjoying the newly fallen snow and thickly iced over lake at its center. Marcus scanned the groups of people as he and the English queen rode down a gentle slope leading to the town. No blue tams caught his eye, but that didn't mean the French soldiers had given up and returned to the coast. They would choose exile over telling Catherine de' Medici that they'd failed to capture Elizabeth. Those who disappointed the Queen Mother didn't live long.

He looked over to the woman riding the large bay horse with the grace of a royal. Damn, but she would attract attention, even in her common wool dress and wrapped hair. Especially riding on the large horse. "We should walk from here," he said and brought them both to a halt amongst the winter-bare trees. He threw his leg over Elspeth and landed in the snow, sinking nearly to the tops of his tall boots. "Let me lead us down farther where the snow hasn't drifted."

"I was about to suggest that," she said.

"Just try not to look so... queenly." Her almond shaped, golden eyes and smooth skin would attract attention on their own, but the grace and courage in how she sat a horse and walked would mark her as royalty.

"I'm just sitting here," she said.

Daingead. Even her voice was musical and refined.

"Round your shoulders forward like a slouch," he said, moving his own shoulders to show her.

She arched her back and then rounded it. "Like this?"

"Aye and keep your eyes and head cast to the ground. Normal people don't stare people down."

"I don't stare people down," she murmured. "Well, not unless they are my foolish advisors."

"The ones trying to get ye to marry?"

"The very ones," she said and cast a smile his way. It lit her entire face, bringing out even more of her rare beauty.

He'd always imagined that the Queen of England attracted so many offers of marriage because of her power and country, but perhaps the princes of Europe wanted her for quite another reason.

"And don't speak if possible," he said.

She frowned down at him. "Even my voice is offensive?"

"Opposite of offensive. 'Tis like the voice of a siren."

She studied him, her frown fading slowly. "A siren?"

He couldn't look away from the unique brown of her expressive eyes and slowed his gait. "Aye," he said. "It calls to people." It certainly called to him. He cleared his throat and turned his gaze toward the frozen lake where a festival looked underway. "And we certainly don't need to call anyone to us."

Marcus led Elizabeth's horse and Elspeth down the slope, his sturdy boots keeping him from slipping.

The queen gasped as her horse faltered, raising his one hoof.

"Bloody hell," Marcus murmured as he turned back. He bent and inspected the horse's foot. "His shoe is partly undone." Several of the pegs holding it in place were missing.

Marcus looked across the square toward an open building where smoke ribboned upward. "There's a smithy. They should have a farrier to fix the shoe, but ye'll have to walk the rest of the way." He reached up, his hands moving through the parting of her cloak to settle around her trim waist. The touch felt intimate, but she didn't pull away or even cast one of her usual frowns at him.

"'Tis lucky that we were here when the horse went lame," she said without protesting about his touch. In fact, she seemed to lean into him.

He lowered her to the snow-covered ground and stared down into her lovely, sculpted features. He tipped his mouth toward her gently rounded earlobe. "I will have to call ye something other than Yer Majesty in town." They stood close together, almost like lovers. He could feel her warmth and smell the slight aroma of flowers rising from her.

She looked up at him without stepping away. Her rose-hued lips parted. "Other than Elizabeth?"

How many princes had those soft lips kissed? "'Twould be best if ye'll answer to another name," he said, unable to look away with her so close. Everything about the queen pulled at him, and she didn't move away. Almost as if she liked having him against her.

"Cordelia then," she said, dropping her gaze to her boot tips sticking out from the edge of her woolen petticoat. Her lashes were dark and long, fanning out under her lowered eyes. "I have a loyal maid with that name. Or Cordy if that's too formal."

"Cordy." The name felt right on his tongue. "It suits ye, Yer Majesty."

With a full breath of the chilled air, he turned away, letting the freshness of the winter morning cool his damn raging blood. He led them across the square to the smithy. An elderly man hammered an axe head, and a lad worked the bellows inside, pumping air to feed the hot fires required. Marcus looped the reins of both horses over a hitching post set up behind the building that remained open in the front.

"Ye can wait with the horses, and I'll be right back." He looked at her sternly. "Don't go anywhere."

"Where exactly would I go?"

"A wolf's den or a French encampment most likely."

She narrowed her eyes at him, her lips pressing tight. Even angry, she was beautiful.

"Right now, I'm yer only guide to get somewhere safe," he reminded her. And currently she didn't know that he planned to guide her north to Scotland instead of south to London.

"I will remain right here," she said and turned to pat the bay horse she'd named Racer.

He moved around the horse to stare over its back directly into the queen's eyes. "And whatever ye do, don't attract attention," he said. He waited for her nod and then strode around the front of the smithy.

A few pennies won Marcus an "aye" when requesting the shoe to be fixed. A few more pennies brought the lad running to water and feed the two horses while Marcus escorted the queen toward the festival goers.

"We'll act like we're enjoying the festival while we wait for the shoe to be affixed," he said.

"And find food and drink," she reminded him, although his stomach gnawed inside, making sure he couldn't forget.

"Just try to keep your hair covered, and if ye see me talking to anyone, walk in the other direction. Hide if ye must. I don't know where the French soldiers regrouped after the ambush."

"They are probably in disguise too," she said and then glanced down at his plaid wrap. "But not you. Maybe you should find some breeches to wear."

He grunted softly. "I will if I can find some." He preferred the freedom of his woolen wrap. In the wet seasons, he didn't have to worry over trews getting soaked, his legs drying faster. And pissing was far quicker.

Stone walls flanked the path, snow capping them except where children had gathered snow to make throwing balls, which they hurled at one another. "Look out," Marcus called as one dropped from the sky toward the queen. He got his arm up before her face where the ball hit, shattering into hard slush.

"God's teeth," the queen yelled, her hands shielding her face.

"Pardon, milady," the urchin called, running away with two of his friends.

Marcus lowered his arm and couldn't help the chuckle. The queen's face was speckled with tiny ice crystals. "Here," he said, his thumb brushing over her cheek. The skin was cool and rose-colored from the cold. *So smooth.* Not at all like what was reported to Lord Morton.

He dropped his hand. "'Tis somewhat like having wash water thrown at ye." He helped her swipe the snow out of her shawl around her shoulders.

"There may have been a stone in it or a bit of frozen dirt," she said. "I've seen that trick done before."

He leaned into her ear. "A queen nearly brought down by a child's snowball."

Without moving away, she tipped her head to meet his gaze. "Without my castle walls, crown to protect my head, and a hundred men sworn to keep me safe, I am merely a woman."

"A woman with the heart of a lion," he whispered and stepped back before he did something outrageous, like dropping a kiss on her rosy, very kissable lips.

Those lips turned upward. "I like the sound of that. King Henry was said to be a lion, so I do have his heart."

Marcus glanced around, but no one was close. "He also didn't know a thing about hiding from the public." He held a finger to his lips to remind her to keep quiet.

They walked arm in arm, stopping at a cart along the lake's edge where a woman sold warm buns from a cart. Marcus had a bag of coin from Lord Morton to make certain the queen wasn't wanting. He bought two buns, passing her one. "It looks like the majority of food and drink is being served out on the ice."

"Aye, Scot," the baker woman said, perusing his attire. "'Tis a frost festival with the lake freezing over, but I prefer to keep these old bones on land."

He escorted the queen, or Cordy as he should call her, to the lake's edge where a platform had been built that sloped down gradually. It allowed them to step evenly onto the rough crystal surface of the ice. Marcus made certain to hold her steady. "The ice has snow from the storm all over it, so it shan't be slippery."

"Splendid," she said, making him smile.

He leaned toward her ear. "Common folk don't usually say splendid."

"There are too many damn rules to remember," she whispered.

He chuckled. "Watch other people. Imitate them."

The queen walked on his arm, and he could see her try to round her shoulders forward, sometimes too much. Then she'd get frustrated and arch her back, thrusting her breasts forward. He leaned toward her ear as they stopped by a pig being turned on a spit. The rich, fire-roasted smell made his mouth water. "Ye look like ye might have something creeping and tickling ye under your clothes with the way ye're wiggling."

She turned wide eyes to him and then huffed, a slight grin growing larger. "'Tis harder than it looks being common."

He chuckled and enjoyed the way her eyes lit with humor. He paid for two sticks skewered with warm, roasted pork. They ate in silence as they walked among the people wrapped in woolens. It was past Christmastide, but everyone seemed jolly with market stalls and taverns being set upon the ice. It was near St. Valentine's Day when lovers gifted each other with spicey gingerbread and confections.

He led Cordy before a hut covered with snow, the awning drooping precariously, deterring people from entering what looked like a wooden toy shop. A short man with a white beard pushed at the awning with the pole end of a hobby horse.

Marcus handed Cordy his stick. "Might I help?" he asked the man.

"Blasted snow is going to be my ruin," the man said, glancing at him and nodding to Cordy.

"Ye wait inside so the snow doesn't fall on ye," Marcus said to the man. Marcus heard Cordy laugh as the man handed him the hobbyhorse with all the seriousness of a page providing his master with a lance. With several gentle lifts, the snow fell off each end of the canvas awning.

"Watch out," Cordy called as some from the top slope gave way.

Marcus jumped inward, but the snow still caught the back of his head and neck. Ice slipped down his tunic like a frigid serpent.

"Mo chreach!"

She laughed harder but hurried forward. The meat sticks in one hand, the fingers of her free hand plucked out the ice around his neck. "Now who has something tickling down their back?" she said, teasing in the lilt of her voice.

Marcus bent forward, shaking his head, which scattered icy water like a dog. Cordy squealed and jumped back, frowning. The shop keep laughed. "You might have won a cold bed tonight, man," he said to Marcus.

Marcus snorted but didn't correct him. Let the villagers think they were married or lovers. Either would help hide the queen. With rosy cheeks and laughing eyes, she didn't look like a queen but a lovely lass with a life of family, freedom, and love ahead of her. But she wasn't. She was the queen of two countries, and he must keep her from Catherine de' Medici's grasp. The thought sobered him.

He handed the hobbyhorse back to the shop keep. The man tried to hand him some coin, but Marcus wouldn't take them.

"Thank you, Scot, for opening my shop." He nodded to several patrons who'd wandered in now that the awning was lifted.

Cordy handed the pork back and took Marcus's arm, seemingly unaffected by his shaking dog impression. They stopped to listen to a group of four musicians who played with drum, lute, vielle, and flute. She leaned into him. "I play the lute," she said.

He smiled down at her. "I would like to hear that."

"I'm actually quite good at it," she said. "My mother had me practice for hours." She let her words fade off as if she was in thought. "I didn't mind too much though. The music is beautiful. Calms the soul."

"Your mother?" he asked. Elizabeth's mother, Anne Boleyn, had been executed when Elizabeth was three years old.

She kept her eyes outward. Only a slight deepening of the rose hue in her cheeks gave away any discomfort. "I mean my governess, of course. Lady Bryan. She taught me to play when I grew older."

Marcus's gut tightened, his instincts picking up on a tinge of deceit to her words. He led her toward a gingerbread stand. Warm cider was also being served.

"For your lady love," the middle-aged woman said beside the cart laden with baked fragrant biscuits. "'Tis said the spice in the gingerbread brings heat to lovers." She smiled at Marcus and then Elizabeth, if that was who she was.

"I had heard that," she said, taking the woman's outstretched treat while Marcus paid.

They walked off together in silence. Marcus chewed the spicy, sweet biscuit quickly, but the queen nibbled. Stopping at a set of benches rooted on the edge of a cleared circle of ice, they sat to watch the children slide around. Some had blades fastened to their shoes to cut into the ice. Others chased each other on worn shoes, slipping, laughing, and tumbling into drifts of cleared snow.

"At that age, they can hop right back up," the queen said.

"At your age…" he leaned into her ear, "Yer Majesty, ye seem to hop right back up too. Anytime your advisors or suitors try to knock ye down."

She turned her face to him. On the bench they were so very close. "But every blow chisels at the heart," she said. Sadness lurked in her brown eyes, authentic sadness. He suddenly wanted to deflect every blow that came at her, like the snowball.

Not my mission. He turned to look out at the children. "Chisels or tempers the steeliness of your heart?" He glanced to her gaze. "I think ye've been honed into a diamond."

She smiled brightly. "I do believe, Marcus Blythe, that you would do quite well at court. The ladies would swoon with your words of courtly love."

He chuckled and caught the back of his neck with his hand. "I do no such thing at the Scottish court in Edinburgh."

"So you frequent the court there?"

"When I'm summoned by Lord Morton to do the king's bidding."

"As a soldier? With extra skills," she added.

"Aye."

The queen held her hands in the sleeves of her cape and turned her whole body toward him. "You mentioned these skills before. What are they?"

What exactly should he reveal? That he was a spy? That he was known to be able to coerce reluctant people to accompany him anywhere? He'd be the siren then, planning to take her to Canonbie Parish to meet Lord Morton on the border between their two countries. Nay, he couldn't tell her that. "Beyond English, I know French, Spanish, Latin, and Gaelic," he said. "I can drink heartily and keep my wits. I can keep my life against four men with swords and pick any lock." Would all this explain why Lord Morton offered him so much for his services? And threatened him if he didn't use his talents for Scotland?

Do your duty, and the king and I will reward you well. Fail and you might as well sail home with the French.

"Ah," she said, softly. "But can you play the lute?"

A soft bark of laughter broke from him. "Nay, I cannot, milady."

"Je peux t'apprendre," she said.

His brows rose. "You want to teach me?" he asked in Latin.

She smiled broadly and spoke in Spanish. "Sí, si quieres aprender."

"If I wish to learn," he translated with a wide grin. But did she know Gaelic? It was said that the queen had not even tried to learn the ancient language still spoken in the west of Scotland.

"An aithne dhut mo chridhe?" he said. Lord help him if she knew what was in his heart.

She tilted her head, and one of her golden red curls sneaked out from the black scarf tied over her hair. "Gaelic?" she asked.

He nodded, lifting his finger to catch the curl.

She seemed to scoot closer. "What did it mean?"

Marcus tucked the curl back under the scarf. It took him a moment to pull his hand away from her face. *Daingead*. He lost his clever, level-headed mind around her. Perhaps she was the one who could bespell men instead of her cousin, Mary Stewart. "Ye can teach me the lute, and I can teach ye Gaelic," he said.

A child's cry stole her gaze, and she turned, standing. "That boy pushed that girl in the snow."

The queen's hands fisted at her sides, and she trudged off, anger tightening her face.

Marcus's gaze moved around the crowd. Elizabeth certainly didn't know how to remain out of view. Halfway across to remind her, Marcus stopped, catching sight of a blue cape near the tent where a vendor sold pancakes to fairgoers. Glancing back at the queen, he saw her raising her arms and kicking one leg out. What the bloody hell was she doing?

Then she reached down and pulled the girl out of the snow, dusting her off and pointing to the ground. The little girl smiled at what must look like the angel the queen had made in the snow.

Marcus turned his face back to the pancake vendor and froze. Captain Noire stared back at him. The wiry, clever Frenchman had found them.

Chapter Five

"...when informed by the Scottish ambassador, Sir James Melville, that Mary, Queen of Scots played both lute and virginals, Elizabeth was eager to know if she had a rival. She asked how well Mary played, and received the reply "reasonably, for a queen".

Later that day, Melville was asked by the queen's cousin, Lord Hunsdon, to listen to music with him. Hunsdon took him to a gallery where Melville heard music that "ravished him" – it turned out to be Elizabeth playing. She coyly told Melville that she had not been expecting him, and did not play in front of gentlemen; but, since he had heard her, perhaps he could tell her whether her playing, or that of the Queen of Scots, was better? Melville was obliged to answer that Elizabeth was the superior performer." *History Extra*

"And the angel will help protect you from your brother," Cordelia said to the little girl, wiping her tears away with a linen cloth that Lord Morton had included with the queen's costume.

Cordelia looked to the boy, who couldn't be older than ten, and frowned. "A brother should look out for his younger siblings, not harass them. You will never be a royal knight when you push your sister in the snow." She nodded to the wooden sword he held.

"A pardon," he said to her and then looked at his sister. "A pardon, Ophelia."

The child nodded and took his hand, cheerful again. Cordelia smiled at them, remembering how she and Lucy would push each other in the snow as children at their home in London. It truly was a lifetime ago. Someday she would be with Lucy again, away from court and away from England. If only she could get through this mission alive.

Frowning at her macabre thoughts, she turned back to Marcus. "God's teeth," she whispered as she saw him on the other side of the benches, surrounded by four men. They didn't wear blue tams, but their breeches and doublets were blue. She'd place a wager that they spoke with French accents.

The festival around her was alive with laughter as children slid across the smooth ice while their dogs barked in glee, chasing them. Mothers cuddled their babes and fathers hoisted older babes on their shoulders as they walked along the market. The sun broke through the heavy winter clouds, and sweethearts walked arm in arm. None of them realized the danger right there in their midst. Foreign soldiers willing to abduct a queen. Soldiers with pistols and swords.

She tucked her hands inside her cape and turned to walk toward one of the taverns set up on the ice. If Catherine de' Medici's men caught her, they'd either discover she wasn't Elizabeth and possibly kill her, or they would think she was Elizabeth and force her to sail to France. Both options were terrible.

She wove into a small group of festival goers as if she were one of them. As they walked past the tavern, she ducked inside. Rugs were thrown over the ice and barrels sat on end like small tables. A man served tankards at a rectangular bar, and a platform with instruments sat across the space against the back wall. Where could she hide until Marcus found her? A woman without a chaperone, family, or husband stood out. If the French soldiers entered the tavern, they'd spy her right away.

I should return to the smithy. Cordy turned to leave and stopped as one of the French soldiers came in through the doorway. She spun away, turning back to the room, her gaze scanning for another exit that didn't exist.

"What can I do you for?" the full-bellied barkeep asked her. She hadn't any coin on her. Without an answer, patrons on either side of her glanced her way.

The best places to hide are in plain sight. Her father had tried to help her when she was abysmal at playing All Hid with the children across the road. His words were from a lifetime ago, but she clung to them as her heart thumped hard enough to make her dizzy.

Plain sight? Cordy's gaze slid from the tables to the long bar to the raised dais with musical instruments propped along the wall.

"Mistress?" the man asked again.

"I…Umm…I'm here to play," she said, nodding toward the stage where a beautifully carved lute sat propped against a stump set to act as a stool.

"I thought the group was visiting the other tents until this eve," he said, wiping his hands and coming around the bar.

"I'm new to the group." She smiled. "They said I could play for a spell this morn. The lute is newly strung, and I was worried it would sound off later when we play together."

The man's narrowed eyes relaxed, and he shrugged. "I guess you can play now. Don't expect people to stop their yammering and listen though. And I'm only paying for the whole group to play together."

She nodded, moving away as the Frenchman asked for a whisky. Her frantic heart nearly turned over in her chest when Marcus walked in with the other men in blue. They sat farther down the bar, talking with their heads close together. She'd have left, but two stood right by the door, studying everyone who entered and departed. Were they searching for Elizabeth?

Cordelia tied the shawl tighter over her head, hiding her hair as much as possible. She walked across the space past several tables with talking men. Picking up the carved string instrument, she sat on the stump, which balanced on the back edge of the platform. She rested the stringed instrument in her lap and plucked softly at the strings. The notes sounded on key, and she ran through a song she'd learned as a child. She could barely hear the soft melody of the plucked strings over the rabble in the room.

"Louder," someone called, and her eyes widened, looking out.

"Shhhhh!" a man called, standing to frown at the patrons in the makeshift room. "I want to hear the girl."

Cordelia looked up, her fingers slipping on the strings as Marcus glanced her way and then back at the captain.

"Go on, girl," the burly man a couple tables back called again. "Play that song louder. Me mum used to sing it to me." Several men at the table with him laughed heartily.

The French captain looked her way, and she lowered her gaze to the instrument. *Hide in plain sight.* Her fingers began to move, plucking with more force so that the notes sang louder from the hollow body of the instrument. She moved through the refrain twice and then began to sing the words with it.

"A wee dove sat a winter limb.
So lovely and pure white.
The fox did circle down below,
But my love, my dove took flight."

Her words rang smooth along with the clear notes of the lute, and the room grew quiet. She didn't dare look up, but instead shut her eyes while she sang and played.

"'Tis a silver moon high above
That lights the world in the blackest night,

The shine it coats my love, my dove,
In the brightest, crystal white."

It was a simple song with clear notes. Cordelia remembered her mother singing it to her and Lucy when they were young. It went on for several more verses, its soothing melody helping Cordelia remain on stage. When the final plucked note faded, she looked out. The closest patrons stared at her. Others whispered, smiling as they drank their ale. The man who'd shushed everyone stood, his big hands slapping together in sharp applause. "Perfectly done," he yelled. His friends also stood, clapping.

Marcus didn't look at her again. The captain, however, glanced her way. He was tall and his slender build looked strong instead of lacking in muscle. Dark hair was clipped short, and he had a dark, trimmed beard around thin lips. He frowned, and his teeth showed when he talked to Marcus as if he were furious. His men, one of them the same broad build and height as Marcus, watched her sing. Did they know they were the fox in the story and she the dove needing to fly away?

Even though that was precisely what she wanted to do, run from the stage to put distance between herself and those stalking her, she made herself stay seated. When the men stopped their clapping, she began another tune that was jollier, a rolling song with a foot-tapping beat. The man who appreciated her the most began to clap the rhythm and several others followed. God's teeth! Could she possibly draw more attention to herself?

Hide in plain sight.

Her fingers plucked the strings quickly, her voice chiming in to sing the fun ode to great King Henry. 'Twas one of the queen's favorites. Elizabeth had her own minstrels, but sometimes she asked her ladies to play in her private rooms. This was often requested.

Cordelia didn't dare look over at the bar, but from her periphery she saw that Marcus was still there with the French soldiers. As she moved into a third song, several men walked in, their gazes going directly to her on the dais.

She continued to play despite their angry faces. Arms crossed, they approached. "What the bloody hell are you doing with my lute?" one said, his voice overriding her own.

"Playing and singing probably better than you," the brawny man said. He and his three friends had moved closer, evicting the two smaller men from their barrel before the stage. He stood, his friends too. "Now let the girl finish her song."

Good Lord! Would she be responsible for a brawl?

There was nothing to be done but sing so she continued to pluck and carry the tune through the tale of a man's lady love and how he died protecting her. As the last note faded, her four most ardent spectators clapped loudly as the rest of the common room followed, except for the musicians who came forward. The one who owned the lute came at her, and she instinctively pushed back.

"You better not have harmed it," he said, snatching the lute from her.

Her backwards push was just enough for the stump to shift, and her weight helped it tip off the back edge of the platform.

"Ohhhh," she gasped as she hit the wooden wall at her back. Luckily the pop-up tavern walls were constructed of wood with tarps stretched above to act as a roof. The bump on her head knocked against the wall as she fell over onto the platform. Even though pain shot through the back of her head, she clutched at the dark shawl covering her hair, trying to keep it in place.

The large man who'd defended her leaped onto the stage. "Bloody hell! You can't treat a lady like that."

"I…I didn't do anything to her," the lute player said, holding his lute before him like a shield.

Cordelia gasped as the big man lifted her around the waist. He squeezed her hard as he righted her, lifting her high enough to set her dangling feet on the floor. He let go and offered her his arm. "Come sit with us, little lady. Did you hurt yourself?"

Her first instinct was to run, but her head hurt, and with her luck she'd run right into the men in blue. She tugged the tie tight under her chin. "I…I am fine. Thank you."

She glanced toward the bar where Marcus stared at her, his face tight with anger. His eyes were slightly wider with dark amazement at her display. The French soldiers watched her right along with every single person under the tent. Her stomach twisted, and her knees felt weak.

Her burly rescuer led her to a chair around the upturned barrel. "My name's Henry. Henry James. And this is Luke, John, and Mathew," he said, pointing to the other three men who bobbed their capped heads.

"You are a lovely girl," said Mathew, a tall but slender man with pale skin and red hair. "And so talented with the lute."

"Aye," said Luke. With dark, curly hair that was much too long, he looked like one of the shaggy cows from the north. He raised his tankard to her as if praising her talent.

John merely nodded, his gaze glancing to the bar as if he were more interested in the French than her. He was the smallest of the group and sported a neatly trimmed beard that he'd waxed to a point.

"Like the disciples in the bible?" she asked and sat, trying to turn her face to keep it hidden from the French soldiers. They hadn't seen her during the ambush. *I'm just another woman attending the fair.*

"Just like them," Henry said, chuckling. He slid his mug over to her. "Here you go. Some mead."

The man meant for her to drink from his cup. Cordelia slid her hand to the table and touched the handle, then switched hands so her lips would hopefully touch on the opposite side from which he'd already drunk. The mead was sweet and cool.

She nodded, setting it down. "Thank you. Quite refreshing."

Mathew grinned. "Quite refreshing," he mimicked. "You sound like the queen."

She looked down at her clasped hands, the queen's rings sitting there on her fingers, the locket ring being the most prominent. She'd meant to take them off, hiding them away. Pulling both hands to her lap, she twisted the locket part of the most recognized ring in toward her palm. The band was still studded with rubies, but at least now it looked to be a wedding band.

"With those rings, perhaps you are our good Queen Bess," Mathew said, studying her.

Cordelia's heart thudded all the way into her ears. She pushed a bit of laughter out from between her teeth. "Indeed," she said, sliding most of the rings off to shove into a pocket through a parting in her petticoat.

"Indeed!" they repeated together and broke into rolls of laughter.

The musicians began a tune on the dais, and Cordelia turned in her chair to view them. Hopefully they would cut off more bellowing conversation that had to have reached the French commander at the bar.

Unfortunately, the musical group did not follow the rules of harmony very well.

"Let the girl back up there," Henry called, his hands braced around his mouth, even though he was loud enough without the enhancement.

Cordelia waved her hand at Henry, shaking her head. "Oh no. I am most happy here sitting."

Henry stood, pulling her out of her seat as if to drag her back to the stage.

"The mademoiselle would rather sit. Oui?"

Cordelia's heart dropped into her belly as the French captain stopped on the other side of her. "In fact, I think she would rather step out of this scene you have caused, monsieur." For a Frenchman, his English was quite clear. If he hadn't used a couple French words, she might not have guessed his nationality.

Henry guessed it easily. "Damn Frog," he said, using the well-known slur.

Luke, the youngest looking of the four, stood too, the fingers of his hands spread as if he readied himself to either draw a weapon or curl them into fists. "What are you doing on English soil?"

Captain Noire smiled, but it did nothing to soften the razor-sharp threat on his face. "A diplomatic mission." Cordelia lowered her gaze, but she couldn't miss the arm he held out for her to take as if he were her savior to pull her away from the riffraff. To turn it down would make Henry think she truly liked him, which could be just as dangerous. So she took it, but smiled at the four locals.

"Thank you for supporting music and being such upright citizens, Luke, John, Mathew, and Henry." She nodded to them and walked beside Captain Noire toward Marcus where he sat with his elbow resting on the bar.

Her plan of not being noticed had failed.

Instead of ignoring her or feigning disinterest, Marcus frowned at her. "Mistress Cordelia," he said and gave a small shake of his head. "I said we would meet later this eve."

She blinked, glancing to Noire who had released her arm. "I…I was here spending my time." She stood tall, raising her chin, and turned back to Marcus. "'Twas you who found me here, so I am not in the wrong." Her words were full of haughty reprimand.

"You know each other?" Noire asked, his brow arching over piercing blue eyes. Some might call him handsome with his angular features, dark hair, and wiry build. But there was a hardness to his eyes that made a shiver raise the hairs at Cordelia's nape.

"She followed me to the frost festival," Marcus said.

Heat rose in her cheeks. "I did not. I came to enjoy the fair before we met later."

"Sounds like the little lady might want to come back over to sit with us," Henry said from behind her.

God's teeth. She was stuck between five French soldiers, four English rowdies, and one grim Highlander. Even the musicians weren't holding the interest of the patrons.

Captain Noire's suspicious look softened to one of amusement. "Perhaps la mademoiselle would prefer to meet *me* this evening. I certainly would make it worth her while." He flipped a shilling in the air as if bragging that he had much more money than either Henry or Marcus.

Cordelia's eyes grew round, and she glanced at Henry and his crew and then back to the French soldiers who grinned. They thought she was a whore. Heat flared up Cordelia's neck. She might be masquerading as a queen who was masquerading as a common woman, but she drew the line at pretending to be someone who was forced to sell sex to survive.

Her tight lips curved only at the corner as she met Noire's gaze. "Only if you have your own lute to bring."

"Lute?" he asked, confusion dampening his smile.

"For your lesson," she said. "That is why we are meeting this evening."

Noire looked to Marcus. "You are learning how to play the lute?" Each word was succinct and filled with disbelief.

"Aye," Marcus said. "And ye better have better payment than a few coins. The lass wants to learn Gaelic in return."

"I know Gaelic," Mathew called, raising his hand. "Several languages in fact. My mum taught me."

"Bloody hell, man," Henry said, rolling his eyes at the man. "Do you have a lute to bring to the lesson?"

Mathew lowered his hand. "I could find one." He glanced at the musicians on stage. Would he steal it right before everyone or wait to accost the lute player in an alley?

Cordelia held her arms out as if to stop the rapid round of ridiculous words. "The Highlander has arranged for me to teach him to play the lute in exchange for teaching me some of his language…so I can journey north to visit a dear cousin." Details added credence to nonsensical words. She thought she'd heard that somewhere.

The French soldiers grumbled and spoke in rapid French

behind their commander's back. "No queen and no women," one said in French. "If we cannot find Elizabeth, the de' Medicis will have our heads."

"Likely our pillows will be laced with poison," another soldier said.

Noire cut the soldier off with a flick of his hand while continuing to stare at her as if he wasn't convinced. "Where north, mademoiselle?"

Cordelia didn't even look toward the soldiers and answered Noire directly. "North of Edinburgh in a village on the Firth of Forth. Culross."

"I would think you would need coin to journey so far," Noire said. "A woman alone." His gaze moved to Marcus. "Or has the gallant Highlander agreed to take you? In exchange for…lute lessons?" His question dripped with carnal indiscretion.

The captain was trying to trip her on the details. Cordelia met his gaze with hard eyes like she did with distrustful, elite courtiers at Whitehall. "'Tis none of your business, Frenchman, but he has refused me, and I have made other arrangements."

Without waiting for a reply or more questions, she turned to Marcus. "Meet me off this ice where we agreed earlier when the sun dips below the trees. And don't forget your instrument."

She turned, hands fisted by her sides, and strode toward the door. Half-expecting some man to catch her arm, whipping her backwards, she nearly tripped stepping outside onto the frosted ice. Her heart pounded so hard, it rivaled the sound of the laughing crowd behind her, who had apparently been listening in. Did they think she was really a whore? Better than a queen, she supposed.

Cordelia kept walking, rounding the toy shop and ducking into another where the clacking of wood made her jump. She whirled toward the frame and set blocks of a printing press.

"Card to commemorate the fair?" the man asked as he inked the blocks.

Not wanting to exit quite yet, Cordelia walked closer. "They are lovely," she said, nodding to the rectangular parchment printed with a carving of skaters on the lake. "I left my monies with my husband," she said. "He should be along soon."

The printer nodded and continued his work. "Stay as long as you want, mistress."

The shop, set on the ice, was cool, but out of the wind. She watched the man set the blocks, ink them, and work the printer. "'Tis wonderous," she said, "to see how many can be made at once."

He nodded. "The printed word is as powerful as the sword in spurring the hearts of mankind." He smiled a toothy grin. "I rather think of myself as a knight when I print out ideas so those who can cipher know things and pass them on. There is no stopping knowledge once 'tis out there."

Cordelia agreed. She'd seen many pamphlets handed out in London proclaiming good and bad about the queen. It could be quite dangerous if printed maliciously. "Pray how do you decide what to print?"

"Whomever pays me," he said with a chuckle.

"What if 'tis not true?"

He frowned. "Then I don't print it. I have me morals."

"What if you don't know if 'tis true?"

"Then I try to find out."

She drew closer. "Because I happened to hear five Frenchmen at the fair discussing trying to capture the queen to take to their mistress in France, Catherine de' Medici."

The man's eyes grew round. "Our Queen Bess?"

She nodded. "They were in the tavern moments ago, speaking in French, which I happen to know."

His eyes squinted as if assessing her. "And who are you?"

Did she lie or tell him her true name? Would he even know truth from lies?

"Lady Cordelia Darby," she said, standing straight. *Partly true.* "Print it if you want to print truth. It might help the queen and have her people be on the lookout for those who would do her harm."

Cordelia peeked out of the tent. No Captain Noire, Henry, or Marcus. Where would she spend the rest of the day without coin? It was a very good thing she'd already eaten the pork, buns, and gingerbread. But now she must avoid at least nine men. Hopefully Marcus would guess that she'd meant the smithy as their place to meet. 'Twas where their horses were. She'd go now in case he managed to get away from Noire.

"A souvenir for your information, milady," the printer said, coming around to hand her a card, the ink dried in simple but numerous intersecting lines showing several men, women, and children skating. There were even several dogs running about.

"The artwork is so detailed and fine," she said.

He smiled, puffing up. "Thank you, milady. I carved it myself. And 'tis payment for your information."

Would he really print what she'd said? She smiled sweetly, nodding, and headed out into the open air once more. She slid the card inside her pocket, hoping the discarded rings there wouldn't scratch it.

Walking quickly but carefully on the rough ice, she crossed to the opposite line of tents, peeking around the edge. A man and woman walked holding hands while two boys raced ahead with a dog, barking happily. The woman with the buns was selling some to several men, and a pair of ladies inspected ribbons at a set up shop of hats and gloves. Despite the cold, the air was full of simple joy. And the absence of men from the tavern helped Cordelia relax. She strode out behind another set of three older boys who tossed snowballs in the air, catching them.

Ducking around the toy shop, Cordelia spotted the ramp where earlier Marcus had led her onto the ice. But before she could take more than three steps, rough arms went around her, and a hand clamped over her mouth.

She struggled. The smell of onions and hard work assailed her nose. The man's mouth moved to her ear. "I've got you, Your Highness," he said.

Chapter Six

QE hated foul smells, especially scented leather and bad breath. After a French envoy left her presence after speaking to her she said "Good God! What shall I do if this man stay here, for I smell him an hour after he has gone!" The envoy was told and left the English court to return to France immediately.
Allison Weir, *The Life of Elizabeth I*

MARCUS WANTED NOTHING other than to charge out of the tavern after Cordy. The queen. The bloody queen of England and Ireland. He shook his head at the muddle in his head. The more he got to know the fiery haired woman, the less she seemed to be the overly dramatic queen he was supposed to fetch for Lord Morton. His pulse raced at the idea that she was an imposter.

"So you failed in taking the queen," Noire said in French, making the barkeep frown, his gaze shifting to him. 'Twas unlikely that anyone other than Marcus also knew French in the temporary establishment on the iced lake. Certainly not the four blokes who'd come to Cordy's defense. Marcus's brows lowered as he noticed that their table had been taken over by another rowdy bunch. The four men had left.

"Where is she now?" Noire asked when Marcus didn't respond to the first accusation. Noire knew that he and his dozen men had failed as well, even more so since Marcus had actually captured the queen, or *not* the queen. *Bloody hell.*

Marcus cast hard eyes on Noire. The man's weak chin and drawn cheeks gave his face a triangular look, like that of a pine martin or ferret. Marcus had no doubt the cunning man could deliver a vicious bite as well. "She may have returned to Whitehall after your ambush," Marcus said. "And put all her close attendants who survived into the Tower since they were the only ones to know of her outing."

Noire's fist tapped the bar top in agitation. "And how did she escape on her own?"

"She is known to be an excellent horsewoman, captain." Marcus took what looked like a leisurely drink from his tankard of mead. Inside, his mind moved through the tents beyond the tavern. Where would Cordy go? Back to the smithy? As soon as he could get away from Noire, he would head there.

"You were chasing her," Noire said. "Where did she go?" Irritation made his words snap despite the French flow.

"Her horse dashed away faster than mine," Marcus said, speaking in French in case anyone overheard. "Her trail was lost amongst the wheel ruts and horse hooves from her entourage earlier. I rode about a mile back but didn't see signs of her breaking off the trail."

"We did," Noire said. "Looked like she tumbled down into a ravine. There was blood in the snow at the bottom."

Marcus sat up straight. "She's injured? We cannot allow the queen to die," he whispered. "That was not part of our arrangement."

Noire shrugged. "If she fell and died, her body would have been there. Someone helped her escape." He eyed Marcus. "You, perhaps."

Marcus snorted and took another drink. Setting the tankard down with a mild clunk he said, "How the bloody hell do I expect to be paid letting a woman like that get away? Perhaps it was the traitor in her midst. Someone who plays both sides of this plot."

Would the captain give the name of the man or woman

who'd informed the she-dragon of the House de' Medici?

"Non," Noire said, the word particularly nasally. "He has met with me and is waiting back at the inn where they stayed before setting out toward Haddon Hall. Just in case she arrives there."

"She's likely moved south back toward London," Marcus said, his gaze scanning the crowded tent. When had the four local men left? Had they followed Cordy?

"We are not leaving England until we find her," Noire said.

Good thing Marcus was taking her to Scotland. Marcus stood from his stool. "I'll ride farther south and see if I can pick up her trail. If she makes it behind the walls of Whitehall, our chance is gone."

Noire cocked his head. "What about your lute lesson?"

Marcus drank and set the tankard back down, giving Noire a wry grin. "Do I look like a man who owns a lute?"

The Frenchmen behind Noire laughed. "I told you he was getting under her skirts," one said.

"You cannot be delayed," Noire said. "If you wish to be paid."

"Of course. I'll be off now."

"I can meet la fille for a lesson," one Frenchman said.

Noire frowned. "We are not here for frost fairs and *lute lessons*. We will ride on to Haddon Hall to make certain she didn't circle around to go where she's expected."

Marcus nodded. "I'll send any updates there." He kept his steps even and slow as he walked across the scattered rugs and straw over the ice and out the flap in the tent. As soon as the doorway fell back into place, his face whipped around, searching out corners and ways between tents and stalls. "Where the bloody hell are ye?" he whispered and strode off toward the smithy.

⋙⋘

For a moment, Cordelia couldn't move. Fear shackled all her

limbs in the tight grasp of the man.

Fight, Cordy! She heard her sister, Lucy, yelling in her mind. *Fight until they're dead or you are.* At the time that Lucy had given her the advice when they'd parted ways, the words had seemed overly dramatic, much like her passionate sister. But considering Cordelia's current situation, there was nothing but wisdom in them.

As if releasing a wild horse from its pen, Cordelia bucked in the man's arms, her teeth coming down on the fleshy hand against her mouth.

"Bloody hell," the man said, yanking his large paw from her face. "Your Majesty—"

She cut off his words by kicking at his legs. Pointy elbows shooting outward, Cordy's entire body transformed into a tempest of legs, knees, arms, and teeth.

"I'll bite your foking face off!" she said, turning on the man.

Mathew from the tavern leaped back, still holding his hand which sprouted big drops of blood. His eyes were wide and his face red. "Your Majesty?"

"I mean it," she said, holding her fingers bent to look like claws. "I'll scratch your bloody eyes out too. Blind and gnawed, you will swing from London Bridge!"

"I…I was but…" He beckoned her to hide with him behind a building and lowered his voice. "One of the French soldiers." He jabbed a finger to the street behind her. "He's searching for you. I think."

Cordelia jumped forward to hide around the edge of the closest tent next to Mathew.

For long moments they stood beside each other. Only the sound of Mathew's heavy breathing and the rush of Cordy's blood hid the fair noises.

Mathew cleared his throat softly. "Pardons, Your Majesty, for…handling you like I did."

She cut her hand through the air to make him hush as she waited, but no Frenchman rounded the corner, sniffing her out.

She turned her face to the large man. "You grabbed me to save me from a French soldier?" she whispered.

Mathew nodded quickly. "Aye. I understand French, you see, and they were talking about trying to find the queen. When I followed you to the printer, he told me the tale of Your Highness being chased by the French." He pointed at her hand where her ring had turned forward again, showing the locket. "Me mum said you wear a ring with your mother's picture in it. Said it looked like a ruby covered locket on your finger with the letter E in diamonds." He pointed at her hair that had escaped the shawl. "You have red hair too." He scratched his face. "And then the frog came out of the tavern looking for you, I think." He looked in her eyes. "Are you our good Queen Elizabeth?"

Cordelia's heart was still racing, her lips parted to draw in breath. She wiped her hand across her lips to get the grimy taste out of it. "You have done a service for your country, Master Mathew," she said, and his eyes widened.

"By God, you are the queen." He doffed his hat and bowed his head. "I wasn't sure. Henry said I was an idiot."

"'Tis a secret that I am away from London," she said. "And I must stay out of the hands of the French. The Highlander is helping me despite his interactions with the French."

Mathew's brow furrowed. "Are you certain, Your Highness? He was quite chummy with the frogs."

Was she certain that Marcus was on her side, or the side of the queen? God's teeth, she wasn't certain of anything except that the man was built to infiltrate her dreams in wanton wonderful ways. "He is a spy for the Scottish, helping the English."

"Well, that's new."

"Lord Morton wants me to proclaim King James the heir of the English throne."

Mathew shook his head. "You mustn't ever die, Your Most Beloved High Queen."

"Your Majesty is fine," Cordelia said with a smile.

His face reddened, and he nodded.

"I want very much not to die anytime soon." She glanced around. "Currently, I must get to the smithy on land and remain there until the Highlander finds me."

Mathew stood taller. "I'll get you there, Your Majesty."

Blood from his hand dripped onto the white frost. "I apologize for biting you," she said, nodding to it.

He grabbed some snow and washed the wound. "No matter." He grinned. "And me mum was right. You are a fighting queen. Spain doesn't stand a chance against us."

Cordelia couldn't help but smile at his confidence. "Your mum is a grand and faithful woman."

"That she is."

"Tell her that her queen thinks she did a fine job raising her son."

Mathew's chest puffed outward as he stood tall. "Thank you, Your Majesty." He acted as if she'd knighted him. No wonder the queen liked to talk with the common people. They appreciated her attention so much.

She held a finger up to him. "But don't go around grabbing women or you'll find yourself gutted one day."

"Aye, Your Majesty," he said and bobbed his head before looking out beyond the edge of the tent. "All seems clear." He turned to her. "I'll get a barrow to hide you in."

Cordelia sighed. Would the true queen be able to withstand all this? Hopefully she was safely out of weather and danger.

Her face pinched. How long had it been since their party was ambushed? Only one night and day? Had anyone gotten word to Her Majesty and Walsingham at Chatsworth House where Mary Stewart was being held prisoner? No one knew she was headed there. No word would have been sent.

"Jump inside," Mathew said, pushing a wooden barrow around the corner. "Under the blanket. 'Tis mostly clean."

"God's ballocks," she murmured under her breath as Mathew helped her step in and crouch into the bottom of what looked like the remnants of a load of turnips. He tucked the woolen blanket over her head, and Cordelia sighed. What she endured for her queen.

MARCUS JOGGED ALONG the tree line that surrounded the frozen lake. The blacksmith and his apprentice were working in the smithy, the horses still tethered. Had they been attended to yet? *Daingead.* If he'd known Noire would show up, he'd have paid the smith to fix the queen's horse faster. He'd intended for them to spend the night here in the one inn and leave before dawn the next day, hopefully while the queen was sleepy so she wouldn't notice the northwest route on which he planned to take her.

"Bloody hell," Marcus whispered. Morton wanted the queen across the Scottish border, saved by the Scots from the French, but taking the queen north instead of south was an act of war against her. Morton would likely blame Marcus when she raged. Would he pay Marcus anyway for doing what he'd been hired to do? Or would Marcus need to make contact with his other patron?

Currently, Marcus worked as a spy in France while his mother and sister, Trinity, were kept in Scotland in modest comfort from his earnings. His father had helped inter Mary Stewart but was held in suspicion by the regents of the king. If Marcus proved that his family was indeed loyal to King James, it would cleanse the Ruthven name no matter what his father had done or did in the future. And getting Queen Elizabeth to name James her heir would do just that. But Marcus had a backup plan, secured in secret twists that would ensure his family survived no matter who came to power.

As Marcus approached the smithy, he saw one of the Englishmen from the tavern pushing a barrow up the street. "What's he doing?" Marcus murmured and ducked behind another building that sat across from the smithy. Wasn't his name

Mathew? The one who wanted a lute lesson. Marcus snorted softly. There was nothing musical about what the man wanted from Cordy.

From his position, he watched Mathew push the barrow behind where their horses were tied. Marcus ran to another spot, trying to follow the man with his gaze. Behind the smithy, Mathew threw off a blanket from the barrow and helped a woman out of it.

"Bloody hell." Marcus's heart jumped into a hard beat. He jogged toward them, making both man and queen pivot to him.

"What…?" Marcus indicated the barrow and Mathew. Thank the Lord, the queen looked sound, although the man had dried blood on one hand. In the shape of… He looked between them, a conclusion rising in his mind. "She bit ye?" What had the bastard done to make a queen bite his hand?

"The French soldiers were hunting for me amongst the tents," the queen said, righting her bodice and petticoats.

"And they bit him?" Marcus indicated the bite mark.

Mathew squeezed the injured hand with his good one. "Her Majesty bit me."

"What the bloody hell were ye doing to her, man?" Marcus walked up to him, his fists clenched.

"I was saving Her Majesty," Mathew said, standing before her as if he were her personal guard. "But she didn't know it at the time."

Elizabeth came out from behind the man, hands out as if to break up a fight. "There's no time for masculine posturing. The French may find us any minute."

"I will throw down my life for you, Your Majesty," Mathew said.

The title registered. "Yer Majesty?" Marcus asked, his voice louder than he intended.

The queen shushed him with a finger to her rosy lips. "This countryman has helped me escape my foreign enemy. I shall be forever grateful for his stealth and strength."

"Did you hear that, Scot? Stealth and strength while you were drinking with the enemy."

Marcus didn't know what to say to that. After a moment, he turned his gaze to Cordy. *The queen.* She must be the queen. Mathew certainly felt she was royalty of the highest rank. How then could Marcus think of her as a bonny woman with soft, full curves and a kissable mouth?

"Many thanks to ye then," Marcus said, his voice low. "Now I must get her away to safety."

Cordy looked at the horses. "I don't know if the shoe's been fixed."

The horses had been fed and watered from the look of it, their saddles and bits removed. But the large bay the queen had borrowed from her guard still held the one hoof at an odd angle.

Mathew looked around. "I'll talk to William. He's the smith. 'Twill be done in no time."

"Don't tell him the queen is here or that he works on her horse," Marcus said.

Mathew tutted through his teeth. "Of course, I won't." He sauntered off around the side of the building.

Marcus walked up to Cordy, his hands resting on her shoulders. "Ye are well?" He studied her closely but saw no marks or fear. Strength radiated from her through her stance, and she showed no signs of trembling.

She nodded, and he exhaled.

He looked closer at her face, meeting her eyes. "Ye…" he drew out, "are absolutely horrid at hiding, Yer Majesty. I said do not attract attention. And instead ye hopped on stage."

She frowned. "I was hiding in plain sight. 'Tis a well-known strategy that usually works." Her words had softened, and she glanced down. "It did not work out the way I'd intended."

He leaned closer. "What did Mathew do that made ye bite him?" He couldn't imagine her perfect mouth pulled back in a snarl.

"He put his hand over my mouth to keep me quiet, because

he thought the French were near." She showed her perfect white teeth. "I reacted."

The white teeth, set in between those full rose-hued lips sent a sizzle of sensation through him. Marcus cleared his throat and looked away before he did something foolish and stepped closer to her. She was the bloody queen of England, the Virgin Queen, and untouchable symbol of England's sovereignty. Aye, she was a woman, a flesh and blood, warm woman. But she was a queen first. *Bloody ballocks.*

"We cannot leave town in daylight," Marcus said.

She followed him as he pulled back against the side of the smithy. If she knew that his mind kept trying to strip her naked, she'd keep her distance.

"Aren't there wolves out at night?" she asked.

"We will go right before dawn."

She stopped in front of him, the horses blocking them from view. "Where will we go?" Cordy…The queen was so close that her skirts brushed his legs.

He hesitated. So far, he hadn't lied to the English queen. "To safety."

She frowned, her head shaking. "We…I…" She looked him in the eye. "We must journey on to Haddon Hall where I am supposed to be."

He shook his head back at her and watched worry push up her brows. "Captain Noire is going there in case the queen arrives after her escape from the ambush. We must go far away from there."

Her eyes widened, and her lips parted, drawing his eye before he could stop himself. She was so damn beautiful. Beautiful and untouchable. But those golden-colored eyes set in the perfect shape of two almonds tethered him to her. It truly must be Elizabeth and not her cousin Mary who bewitched people. Because Marcus was feeling flushed and bewitched to his core.

He glanced down to see her fingers curled in the sleeve of his jacket. "We must go to Haddon Hall," she whispered, her voice tight and earnest. "Any of my group who survived will go on there to receive help from Lord and Lady Manners. They will already wonder where I am, and we must warn them about the French."

"My mission is to get ye to safety, Yer Majesty, and I will not risk yer life on alerting anyone else," he said.

The woman dropped his sleeve, her hands going up to run down her face over her smooth cheeks. "Marcus, we must go to Haddon Hall."

He shook his head, but she grabbed him. "Listen to me," she said, coming closer.

"Ye have my full attention, Yer Majesty," he said, looking down into her mesmerizing eyes.

She took a full breath and let it out, keeping his gaze. "Marcus…There was this mission, a secret one."

"Aye, no one at Whitehall knows ye're even up here."

"No, well, yes," she said. "Just listen to me." She waited for his nod, although he was having a hard time concentrating on her words when she flattened her hands over his chest. She moved them there, making this jack twitch.

"There was a mission within a mission," she said. "First a group of eight came up to the inn. From the inn…Queen Elizabeth and her spy master, Francis Walsingham, traveled on to Chatsworth House."

"Chatsworth House?" Marcus murmured, frowning. "Where Mary Stewart is being held prisoner."

"By Lord Shrewsbury, yes," she said. "Only four of us knew of this side trip, me being one. The queen and Walsingham are planning to catch up to us at Haddon Hall before going back to London. Without any knowledge of the ambush, they will still go to Haddon Hall after visiting at Chatsworth House. The French will be waiting at Haddon Hall. They will capture her."

"The queen?" he asked and watched her face tighten. He held his breath.

"'Tis the biggest of secrets," she said, her eyes imploring him to understand. "She parted with her beloved ring so the others would be fooled when I came among them veiled."

"So…" He inhaled, letting the words out in a rush. "Ye are not Queen Elizabeth."

She shook her head. "I am Cordelia Cranfield, the queen's lady."

Heat flushed up through Marcus's chest and neck into his face. It should have been from anger. He'd spent the last two days saving and protecting an imposter. She'd lied to him through it all. He should be furious. He should leave her and ride off toward Chatsworth House now. He should curse and rethink his strategy. But all Marcus could think was, *Bloody thank you, Lord.*

Marcus's hands lifted to capture her face between them. "Ye are Cordelia, not Elizabeth."

Her lush lips sat parted, her breaths coming shallow, and the black spheres in her eyes had grown larger. She gave the smallest nod, but it unleashed a huge wave of relief and heat through Marcus.

He bent his face, and his lips fell upon hers.

Chapter Seven

"I thank God I am indeed endowed with such qualities that if I were turned out of the realm in my petticoat I were able to live in any place in Christendom."
Queen Elizabeth I of England and Ireland

Surprise made Cordy's eyes widen. Marcus's body felt like warm granite wrapping around her, but his lips were soft. His hand came up to cup the side of her head, tilting her face to deepen the kiss. Her eyes fluttered closed, and she let him.

In the barrow pushed by Mathew, the cold had replaced the heat Cordy had felt from her dodging the French. And now that cold melted away under Marcus's touch. She'd expected his anger but not his kiss. Nor had she expected the dam she'd been holding on her own heat to shatter under it.

She was no timid virgin, but she'd never been held like this before, touched with such unleashed passion. The heat boiled up through her, making her ache in all the places that seemed suddenly so very neglected. What would it be like to lie with a man like Marcus Blythe? A warm mountain of a man with chiseled muscles? A spy? An honorable rescuer trying to save the queen?

The thought spurred her kiss, and she pressed against him so that his knee rode up between her legs. Hampered by her petticoats, she could still feel the hardness of his thigh against her mound, against the ache that began to pulse there in time with her heart.

His hand raked up through her wavy tresses so that the shawl fell off, letting the coolness of the afternoon air infiltrate her hair. He was careful to avoid her stitches, although she probably wouldn't have felt any pain, not with all the pleasure rolling through her.

Cordelia's palms lay flat against his strong chest, and she stroked them downward, pausing at the boundary of his leather belt. But then she dared to move lower, instantly feeling his raging erection under his plaid. Her hand molded around it through the wool, and Marcus groaned low against her mouth. His clothing was so much easier to work around. Cordy moved one hand against his yard while her other rucked up the edge of his wrap, her fingers finding the hot skin of his arse underneath. She squeezed the muscle there.

Marcus made a noise like a growl and turned with Cordy, pressing her back against the wall of the smithy. The kiss became wild, sliding and tasting against each other's mouths. Collecting her hands, he lifted them up over her head, using his pelvis to pin her to the wall. How easy it was for him to overpower her. The fleeting thought should have triggered alarm, but instead it washed a deluge of heat and want through her body. She gasped softly as his mouth left hers to kiss a trail along her neck as he pressed his rigid yard against her through the layers of clothes between them. She pressed back, her eyes still shut against the onslaught of sensation as his hot lips traveled down her neck to the swell of her breasts at the edge of her neckline.

"Where are ya?" came a hushed voice from the other side of the horses.

The heat from Marcus's mouth was suddenly gone, the dampness of his kisses left a coolness on her skin. He released her arms, and she opened her eyes. Marcus's breath came quickly from parted lips, which he held a finger before to keep her quiet. She nodded, glancing down to make sure her breasts were still tucked away, and then back to him. Marcus slid his dagger free from its hiding place in the folds of his wrap.

Cordelia tried to catch her breath to calm her racing heart. She lifted cool hands to her hot cheeks.

"Your Majesty? Highlander? Where did you get to?" It was Mathew.

The dagger in Marcus's hand disappeared once more in the folds of his wrap, and he quickly adjusted his jutting yard before stepping from around the rump of his horse.

"We are over here," he said.

Cordelia wasn't recovered enough to speak, so silence made the scene awkward when Mathew came around the animals, looking between them.

"Why are you both all rosy in the face?" the Englishman asked. "Like you've been running." He glanced around, lowering his voice. "Are the frogs hopping close?"

"Nay," Marcus said, clearing his throat. "What did ye find out about the horse?" he asked.

The banal question distracted Mathew from their flushed appearance, and his brows softened. He bowed his head to Cordelia. "The smith's apprentice will come out next to reshoe your horse, Your Majesty."

Did the title grate on Marcus now that he knew the truth? Now that she wasn't kissing all the angry thoughts about her duplicity from his head?

"There's an inn up the road," Mathew said. "The Golden Goose. Madge will take you in for a hot meal before you head back to the safety of London." He bent at the waist in a deep bow. "Your Majesty."

The man straightened. "Henry, Luke, John, and I could go with you to assist in your protection against—"

"Nay."

"Not necessary." Both Marcus and Cordelia cut in.

Cordelia smiled at Mathew, her mask of serenity back in place even though her heart still hammered under her breastbone. "Master Blythe will secret me to safety thanks to your help." The man grinned, bowing his head. "You have earned my gratitude and a reward," she said, and cocked her head at Marcus and then indicated the Englishman.

Marcus grumbled something under his breath and passed Mathew a gold coin. The man's eyes lit, and he pocketed it quickly. "Thank you, Your Majesty."

Mathew seemed reluctant to leave. "Again," Marcus said. "If we have need of your assistance, I'll send word."

The man nodded and walked off, leaving them alone once again. Neither Marcus nor Cordelia moved for a moment.

"So…ye are truly Cordy?" he asked, his voice harder than before.

She gave a brief nod. "Most know me as Cordelia at court." Her stomach tightened, waiting for his anger to explode.

He ran a hand through his thick hair and glanced at the sky as if asking for divine intervention before meeting her gaze. The heat that had flooded his gaze minutes before was replaced with suspicion. "What is your family name?"

She breathed in long through her nose. "Cranfield. Cordelia Cranfield."

"And ye're a lady of the queen's bedchamber?" He said it like an accusation.

She crossed her arms over her chest. Yes, she'd lied and deserved some reprimand, but she had been doing her duty to the queen. "I was a lady of the bedchamber until my mother tried to kill the queen. I'm still a lady of court, but…I am not entirely trusted. My family name is…soiled."

His lips tightened. "Your family name," he murmured. His face leaned closer, but this time there was no sign that he might kiss her. "Ye are trusted enough for the queen to give ye her ring, or is it a forgery too?"

She narrowed her eyes. Here was the anger, leaking out in his words despite the kiss. "No, 'tis real. I'm to protect it with my life. I almost feel 'tis some sort of loyalty test."

"Loyalty test," he repeated, his hand going to the back of his neck. The sharpness in his face softened. "As a spy going between Lord Morton and the French, I'm rather familiar with those."

She folded her fingers into a fist, locking the ring firmly on her hand. "Which is why I must go to Haddon Hall to warn the queen that she could walk into Noire's men there. They will entrap her and ship her to France and untold torture." And everyone at court would think she, Cordelia Cranfield, daughter of the traitor, was part of the scheme.

Would the queen think that too, even though she was the one to choose Cordelia to masquerade? Would the court advisors even ask Her Majesty, or just execute Cordelia before the queen was ransomed?

She wet her lips. "What will happen to the queen if she's taken to France?"

Marcus tapped his fist against his forehead as if he were thinking and wished to make his brain work better. "Catherine de' Medici will try to get her to wed a Frenchman of her choosing. Even if the council won't call him king, he will have influence."

"Elizabeth Tudor will not be forced into marrying."

"Then she will likely be executed," Marcus said. "Opening up the throne for Mary Stewart to return England to the Catholic faith."

"No European sovereign has ever been executed," Cordy said with the briskness of a fevered prayer.

"Catherine de' Medici has no problem assassinating anyone."

CORDELIA CROSSED HER arms, warming her hands under her cape. "If Elizabeth dies, I will be held responsible, and the entire country of England will suffer for it."

Marcus rubbed his solid jaw. So far, he hadn't talked about the kiss, and she wouldn't either. Somehow talking about treason felt easier right now.

"Then...we must intercept her at Haddon House," Marcus said.

Cordelia's eyes closed as she exhaled her relief. She opened them to find Marcus staring at her. "Thank you for realizing that too."

Anger tightened his mouth. "My mission, in the name of King James, is to protect the Queen of England." He paused.

She swallowed. "And instead, you've been protecting someone with no royal value at all." She wouldn't say she had no value at all, because to her sister she did. Lucy would be devastated if Cordelia was killed, the same as she would be if something lethal hit Lucy. But in royal eyes, Cordelia was expendable.

Marcus's face was a mask, hiding his emotions except mild anger. "I don't like to be lied to." He took a step closer to her, making her back against the wall once more.

She gave him a dark smirk, tilting her face up to his. "You're a spy, Marcus. You live in lies by choice. Don't be surprised when others lie to you in return."

His arms came up to lean on either side of her head, but he still didn't touch her. At least not physically, but his eyes, his very essence seemed to grip her. "Was the kiss also a lie?" He didn't close the small distance, instead waiting for some indication from her.

She should turn away, push him backward, escape. Tangling with a man who lived on deception was not a good idea. Lucy would surely tell her to run or that she was dangerously foolish when it came to men. Hadn't Cordelia already proved that with Johnathan Whitt, a man who ended up being a traitor, almost dragging her down with him?

But instead of listening to her demands for caution, she set her hands on his shoulders, tugging him closer so that they were mere inches apart. "What do you think, Highlander?"

Her hand slid behind his head, and she pulled him down to her mouth almost roughly. He grabbed her to him, passion mixing with his anger, building the flames even faster than before.

Cordelia's heart thudded with her audacity as sensations ricocheted through her body, making her knees feel weak. But

Marcus held her up, his strength all around her. A familiar ache stretched down from her abdomen to the crux of her legs. 'Twas the same she'd woken to when she'd suffered the carnal dream about him in the cabin. But this time it was real, and she was lost in the tempest of it. And all of it served to wash away the frantic worry swirling in her head, at least for a moment.

Marcus stiffened, his mouth pulling away from hers. The cold air slaked across her damp lips. "Daingead," he murmured.

"Matt said you two were in a hurry," said a voice behind her. "But it looks like you'll be wanting to stay overnight at the inn."

Cordelia turned to see the smithy and his apprentice looking at them next to the horses. The boy had a grin across his young face, and the smith frowned.

Marcus said something in Gaelic under his breath. "We will leave before dawn if the horse is reshod by then?" There was a question in the statement.

The smith nodded. "Phillip here is good with the horses."

"I can do it now, Scot," the boy said. He ran his hand over the side of Lord Oliver's horse. "What's his name?"

To admit not knowing the rich horse's true name would cause suspicion. "Racer," she said.

"Oi, he's a fast one, ain't he?" Phillip said, sliding his hand down the back of the beast's leg to lift the foot. The horse dutifully obliged for the boy to inspect. The boy glanced up at them, a frown pinching his face. "He wasn't shod right. I should check the other hooves too. Who did this? 'Tis poor work."

Marcus walked over to look at the bottom of Racer's hoof. "Some of the nails came out?"

The boy walked around to another hoof, sliding his hand down with a gentle pinch that signaled the horse to raise his foot. Phillip looked at Marcus. "Or there weren't too many nails to begin with."

"How many nails should there be?" Cordelia asked, coming to spy over Marcus's shoulder.

"Five to eight, mistress," the boy said, letting the smith take a look.

The smith *tsked*. "Only two on this one. 'Tis a wonder it didn't fly off."

The boy pulled a tool from the belt slung around his narrow hips and went back to the loose shoe. He tugged and lifted the tool, showing an extracted nail. "And the nails are too short to hold." He looked at Marcus "I'd say the last farrier tried to disable this mount."

"Disable?" Cordelia asked, frowning deeply.

"Aye," Phillip said. "The bay could have lost a shoe when galloping and tripped, falling and throwing the rider." He shook his head. "Shoddy work could kill a man."

Marcus looked at her. "Or a woman," he said.

Or a queen, she thought.

⇶⇷

WHAT THE BLOODY hell was he doing? Queen or masquerading court lady, he certainly didn't need the complication of a liaison, especially on a mission he'd fouled up so terribly. Why hadn't he listened to his gut when it said that Cordy was too young and beautiful to be the English queen?

Because I needed her to be the foking queen. His mother and sister depended on his success, and without another woman in sight who could be the queen, he'd latched onto the closest to it.

"Daingead," he murmured the curse as he walked briskly from the inn where he'd paid for a private bedchamber, leaving Cordy inside. Marcus stopped at the side of the village church to retie his boot lace. It had been perfectly tied, but he needed the chance to glance about. He released his breath as he stood. No Captain Noire.

Marcus continued to the smithy where the master smith was hanging up his tanned smock. The lad covered the banked fire with a stone to keep any embers from floating out to burn the smithy down during the night. He nodded at Marcus when he caught sight of him.

"Racer's shoes are re-nailed, and I cleaned out his hooves."

"Thank ye," Marcus said, handing him several shillings for his work.

The boy pocketed half the fare and held out the other half for the smith to take. The old man nodded at Marcus. "You can keep the horses here for the night." He glanced out at the growing shadows.

Phillip stroked the long white nose of Marcus's horse. "Wolves roam about in the dark, and with the snows, they'll be hungry," he said, worry in his tone. "These fine animals wouldn't survive an attack."

"Appreciated," Marcus said.

"Where be the lady?" Phillip asked. He seemed especially taken with Elspeth.

"The innkeeper lent out a room at the Golden Goose," Marcus said, tipping his head in the direction of the inn. "She's warm and well."

"Like her horse," said Phillip who threw a blanket over Elspeth before turning to do the same for Racer.

Marcus ran a hand down Elspeth's long nose, touching his forehead there before turning to stride back to the inn. The smell of roasting meat, ale, and sweat assailed him as he entered the main room where the musicians from the frost fair were setting up to play in the corner.

Cordy stood talking with Madge at the bar. "We are much obliged, kind lady," Cordy said, a graciousness in her tone that bespoke a royal upbringing. She'd probably had the same schooling as royalty with lessons in diplomacy, secrecy, and grace. No wonder she could easily play the part of the red-haired, fiery-tempered Queen Elizabeth despite her youth and skin so smooth she needed no makeup.

Fool. Marcus huffed and stopped by the bar, ordering an ale.

He thought of his mother and sister living in their comfortable home in Edinburgh. They depended on him since his father had been locked up. Even though he'd been released, no one would employ him.

"I'll have the lads bring the bathing tub up within the hour," Madge said, setting down a tray laden with two bowls of stew and plates of oatcakes. The woman turned to stride into the back where the kitchen sat.

"The horses are ready to ride come morning," Marcus said in greeting.

She nodded, carrying the tray toward a small wooden table near the staircase away from the stage. They both sat in the rickety chairs, Marcus's threatening to topple if he did much more than sit straight on it.

"'Tis best we aren't sleeping outdoors tonight," she said, with a tone of thankfulness. "With the wolves and snow."

He took one of the bowls of stew, blowing on a steaming spoonful before eating it. The spice was nicely balanced with the broth. There were carrots, turnips, and chunks of beef in it.

Cordy glanced around at the small crowd of men, most of them locals looking to spend the evening with a pint and friends. "Won't Captain Noire and his men be staying at the inn?" she asked. "'Tis the only one in town."

He swallowed down more stew before answering. "They were headed out earlier this afternoon."

Her eyes widened. "To Haddon Hall?"

He nodded, exhaling through his nose.

She leaned forward, and he ignored the swell of her creamy skin above the neckline of her bodice. "We must intercept the queen before she and Walsingham reach there," she whispered. Her small hands fisted on the table, showing her determination. At least they had the same mission now.

"We will hide there and intercept them before they are seen and captured," he said. "The estate is large. I've thoroughly scouted it."

Cordy released a breath, straightening, her features softening.

"'Twould be even better if we could stop them on the road so that we don't run the risk of encountering Noire."

"I agree, but 'tis quite possible that with the heavy snowfall, they may not remain on the road. And Walsingham might keep them riding through the vast forest to get to Haddon Hall. To remain hidden. The man is wise enough to know that if he and the queen were set upon by anyone, he might not be enough to defend her. 'Tis odd enough that they went alone."

"He may have employed some of Lord Shrewsbury's guards to accompany them," she whispered, looking around.

"If he has sense," he murmured.

She leaned forward again, resting her breasts on the edge of the table. Bloody hell, the woman had no training in espionage. Every time she leaned closer to whisper, she drew attention, not only making it look like she shared interesting secrets but the lowness of her neckline and beautifully distressed features drew the patrons like a beacon. Some may be lecherous while others may be chivalrous. Either way, she drew attention.

"If any of the guards survived the ambush, they may have ridden to…" Her words faded. "They don't know she went to Chatsworth House. Even Lord Oliver, who loaned me his horse, thought I was the queen." She leaned back in her seat with a huff.

"Eat something," he said and crossed his arms as he met the gazes of at least four too-interested men.

She sighed with exasperation and picked up her spoon. "Such a tangle." She brought the utensil to her lips with graceful ease. The patrons of the Golden Goose had likely never seen a royal eat and preferred to shovel their stew into their gullets.

"Daingead," he murmured.

"What is it?" she asked.

"Bring your stew," he said, standing.

"Where are we going?" she asked, sliding the remaining oatcakes into a square of linen set with the meal on the tray.

"Above before I have to fight off a horde of admirers."

Cordy's eyes opened wider, and she looked out at the men.

Even though the musicians played, most of them followed her with their eyes. "Yes, husband," she said, her voice artificially loud. "Let us retire for the night."

She carried her stew before her, her gaze set on the stairway above. Marcus followed her, turning back at the foot of the wooden steps to scowl at the other men in the tavern room. "And we have bought the private room," he said, in case any of the patrons thought to purchase a night sleeping next to them in a large common bed.

One hand holding his stew, he rested the other on the hilt of his sword, standing there for a long moment, taking in the stares in the room. Turning he followed Cordy up the stairs in the dim light of a sconce. He needed to get her into a room, a room with a lock and a window for escape if need be. *And a bed.* Damn unruly jack.

Despite the kiss outdoors, Marcus wasn't about to jump upon the lass. But it was more than his carnal response to Cordelia Cranfield that drew him. She was beautiful and lushly curved, but it was her courage that claimed his thoughts more than they should. She'd ridden away with brave intent at the ambush and tried to escape from the cabin. Then there was her performance at the frost fair. A timid maid would have hidden somewhere, but not Cordy. She "hid in plain sight" as she called it. Perhaps that would have worked if she was indeed plain, but she was far from it.

Cordy was polished and soft with intriguing brown eyes and brilliant red hair. Where the queen's hair was rumored to be gray and hidden by a wig, Marcus knew that Cordy's was as real as his desire for her. And now he must stay the night with her in a tiny room with a huge bed. If she touched him again, he might explode for want of her, and he couldn't form any attachments. Being a spy, moving in and out of political circles, made the possibility of attachments ludicrous.

"Let me check the room," he murmured at the door, and she stepped aside to let him in first. A fire was started in the hearth where water perched on a sturdy iron spider. A wooden bathing tub sat between the fire and a privacy screen, leaving only a couple feet between it and the bed.

"Hopefully there are no bedbugs," Cordy said, sweeping in behind him. She went directly to the bed, pulling back the woolen blanket. "Thank the Lord, the sheets look fresh."

That's because he'd paid extra for it. Usually, this room was let to four people who had to fend off the bugs that called the sheets home. But Lord Morton wanted to give the English queen excellent accommodations while Marcus brought her back to Canonbie, Scotland.

"Mo chreach," he murmured. He'd completely fouled up this mission. He should leave Cordelia Cranfield immediately and ride toward Chatsworth House in order to intercept the true queen, confusing her with misdirection and taking her northwest to meet up with Morton.

"What is it?" Cordy asked, her tone tight, showing she was on alert. She held one of her boots in a hand, her gaze scanning the shadows. "Is it a rat?"

"Nay," he huffed, busying himself with the fire. "The inn has a number of mousers slinking along the halls," he said. "No vermin."

She set her boot down and sat on the bed to untie the second one. "What is it then?"

He watched her strong, thin fingers loosen the laces down the front of her foot. Marcus could imagine loosening the laces of her bodice. He cleared his throat. "What happened outside the smithy..."

"Oh," she said, sitting straight on the plump tick. The one word didn't hold anger nor any indication of her feelings on the matter. She pulled the pins from her hair, letting the thick braid drop to lay over one shoulder.

He shook his head. "We shouldn't...I mean...I work for Lord Morton and ye work for the Queen of England. Nothing can come of a dalliance between us."

"Very well," she said, her face looking lovely but tighter.

The fire crackled as he added another square of dried peat to it. Behind him was silence. It stretched uncomfortably. Finally, when there was nothing left to do with the fire, he stood.

"Why did ye agree to play the queen?" he asked, turning. "Gold? Loyalty?"

She looked up at him, and he watched the firelight reflect gold over her face. It made the red in her hair shine like twisted steel glowing in the fires of a smithy.

"Freedom," she said. He stared at her for a long time, but she didn't elaborate. She didn't look like a prisoner of the English court, gaunt from being kept at the infamous Tower of London.

"Are ye a political prisoner? A courtier put in The Tower?"

"I might as well be living there, but no. I have accommodations at Whitehall Palace appropriate for my status as the daughter of a baron and lady of Elizabeth's bedchamber. But my mother was a traitor, and everyone expects me to follow suit. My sister, Lucy, was allowed to marry and move to your country. For me to follow her, I was asked to do this last mission for the queen. To prove my loyalty."

He knew the name Cranfield. It had been discussed at the Scottish court with Lord Morton sending another man down to Whitehall around Christmastide with a warning. He crossed his arms, watching her sit primly on the edge of the bed. "Ye could leave for Scotland from here. Escape the queen and your mother's treachery."

She glanced down, her brow furrowing. "If I go north with you, it will be assumed that I was part of the plot to take the queen."

"Even if you were captured and taken against your will?"

If his words worried her, she didn't show it. Did she trust him not to abduct her?

"For what reason?" she asked. "You wouldn't need me once I was discovered as being only a dead baron's daughter. Elizabeth's advisors would have hardly a care whether I lived or died."

Daingead. She'd come to the same conclusion as he.

A soft bark of laughter escaped her wry mouth. "They would likely celebrate their good fortune of being rid of the Cranfield heiress and confiscate our small estate in London." She folded her hands in her lap. "I will not be there to prove I tried to help the queen. My abandonment of my post acting in her stead would be seen as an act of treason." She looked up at him. "So I must continue on this mission even though it is vastly different from the one to which I agreed. Then I can leave England behind with the monies from my estate and more importantly, I will cleanse the Cranfield name."

Cleansing one's family name was something Marcus was very familiar with, or at least the attempt to do so. What amount of proof could he give to Lord Morton to wash away the taint of being his father's son? The tests on Marcus's loyalty seemed endless. If his mother and sister didn't depend on him, Marcus would find a remote isle to live upon with sheep, goats, and a dairy cow for company.

Cordy's gaze shifted to the hearth. "I think the water will be warm enough for bathing." She nodded to two more buckets of cold water sitting beside the tub. The water over the fire was sending up tendrils of steam. "I will bathe quickly so the water is still warm for you," she said.

She would share her bath with him? Of course, not at the same time. There wouldn't be room, and they'd both be naked and slippery and hot.

Marcus swallowed past the dryness in his mouth, wishing for an ale or perhaps a smooth whisky. "I'll wait in the hall and make sure ye aren't disturbed." Remembering the lump of sweet-smelling soap Lord Morton had included with the clothes, Marcus pointed to the satchel. "There's some soap in there."

She offered a slight smile. "Lord Morton thought of everything."

"Only the best for the Queen of England," he said, and her smile faded.

"I'll be quick," she repeated, sliding off the bed to untie her petticoat, letting it drop to the floor leaving a second petticoat over her smock. She began to unlace the bodice, loosening it over her breasts.

Her gaze met his as her fingers continued to work. She didn't ask him to leave. He watched her widen the stays of her bodice until she could raise it up to take over her head. Her breasts jutted outward as she arched her back, her nipples hard against the linen of the smock Lord Morton had provided. The sight went directly to his groin.

Without another word, which might come out like a groan, Marcus left the room, shutting the door behind him. He stood in the dark hallway, leaning against the wall beside the door. He adjusted his jack. The night would be long and uncomfortable at worst. *Or it could be bloody fabulous.*

Chapter Eight

"I do not want a husband who honors me as a queen, if he does not love me as a woman."
Queen Elizabeth I, who never married despite hinting that she would for two decades.

Cordelia stood out of the still-warm water. She'd hurried through the bath, not wanting the water to grow cold before Marcus had a chance to use it. Growing up, she and Lucy took turns sharing a bath, and if they were having a spat, the first girl would lounge in the water until it was cold, something that would keep the spat going. That was until their father made them sit in his study in a forced hug until their glares turned into giggles. If only quarrels and hurts were so easily solved as adults.

Her hair was a heavy, wet mass that she held dripping over the tub while she used the bathing sheet to dry away the chill bumps across her arms and legs. Wrapping the linen sheet around herself, she squeezed as much of the water out of her hair as she could. It smelled of the jasmine soap, and she hoped Marcus wouldn't mind the scent in the bathing water.

She hurried to the door. It looked newly set as if the old one had been kicked in or fallen apart. "Marcus?"

"Aye," he replied through the sturdy pine wood.

Her heart sped at the simple fact that she was nearly naked and about to let the brawniest, most honorable man she knew into her private room so he could get naked too. She took a full breath. "I'm finished bathing, and the water is still warm if you hurry."

She lifted the latch, pulling the door inward. The hall was dark, and music and bawdy laughter filtered up from the tavern below. More chill bumps blossomed on her arms with the slight breeze that came through the crack that she widened.

Marcus stood there looking ruggedly handsome and fierce with the firelight casting him in gold. "Ye…aren't dressed."

She glanced down even though she obviously knew what she was wearing. Frowning, she met his gaze. "If you want to bathe in cold water, by all means stay out there until I'm fully trussed up and under the covers." Maybe his kiss before in the smithy's yard hadn't warmed him like it had her. Actually, *ignited* was more accurate, a scorching fire that still simmered under her skin. She'd been kissed before at court, but even with Johnathan she hadn't felt such immediate heat. And yet Marcus stood there looking anywhere but at her.

Cordelia turned away. "I'll be on the other side of the privacy screen dressing." She tugged it slightly over to block his view of her. She stood still there, her cool palms resting on her flushed cheeks, her elbows squeezed in to hold the towel in place. The door shut, and she heard a bar fall across. At least he'd come inside.

She pivoted and sat on the edge of the bed. Would he sleep on the floor, or did he intend to sleep next to her? What would he do if she attacked him with wild kisses during the night? Cordy wasn't a virgin, and she wasn't a queen. When she reached Scotland, she could pretend to be a widow. A wealthy, amorous widow without a need to remarry. So there was nothing stopping her from giving into the wildfire threatening to blaze up inside her. Nothing except the apparently reluctant Highlander on the other side of the privacy screen.

The heat from the fire was blocked by the screen, and Cordy shivered as she dropped her linen sheet to throw on the fresh smock she found rolled up in the same satchel that held basic toiletries. She'd clean the first one, letting it dry overnight. Sitting back on the bed to squeeze more water from her hair, Cordy glanced at the screen. Her hands froze clenched around her gathered mass.

Marcus's silhouette was clear with the fire behind him. Her mouth went dry as she watched him yank the tunic off over his head. He pulled the tongue of his belt until it was loose, and the subsequent thud of it dropping on the floor almost made her gasp as she watched the heavy plaid wrap slip down off his hips.

Cordelia's cool fingers pressed against her lips as the lines of his shadow became crisp when he walked up close to the screen. Could he see her staring at him? Sense it? Because with the darkness on her side of the screen, he shouldn't be able to see her at all. But Lord, could she see him. Her imagination created the tanned skin over the outlined muscles and wavy hair and clever brown eyes.

Her breath caught in her throat as he turned to the side, and she saw the silhouette of his jutting yard standing straight up against his abdomen. The heat from before, poured down through Cordelia at the evidence that he wasn't disinterested. She shifted where she sat on the bed, her legs clenching against the ache at their crux. Her hand came up to brush against her hardened nipple, making her feel deliciously wicked.

Marcus stepped into the tub, the water sloshing inside with his bulk. "I left the soap there," she said.

"Thank ye, but I have my own. I doubted the queen would want to share." His pleasantly deep voice was like a caress against her, feeding the fever growing inside.

"Of course," she said. What scent did he favor? She inhaled, trying to catch it, but didn't smell anything yet.

The fire behind the tub gave her the perfect view of Marcus's bath. He rubbed the soap over his arms, face, neck, and hair, dipping down into the water to rinse. "I hope I didn't perfume the water too much," she said.

"'Tis well and good."

"And still warm?"

"Aye, a bit. Better than a frigid mountain stream or melted snow."

"Or cold wash water being thrown from a bucket?" she asked.

He snorted. "Aye. Thank ye for sharing. The warm water, not the wash water."

She smiled softly behind the screen, her gaze continuing to follow the rub of the soap as he bent forward to wash each leg. He used his hands to wipe across his back, and she found herself gripping the edge of the mattress when his hands dipped below the water. Was he touching himself? Rubbing along his length? Her lips opened on a shallow breath. What would he do if she walked around the screen?

Cordelia stood but didn't walk forward. Her hand slid down her breasts and stomach, making her skin prickle under the brushed silk smock. "Marcus?" she said, his name making her rub her lips together.

"Aye?" he asked and she saw him turn in the tub.

"Do you mind if…I dry my hair before the fire? I won't look." Heaven judge her as wanton, because she'd certainly been looking from behind the screen.

"Ye should get it dry before sleep," he said. "Come around or move the screen completely. I'm not shy."

She grabbed the light screen, setting it before the closed door. Her gaze flicked over to him, his neck against the back of the wooden tub. Taking the drying sheet, she hurried over to the fire, stirring it first with the iron poker and adding a square of dry peat. The fire crackled as it caught, and the heat from it added to the heat flushing her cheeks. The feet of a small chair scratched against the floor as she slid it over, sitting in it and splaying her wet hair out to catch the radiating heat. Tipping her head forward, she let it slide so the underneath was exposed.

Beside her, she heard Marcus move in the water. "Close your eyes if ye're shocked, but I'm getting out."

Cordelia blinked and lowered her lids. Tilting her head to the side, she continued to work her fingers through the damp snarls. Her eyes edged open. Only enough to catch a glimpse of bronze skin over a muscular back down to the paler skin of his perfectly formed arse.

God's teeth, his form was perfect, like chiseled marble. Sculpted muscles ran from his shoulders, down his broad back which narrowed at his waist and hips. And Lord, his arse! No doubt he trained with weapons and horse, and it showed in every angle of his body. Her gaze slid the rest of the way down his well-shaped thighs and calves.

He turned and she snapped her head toward the fire before he could catch her ogling him. Should she admit her sin? Once again her mouth opened but nothing came out.

"'Tis thick and long," he said.

Cordelia choked on her inhale and coughed. When she turned to him, he had the bathing sheet wrapped around his hips. "What?" she asked, the word coming out like the squeak of a mouse that had been pounced upon by a tiger.

"Your hair. Thick and long. Must take a lot to work the tangles out."

"Oh…yes," she said. "Could you please pass me the comb from the satchel?"

She looked up at him as he handed it to her where she sat before the fire. His gaze lingered, connected with hers, but then he turned away. Cordelia closed her eyes. If only she were braver, she'd tell him that she wanted him, that she was already a ruined woman and didn't need to guard her maidenhood. Instead she ran her fingers through the damp tangles. The comb had widely spaced teeth at one end and fine at the other. She worked the wide side through her hair, catching every few seconds on a knot, but she continued to work, trying to ignore the half-naked, statuesque man behind her.

A prickle climbed her spine as if he watched her. Was it his gaze that washed warmth against her back?

"I can help," he said. She glanced at him, noticing immediately that he was still only in the bathing sheet. It was tucked around his waist to stay up. "If ye give me the comb, I can help get the tangles out."

Without a word, she set the tool in the large palm of his hand. He made a circle motion with his finger. "Turn around. I won't hurt ye."

She swallowed, ignoring how tight her nipples felt jutting against the silk smock. "You know about women's toiletry?"

"I have a sister," he said. He touched her hair, and she closed her eyes at the ripples of sensation that shot through her from a simple touch. "I used to help her comb the snarls out when our mother would have punished Trinity for untying her braids while playing out on the moor."

The image of him playing with a little sister and then helping her right her hair filled Cordelia's heart. "I have a sister too, but we didn't help each other with our hair."

Marcus pulled her hair to one shoulder, exposing her nape. Before she could pull some back, she felt him slide a finger over the scar there. "What is this?" he asked.

The embarrassment cooled some of the heat coursing through Cordelia. "'Twas a spot that was burned when I was a child," she said, matter-of-factly. "'Tis nothing." Really, it wasn't anything compared to the scars her sister, Lucy, had received from their mother's brutal ways.

His finger slid down one side of her neck. "How could ye suffer a burn on the back of your neck?"

She exhaled. "My mother thought I had a witch's mark, so she burned it off. I am lucky it was somewhere easily concealable."

He paused for a long moment. "Does it pain ye?" he asked.

She shook her head, her gaze watching the twisted dance of the flames in the hearth. Cordelia held her breath as his fingers grazed her skin. The sensation sent chill bumps down her arms and chest. Her eyes closed when she felt his breath on her neck, and then his warm lips brushed against it. The touch coursed directly down through her body, making the crux of her legs clench with such an ache that she reached in front of her, pressing against it through her smock.

Marcus's mouth moved to her ear, and she shut her eyes as he kissed her below her ear. "I can't stay away from ye, lass," he whispered, and Cordelia's heart leapt. He dropped the comb in her lap and backed up as if burned. "I will find another place to sleep tonight," he murmured.

"Don't," she whispered, tipping her head. "I am no maiden, Marcus." She turned in the chair to stare up at him where he still stood close. In the small room, there was nowhere to retreat.

Cordelia's heart ticked quickly inside her as her breath came shallowly. The quiet in the room was broken only by the crackle of the fire and the rise and fall of laughter and music below in the tavern. "I would have you stay. With me," Cordelia whispered. She stroked a hand down over one of her breasts and watched him follow with his gaze.

His lips parted as if he wished to taste her. The light from the fire warmed her from behind, but the heat from Marcus's stare scorched her front. She stood, knowing the firelight behind her would light her form from under the silk smock, and turned to him, only the chair separating them.

"We can have no attachment," he said, touching one of her clean, dry curls along her shoulder.

The warning did not worry her. Cordelia's plans involved following her sister, not a spy. "I expect none," she said with a little shake of her head.

"What is it ye want?" he asked. "I don't want to mistake…anything."

At first, she couldn't make the words come. How she wanted him inside her. Instead, she lifted her finger and touched the tip in the middle of his chest. "I want to be right here," she whispered, watching him take in her words and tone. Sometimes the slowest, softest touch could turn stone molten, but he still didn't pull her into his embrace.

"I would not do anything ye don't intend, Cordy lass," he said, catching her finger and kissing the tip that she'd run down his chest.

She wet her lips. "Right now I want you to stop this ache in me." She pulled her hand from his grasp and slid it down her smock to her sex, touching herself through the silk. He watched and slid his own hand under his wrap to grip his rigid length.

"I want you, Marcus," she whispered, "to thrust into me over and over, to flood this fire you've started in me."

Her words made his lips open wider as if a delicious surprise left him famished. The chair toppled as he shoved it out of the way, grabbing her to him. Giddiness fluttered through her as his control seemed to shatter. His mouth found hers already open, and he kissed her. A hot, wild, kiss of abandonment, abandonment of morals and obligations and missions.

Their hands slid up and down each other's bodies. His bare chest had a sprinkling of hair over it, making him even more masculine, if that were possible with the thick cording of muscle underneath his hot skin. Cordelia clung to his shoulders, pressing her breasts against Marcus. She untied the ribbon at the neckline of her smock, letting it part. With a back-and-forth shrug of her shoulders, the silk fell, catching briefly on her breasts before slipping down her naked body to the floor.

"Mo Dhia," Marcus murmured in awe as his gaze followed the path of the silk, resting on her full breasts with rose-hued circles around peaked nipples.

Cordelia pressed against him, letting her nipples be teased by the curls across his chest. His hot length pressed against her stomach, and she realized that he'd dropped his bathing sheet upon her smock in a heap at their bare feet.

He kissed her, and she opened fully under the pressure of his lips. He tasted of something minty with which he must have washed his teeth. No wonder they were white and whole. His large hands stroked sensation down her spine until he reached her arse. He lifted under her, pressing her against his yard, and she couldn't help the moan that broke from her. He rubbed the sensitive nub at the crux of her legs up and down against him, stoking the fire that was already burning brightly through her. She felt awash in heat.

She reached around to find him long, thick, and hard as granite. It made her shiver, and he kissed over to her ear, letting her suck in shallow breaths. "I won't enter ye if ye worry."

She shook her head and pulled back to reach his gaze with her own. "I said I'm no maid, Marcus."

"That doesn't give me any admittance to your body, lass." He caught her cheek in his palm. "'Tis your choice. We can do other things that bring ye pleasure."

She blinked, his words pressing on her heart, and moved her lips together. "Oh, I want to do all those things." She leaned up on her toes to his ear, pulling him down slightly. "But I also want you to ride me hard, Highlander."

She met his gaze and smiled at the slackness of his jaw even though her cheeks flushed. "And if that's not clear enough," she said, "I'm not letting you leave this room without you first entering this very willing body. Fully." She touched his bottom lip with her fingertip.

A grin turned up his mouth with just the right amount of luridness to make her insides tremble with anticipation.

"Aye then, lass," he said with a slow nod. "I can see to that."

Before she could fully smile, his lips descended back to her lips, his fingers stroking up and down her spine. She clutched behind his neck, stretching against him fully. His fingers dipped down her arse to touch between her legs from behind, and she spread her stance as best she could on tiptoe to accommodate him.

"Och, but ye are soaked," he murmured against her lips, and then his fingers entered her, making her gasp in swoony pleasure. His mouth dipped down to her breast, pulling her nipple into his mouth and sucking. A line of pleasure seemed to tether her core to her nipple, pulling taut as he played her, first from behind and then from the front. His fingers were magic, working inside and against her outer nub. Each stroke and tease pushed her higher and higher toward something that seemed just out of reach.

Suddenly her toes lifted off the floor, and he carried her, setting her on the bed. She took a moment to look at him, framed by the firelight from behind. A godlike form of muscle stretched from shoulder down his chest and legs. "Heigh, my heart," she murmured, her gaze sliding back up to reach his face. "I may burn to ash merely looking at you."

He climbed slowly over her to lay on one side. His hand flattened on her collarbone. "Watch me looking at ye, lass, tasting ye."

Her breath caught as she followed his instruction and watched his gaze fall over her breasts. His hand followed, cupping each one while gently pinching the nipple. Her legs moved restlessly against his shins as his mouth followed, his tongue circling each peak.

"Oh god," she whispered as his hand slid down over her stomach and abdomen, his mouth following in a hot trail of kisses. He deviated to the side to stroke her hips, stopping on the bones, grasping them. On their own accord, as if her hips were some magic lever, her legs widened, leaving her even more exposed. She clenched with wet heat as she watched him fully view her sex, touching her there, parting her there. Her eyes grew wide as his mouth descended on her, and she gasped.

Watching him love her with his mouth and feeling his teasing touch was the most erotic thing Cordelia had ever seen or even imagined. His dark head moved between her legs, and she moaned out her pleasure. The pressure grew until she threw back her head on the mattress, her hands fisting the blanket at her sides. Waves of pleasure swamped her, making her bones feel like they were turning to molten liquid.

Marcus slid up her clenching body, moving over her. Her legs opened wide as she felt the head of his yard press against her throbbing core. "Ye're sure," he asked through gritted teeth.

"Oh god, yes, Marcus."

It was all he needed, and he thrust into her open body. She gasped at the fullness as he plunged deeply, and he answered with a groan of his own. He pulled back and thrust again and again. "Yes," she crooned, trying to keep her voice lowered else the whole inn hear her. "Oh my god, yes."

Their rhythm built hard and fast. Her nails raked across his back as she clung to him. The sound of their gusty breathing, the slide of their skin against each other, the sounds of pleasure escaping their parted lips…The hot waves of rapture swamped her, ridding her of all reason. She knew only one thing. She must have all of him, all of Marcus Blythe.

"Mo Dhia, Cordy," he breathed in her ear as if he too tried to contain his yell. "Good bloody hell." He thrust over and over inside her, and she felt him slide higher on her body so that he rubbed against the sensitive spot with each thrust. It was enough to throw her over the edge of reason, and she moaned loudly. He captured her mouth with his, swallowing her yell. She felt his muscles clench, his chiseled body tensing as he released into her still throbbing body.

For long moments they rode the waves together as they slowly floated back to reality. Neither of them spoke for long minutes. He held her, and her legs lay tangled with his. She breathed in their combined smell, mint and jasmine mixed together with their heat. Wrapped in his arms, warm and hidden away together in the darkness, Cordelia wished to stay there forever.

CHAPTER NINE

Descriptions of Queen Elizabeth I
"Her face is comely rather than handsome, but she is tall and well-formed, with good skin, though swarthy; she has fine eyes."
Venetian Ambassador, Giovanni Michiele, 1557

"…her face oblong, fair, but wrinkled, her eyes small, yet black and pleasant; her nose a little hooked, her lips narrow and her teeth black; her hair was of an auburn color, but false; upon her head she had a small crown. Her bosom was uncovered, as all the English ladies have it till they marry. Her hands were slender, her fingers rather long, and her stature neither tall nor low; her air was stately, and her manner of speaking mild and obliging."
Paul Hentzner, German visitor to Greenwich Palace, 1598

MARCUS LOOKED DOWN at the naked nymph stretching in the bed. *Bloody hell.* All he wanted to do was fall back amongst the sheets that smelled of their tupping and take her again before dawn flooded the world with responsibility and harsh reality. He closed his eyes. *Duty comes first.* The picture of Cordy lying there was replaced behind his eyelids with the faces of his sister, mother, and despondent father. Aye, he must finish his mission. He rubbed the back of his neck at the tension there.

"Is something wrong?" Cordy asked, pushing up on one elbow. Cast in gold by the fire he'd rekindled, she was a glorious siren, barely hidden by the sheets, the curve of her hip obvious under the quilt, one full breast swelling out the top.

"We should leave," he said, continuing to strap on his belt despite his jack rising against his heavy wool wrap.

Cordy held the sheet to her breasts and sat up, looking toward the dark window. "'Tis still night."

"Dawn will be up before long, and we have a full day's ride to reach Haddon Hall. The few hunting shacks I know on the route are closer to this end of the journey with nothing close to Haddon Hall. So we must get there before dark to avoid the danger of wolves."

She swung her long, shapely legs off the edge of the bed. "If we must." She looked as forlorn to leave their nest as he did. They hadn't had time to explore each other or pleasure each other more than the first time before she had fallen asleep.

"I could push ye up into a tree if we were tracked by a pack, climbing after ye, but Elspeth and Racer would be left to the wolves," he said, more to convince himself than Cordy that he mustn't yank his belt open and push her back down in the warm bed. They must reach shelter before that night, and a delayed start, no matter how delicious it would be, would make that impossible.

She nodded. "Of course," she said, and stood, using the sheet as a robe.

He came closer, his hands taking hold of her upper arms, and he whispered, "I would rather remain in that bed with ye if I could."

Her lips turned upward in a smile that warmed him. "I would too."

He pulled back, the cold in the room cooling his blood. "I'll use the public privy down the hall and meet ye below."

They both stared at each other for a moment, as if they were trying to fight against the pull of the warm sheets and the promise of pleasure. *Daingead*. Where was his discipline? *You damn idiot.* All he could think about was the way her skin felt soft and warm against his. Her smile disappeared, replaced with a questioning frown.

Without a word, he nodded, turned to the door, and walked out into the dark, cold corridor. He released a muted sigh. When he'd thought that his mission couldn't possibly go more wrong or be more complicated, he'd gone ahead and had the most amazing tupping experience of his life. "Bloody foking hell," he whispered and walked silently down the hall to find the privy.

Some said that King James's exiled and imprisoned mother, Mary Stewart, was a witch who could bespell people, wrapping them in her siren's song. Marcus had always thought that was a pile of *cac* but now he wondered if Cordelia Cranfield didn't possess some such power.

Marcus washed, dressed, and headed below to the quiet, cold tavern. Dawn hadn't yet broken, and the room was only lit by the remaining coals from the fire. He splayed his hands before them.

"I am ready," Cordy whispered, coming down the stairs. She was dressed in the woolen gown that hugged her curves in the most tantalizing way. She carried her cape and the satchel that held the basic toiletries he'd brought for her. Well, not her, but Elizabeth.

The reminder made his teeth clench. "I have food and ale. Let's retrieve the horses and head out."

"Will the sun rise soon?" she asked, setting the satchel down to throw her heavy cape on over her shoulders.

He glanced at the still dark window. He hoped it would. Perhaps it was earlier than he'd thought. "Aye," he said with confidence. "Come along." He turned, barely waiting for her as they stepped out into the cold gloom.

"The horses are inside the smithy," he said. "Phillip sleeps there with a firearm to keep horse thieves away."

"And wolves," she said.

"Wolves don't rampage through towns. Too many people

and too much fire."

He led her across the still sleepy square. No one yet moved about, but the horizon looked dark blue instead of black. Dawn was coming. Slowly.

"Phillip," Marcus called outside the smithy. "'Tis Marcus Blythe come to claim our horses."

The blurry-eyed lad opened the latch, letting them inside the warm, closed-up smithy. A heavy pistol was wedged under one armpit. With the horses and the smithy fires banked to keep embers lit, he had a cozy warm place to sleep. "Oh," Phillip said. He set his gun down immediately. "I didn't know Your Majesty was with you. I'd never have held a gun in your presence, Your Highness." The lad babbled, nearly falling over a stack of peat squares for burning. Apparently Mathew had informed Phillip of Cordy's false identity. Would the lad or the smith tell others about the queen kissing a common Scot?

Marcus tossed the boy a gold coin. "Make sure ye and your master keep silent about the queen's visit, every bit of it." He met Phillip's gaze, and the lad nodded, looking quite serious. "Any information given out would be treason," Marcus added.

The lad nodded vigorously. "I'll say naught about anything," Phillip said.

Marcus nodded, satisfied, and walked to the horses where Cordy was already stroking Racer's long neck. Both beasts looked alert, feeling dawn coming soon. He checked Racer's hooves.

"They be all in place, hammered on good," Phillip said with pride in his voice. He offered Racer an apple and then went over to Elspeth to do the same. "Strong steeds, these two," he said.

Cordy smiled at the boy. "And not a peep about my visit, Master Phillip," she added, apparently not hearing Marcus on the other side of the smithy.

Phillip looked solemn. "They could rack me, Your Majesty, and I wouldn't tell them you were here."

"Heavens," Cordy said, the gentle curse sounding elegant. "Let us hope it doesn't come to that." She came closer. "In fact, if it comes down to torture or losing your life, you have my permission to say I was here before heading home to Whitehall."

Phillip nodded and bowed with his front knee bending so much that he skimmed the hay-strewn floor.

"The horses are ready," Marcus said, feeling a wee bit of irritation. Cordy certainly played the queen well. She was a very convincing actress, an actress who had fooled him, someone who was a professional liar. His jaw tightened, anger at his hypocrisy. He had no right to be cross with her because he'd allowed himself to be thoroughly tricked. Being a spy between Scotland and France meant Marcus lied all the time. He still hadn't told Cordy about his true mission.

The orneriness within him grew. It was dark and cold, with a fierce breeze that blew through layers. And now, instead of riding to Canonbie with the queen, he was riding to Haddon Hall where the enemy waited. All the while, he'd rather be tucked in bed with a blood-heating siren.

He led the horses toward the double doors that would be swung open for the rest of the day once the smith arrived at work. Weaving his fingers together for Cordy's foot, Marcus helped lift her onto Racer's back. Without thought, he slid his hand along the curve of her calf, but then yanked his hand away. Turning he released his breath that Phillip had been occupied and missed the telling sign of their intimacy.

As he walked around front of Racer to open the doors, Marcus could feel Cordy's stare on his back. What was she thinking? He barely knew what he thought. He was a fool to let himself get tangled up with a complicated Englishwoman or any woman while he was on a mission. But Lord knew, if given the chance, he'd do it again. And again. And again.

Mo chreach. He ran a hand down his face as he led Racer out of the barn. He clicked his tongue to get Elspeth to follow. The warm feeling of Cordy's gaze remained as he mounted, and he looked back at her in the shadows. She was wrapped up in her warm woolen cape that engulfed her, hiding her from curious eyes. Cordy's smooth face peered out from the depths of the hood, whisps of her red hair breaking the boundary to move across her cheek before her long fingers captured them to tuck inside. She stared at him like he'd known she did. Questions sat in her golden-brown eyes.

"If we leave now, we will reach safety by nightfall," he said, as if reminding both of them why they weren't tumbling together in a warm bed right then. Lord, he must try to put some distance between them, or he'd lose all discipline. And too much depended on him keeping his head.

She nodded regally without any outward emotion, and they began to ride along the snowy path that led out of town. Dawn battled against the heavy clouds, so darkness lingered under the trees, making it seem as if night was still ruling the world. Marcus pulled back until they rode side by side, the horses' hooves crunching on the snow that had iced over during the night. He broke into a trot on the straight paths, and Cordy followed. They'd traveled nearly an hour and darkness still clung under the clouds that released snowflakes. They glided down between the naked limbs of the winter trees like leaves in the autumn.

Marcus pulled Elspeth to a walk, and Cordy slowed next to him. "You are angry," she said.

Well hell. Aye, he was angry, but he didn't want her to notice.

She continued before he could say anything. "But I can't figure out if you're more angry that I am not Queen Elizabeth or that I seduced you last night. Or perhaps you wish your mission was complete and you were truly headed home. Or perhaps you're just an ornery bastard who is stupid enough not to know you should speak more than a few words to a woman after laying with her. Maybe even kiss her. Or maybe—"

"I am a fool," he said, interrupting her. He glanced at her, but she stared straight ahead over her horse's twitching ears. Could Racer feel the tension between them?

Marcus released a full breath through his nose. "I am a fool because all I want to do is forget about my bloody mission and carry ye back to that inn or any other safe, warm nest to kiss every inch of your delicious body, Cordy."

Her face snapped to him, lips pursed. She swallowed. "So you are punishing me." Although her words were terse, there was a softening in her eyes.

"Nay...I know not." He huffed. "Cordy, my mission... There are consequences for more than me if I fail at bringing Elizabeth up to Scotland."

"Up to Scotland?"

Foking hell, he hadn't meant to tell her that. What had happened to him in her arms? He'd once been a hardened spy, easily playing any part, and keeping secrets to the grave. He'd slept with women before who'd tried to pry secrets from him, but he'd revealed nothing. And yet this cunning Englishwoman had done just that by showing her ire.

He looked back out over Elspeth's ears, which had also started twitching. She raised her head, sniffing at the air.

"My sister and my mother live outside Edinburgh with my father, who can earn no monies after his involvement with Mary Stewart. My missions support them, so my sister doesn't have to toil outside the home. 'Tis a responsibility I took on when my father was arrested five years ago. Once I started working for Lord Morton, and doing well at this bloody game of secrets, he made it clear I must continue or lose all support for my family." And perhaps his own life.

"Your mission was to take the queen up to Scotland?" Cordy asked, some of the sting out of her tone. "For what reason?"

Flaming ballocks. He might as well tell her now. It was unlikely he'd be able to carry the true queen north without her figuring it out and fighting against him. Then Lord Morton would have to charge him with mishandling a queen and take his land and his head. Either way, he'd failed the moment he'd saved the wrong woman.

"Only across the border at Canonbie. Lord Morton wishes

her to know that King James and his advisors have her best interest in the forefront of their thoughts and plans. So King James would have sent his best spy and warrior down to thwart the French in taking her. I would ride her to safety across the Scottish border where Lord Morton, in the name of King James, could then surround her with an army to escort her back to London."

"She would be ever so thankful and name James her heir," Cordy said, her voice soft as if she spoke only to herself. She looked over at Marcus through the dim light the trees and clouds barely allowed. "This is the scheme of a regent, not the young king."

"Aye, although James has probably been convinced of it working."

Cordy shook her head. "My queen will not name an heir until her last breath. If she did so before then, those who are disgruntled with her rule would rally around the heir, threatening to push Elizabeth out before her time."

"She has the strongest rule of woman or man," Marcus said, although he agreed.

"One person can never make every citizen happy." She huffed, looking forward again. "So you were sent to abduct the queen, not save her from the French."

Elspeth nickered, tossing her head, which stopped the denial on Marcus's lips, a denial that would be useless against Cordy's perspective. Racer answered Elspeth, his ears flicking and nostrils raising to the breeze.

"There's a hunting cottage along this road to the east," he said, pointing ahead. "We must ride there now."

"First answer—"

"*Siuthad!*" he yelled as the forms appeared alongside them. *Daingead!* On both sides. "Wolves!" His heels pushed into Elspeth's flanks, and she shot off like a bullet in the dark. They'd departed the safety of the village too early with the clouds obscuring the rising sun. *Shite!* With the heavy snows, the wolves would be ravenous and not willing to crawl back into their dens with empty bellies.

"Ride, Cordy!" He glanced back at her where she leaned over Racer's neck. Her hood had blown back, letting her hair flow behind as she followed him. The shadows masked her face, but he saw large eyes to match those of the horse who carried her. Marcus had trained Elspeth to survive battle. She was brave, nimble, and fast. Racer had bulk, slowing him down. The wolves would focus on him.

Marcus slowed so that he raced beside Cordy. "We make for the cottage," he yelled. "Follow me if I race ahead."

She didn't speak, concentrating on keeping her seat on the fleeing horse. The wolves revealed themselves, trying to get ahead to cut them off, but the horses were faster with fear making them fly, snow and pebbles kicking up behind them. Some beasts barked behind while others kept even with them. One snapped at Racer's leg, making the horse screech. Marcus slowed Elspeth enough that Racer got in front to switch sides by pushing forward again. The wolf snarled, but Elspeth's lethal hooves nearly trampled him until he scooted off the side of the road into a drift of snow.

"There!" Marcus yelled to Cordy. "Follow me." Giving Elspeth her head, the mare surged ahead of Racer. "Don't stop," he called back and diverted around the bend, leading them toward the hunting lodge. He could make out the dark shape in the distance with the muted sunrise.

There was no time to explain his plan, what must be done to beat the pack of at least eight wolves. Marcus bent low, heading straight for the wooden door on the low porch. Hopefully no one was inside, locking it.

"Marcus!" Cordy's yell from behind caught at his gut, but he was almost to the door. Just before it, he yanked back on Elspeth's reins, making the horse stop short like they did in training. Instead of Trinity's apple for a reward, the horse hopefully got to live.

Marcus leaped down from the saddle, hitting the door at the same time he pressed the latch. The door swung inward.

Elspeth knew an escape without him leading her inside. As soon as she was in, he looked out to see Cordy and Racer headed his way. The wolves wove together, running after them. They were only about ten feet behind their prey.

Marcus waved his arm to the open door. Cordy's eyes were huge, her face tense with a mix of fear and determination. He would have to time this right. Thundering hooves flew through the snow-heavy yard. The height of the drifts slowed the shorter wolves, while Racer's feet churned right through the snow. Marcus stood inside the door, his face snapping between it and Elspeth who was luckily standing to the side.

Racer leaped up the porch, barely low enough to barge through the cottage door. Cordy screamed as she ducked low, flattening along Racer's neck, so as not to be plucked out of her seat by the lintel. Marcus slammed the door shut, throwing the thick bar over the holders on either side and added his own weight against it.

Bodies hit the door on the outside, and yelps cut through the thickness of the oak. Barking and frustrated snapping sounded, but the door and walls of the cottage were sturdy. Marcus turned to the room, his arms outright, blood surging.

Cordy still lay over Racer's neck. Elspeth watched from before the cold hearth. Windows were cut up high in the walls, but the glass had been removed. Only leather skins were stretched over them, with a couple open to the wind. The growing daylight showed Cordy breathing hard, her back and shoulders rising where she draped over the heaving horse.

"Cordy, lass." Marcus left the door, going to her. He touched her leg and felt the tremors. "Look at me."

She kept her face turned away. Her hands were still gripping the reins so hard that they looked bloodless. They were cold as he pried them away from the leather leads. "Come down now. Ye're safe in here. We all are." He reached up and pulled her toward him. She didn't resist, but she didn't help. She was like a blanket being dragged off Racer. The horse shook his head and mane.

Her boots hit the floor, but Marcus didn't dare release her. She shook in his arms. "Ye're safe," he whispered. "We won't go out until 'tis bright and we have a torch with us." He heard her sniff and wondered where he'd stuffed his handkerchief.

His heart hurt for her, the fear that made one unable to function. He'd seen it in his mother when his father was dragged away by castle guards.

Marcus ducked his face to look into hers. Tears stained her cheeks. "Cordy?"

"I thought…I thought you might have decided to leave me, leave us."

Anger shot inside him like a pistol being fired, but he pulled her into his arms, hugging her to him, absorbing her tremors. "Has that happened to ye before, Cordy?" he asked. "Someone leaving ye in danger to save themselves?"

A small sob escaped her, and he knew his guess was near the mark.

He tipped her chin up so that she met his gaze. Her beautiful dark eyes glistened with tears. "I would never…" He leaned in closer so that mere inches separated them. "Absolutely never, Cordelia Cranfield, I would never leave ye to fight danger by yerself. There was no time to explain that I had to get the cottage door open before ye reached it so ye could run inside."

She swallowed, staring up at him.

"Do ye understand?" He shook his head slightly. "I will not leave ye to the wolves." His words held the tone of an oath, because he meant every one of them. "Trust me that I will never let harm come to ye as long as I breathe."

"I am not your mission nor a queen," she whispered.

His mouth hardened. "And I am not some bloody bastard who would leave someone to fight wolves to save himself." His words were terse, but he didn't let go of her because that would be abandonment as well.

She kept his gaze, holding onto him. "There are quite a lot of those bloody bastards at court."

He exhaled long, pulling her against his chest, and rested his chin on the top of her head. "Sounds like the English court is very like the Scottish and French courts. I've met a few of them myself, but I'm not one of them."

Slowly her arms slid around his middle, hugging him back. They stood in the quiet of their breathing, and Cordy's shaking subsided. He widened his arms as she pulled back, but she didn't step away. Instead, her hand slid up to the back of his head, and she pulled him down to her lips.

Any resistance melted with the first touch. With a low groan, as if a vaulted door was opened and the air escaped, Marcus wrapped his arms back around Cordy. Their kiss wasn't frantic like last night, although it seemed it could tip that way quickly. Instead it was slower, as if they both needed the joining to remind them that they'd survived and were indeed alive.

Cordy sighed against his lips, her hand raising to his stubbed jaw. She pulled away. "We shouldn't. The mission…"

He inhaled and nodded, loosening his hold on her. "We must focus on the mission."

"Which is?" she asked, and he felt her withdrawing even though she didn't move.

"To save your queen from the French." And then he'd still take Elizabeth to journey to the small border town.

As if she'd seen the thoughts behind his eyes, she stepped back, dropping her arms from him. He felt the absence like the embrace of icy wind. "I don't hear the wolves outside," she said and walked toward the door. It gave him time to inhale and adjust his jack before turning. *Shite, shite, foking shite.* If he'd only met Cordy before this damn mission.

"Could the beasts be out there waiting for us to open the door?" she whispered.

"Let's give them time to fully retreat or catch the scent of some other prey," he said.

She nodded, her eyes blinking and too wide. Fear. At least her fear of wolves was one he could battle. Battling worry about losing one's home and starving through the rest of the winter was different, and the only way he could beat that back from his mother and sister was to keep Lord Morton happy.

But he was without the English queen and unlikely to trick her into traveling northwest after this plot to capture her. After this failure, suspicions from Captain Noire would also make it impossible to take his mother and sister safely to France. He exhaled over Cordy's head. He could save Cordelia Cranfield from the wolves of the forest but not his own family from the wolves of court.

Chapter Ten

"Following the highly influential writings of the ancient Greeks Hippocrates and Galen, physicians believed too little sex could be bad for your health, and even endanger those around you. According to them, both sexes produced 'seed', the means by which new life was created, and good health required maintaining a balance of this in the body... For women, "retention of seed" could lead to convulsions, fainting spells, breathing difficulty and even madness."

The Tudor Sex Guide; History Extra

Cordy kept her gaze scanning the winterberry bushes that flanked the snow-covered road north toward Haddon Hall, but she hadn't seen any more wolf tracks after leaving the hunting lodge. The tracks showed the wolves circling the cabin before running back the way they'd traveled from the south.

When Marcus had sprung ahead, leaving her behind, panic had prickled within her even though he'd said to follow. Johnathan Whitt had acted the lover until he'd dragged Cordelia into the Ridolfi Plot against Queen Elizabeth. He'd ordered her to spy and report and help lay a trap for the queen despite Cordelia's resistance and fear.

Marcus isn't Johnathan.

Cordelia glanced at the Highlander riding next to her. *I am a fool because all I want to do is forget about my bloody mission and carry ye back to that inn or any other safe, warm nest to kiss every inch of your delicious body.* She remembered each of his wonderful words from before the wolves.

The man had made her feel things she hadn't known existed. She was no maid, but Johnathan's loving had been fast. Now that she knew the pleasure that could be had, Cordelia realized that Johnathan had been lacking. Was that type of wild tupping what Lucy and their friend, Maggie, had been basking in with their Highlander husbands? Jealousy tightened in Cordelia's belly. Had it just been that one magic night with Marcus, or would another session be as thrilling? Would she ever find out?

Cordelia watched Marcus as he studied the road for tracks, frowning over the hoof prints made by passersby the day before, probably Noire and his men. And then there was Marcus who wanted to steal the queen away to Scotland. If Cordelia helped him, wouldn't that be treason, something she was desperate to expunge from the Cranfield name? But he was saving the queen from the French. Lord Morton wanted the queen to be grateful.

Cordelia cleared her throat. "If you save the queen from the de' Medicis' plan, she will be grateful to Lord Morton for sending you south and infiltrating Captain Noire and his men. You don't have to take her to Canonbie, Scotland. In fact, she will probably despise the Scottish more if you force her north."

"It was not to look forced, Cordy."

"Unless the French are chasing you north, it will look forced," she said.

They rode in silence for a bit before she spoke again. "You will have to abandon that plan, or do you intend to continue this farce by helping Captain Noire?" Just her knowing about it made her an accomplice, unless she confessed the plan to the queen when they intercepted her.

"I have not had ample time to decide how I shall act, but for now we will stay hidden from Noire and intercept the queen before they can capture her."

Did she believe him? She sighed. "You say you have a mother

and sister who depend upon you," she said, listening to the crunch of the horse hooves on the frozen ground.

"Aye." His face looked shuttered. "They have no income without me, because my father is not trusted to work in Edinburgh. He has no other source of monies, so I provide it. Without the favor of Lord Morton and King James I have no source either."

"You could take your family to England. London perhaps."

He snorted, his handsome face tipping toward the sky. "My mother is even more against England than me. She will not move away from her home. She's a stubborn woman."

Like mother, like son.

Snow dropped in clumps from the trees as the sun warmed the day. "Marcus," Cordelia said, breaking the silence that was stretching, "only my sister calls me Cordy."

He looked at her, his eyes not as dark. "Ye don't look like a Cordelia dressed in comfortable wool and bonny plaid with your hair down." His smile was genuine, and she felt her spirit lighten from the truth in it.

"Cordy," she repeated. "Perhaps that is who I am without all the royal trappings."

He snorted. "Trappings is right. If I could, I would live away from Edinburgh."

Cordelia smiled, remembering her sister's last letter. Lucy and Greer had just arrived at their own cottage in Culross, moving apart from Greer's mother. They had bought a baby goat, and Lucy was in love with it. She'd sounded so joyful about the animals they would soon add to the dogs and two roosters she and her three adopted children had brought with them from London. "I would have a goat," Cordelia said. "My sister has a baby one, and she's knitting it a jacket to keep it warm during the winter months."

Marcus stared at her. "A jacket? For a goat?"

"A baby goat. I believe they call it a kid." A small clump of snow fell on Racer's head, making him twitch his ears. "Horses have saddle blankets. Little goats need to be warm too but they're more active. Lucy says her little one hops around."

"So ye want a cottage with a goat. In a jacket." His voice was full of laughter. "Anything else? A cow with breeches perhaps?"

Cordelia snorted. "A gaggle of chickens for eggs and the cocks for meat." She nodded. "I would like that."

"'Tis called a flock of chickens," he answered, "not a gaggle. And I don't think jackets would work well over their wings."

Cordelia grabbed some snow off a low branch and threw it at Marcus. He dodged it, but his head brushed another branch, which delivered a freezing shower of wet snow. Cordelia swallowed her loud laughter as much as she could to keep her voice from carrying in the empty forest.

"That is what you get for making my dreams out to be jests," she said, her smile wide.

"Dreams?" he said, meeting her smile. "Ye dream of goats in jackets and chickens?"

"And other things," she said, looking forward over Racer's ears. "A horse of my own. Children one day. Love." The last trailed off, and silence again claimed the space between them.

Marcus cleared his throat. "The children will probably appreciate the knitted jackets more than the goat."

A laugh burst from Cordelia, and she met his gaze. "Marcus Blythe, you are a jester at heart."

He kept his smile, but some of the happiness left his gaze, and he looked forward again.

They rode on throughout the morning and into the late afternoon, stopping only to water the horses and refill their own flasks at a stream where snow curved over the banks, falling in easily. They even ate their provisions while in the saddle. Cordelia wouldn't complain at the pain in her arse and back. She shivered over the thought of wolves rather than from cold. In the winter night came too early.

"Is it much farther?" she asked, watching her breath puff out before her. "I worry over us finding shelter for the night."

"We lost the time I gained by leaving early to the damn wolves holding us captive," he said. "But it shouldn't be long before we come up to the stone chapel archway, and then the hall is but another short ride."

"You've visited Haddon Hall already?"

"Before meeting Noire, I scouted the place." Marcus pointed. "There."

Cordelia saw a stone structure ahead through the thin trees that crisscrossed upward like spears stuck in the white snow. The horses, sensing an end to their journey stepped briskly around the copse, weaving between the older oaks and birches.

Marcus halted them before a paired set of arches covered in the brilliant crystalline white. They led down a short flight of steps into a sunken chapel, but most of the slate roof was missing. Weather had free rein within the remaining weather-beaten stone walls. The decorative colored glass, which had probably added a holy beauty, was missing, leaving empty arched windows. But the whole structure was eerily lovely as nature overtook it, freezing it in white and darkening shadows like an ancient, lost religion.

"'Tis completely open to the elements," Cordelia said.

"There's a small closet inside that still has a roof, but otherwise 'tis a ruin," Marcus said.

"A beautiful ruin," Cordelia whispered, feeling the reverence of the place.

Marcus guided his horse around the outside of the chapel to continue past, and Cordelia followed. They clopped over a bridge that spanned a narrow river, and a gray stone castle loomed ahead.

"Haddon Hall," Marcus said, his words soft. He scanned the landscape, but there was no movement outdoors on that side of the building.

"'Tis massive," Cordelia said. "More like a castle than a hall or manor house."

"Quite comfortable for a queen." Marcus glanced at her before continuing to watch the open areas around the castle. "We must keep ye hidden. They may recognize ye from the village."

"What about you?"

He rubbed his jaw. "I've been thinking that I should meet with Noire, keep up the pretense of helping him so I can learn what he knows of the queen's whereabouts."

Cordelia huffed. "After the failed abduction, wouldn't they go back to France?" She indicated the hall. "Maybe they're not even here."

Marcus shook his head. His quiet confidence was both admirable and vexing. "Catherine de' Medici reacts to failed missions with deadly vengeance, and Noire knows that. He won't leave these shores without the queen."

"Then he must die," Cordelia said, winning a look from Marcus.

His mouth crooked up at the corner. "Bloodthirsty. I like it."

She snorted softly but couldn't help but grin in return. She'd never been called bloodthirsty before. Away from court, a whole new Cordelia was emerging. Wanton and bloodthirsty and known as Cordy.

He looked back at Haddon Hall. "Let's get ye inside before night falls."

"How?" Would he roll her up in a tapestry or find a barrow to carry her inside like a load of turnips?

He tipped his head as if judging her attributes. "How are ye at baking bread and churning butter?"

⇶⇷

MARCUS DISMOUNTED BEHIND a hedge of holly bramble near the rear of Haddon Hall and helped Cordy down. His hands lingered around her waist under her cape. The warmth emanating from her filled his inhale with jasmine. She didn't seem eager to pull away either. The fire between them rekindled easily despite their contrary missions.

They both wanted to protect Queen Elizabeth, but Cordy wanted to ferry the royal back to London while Marcus must bring the queen north to meet Lord Morton. The man had rallied a battalion to wait in Canonbie at Gilnockie Tower. The divergence between their missions drove a wedge between Cordy and him. *Which suits me.* Maybe if he told himself that lie over and over it would become true.

Just outside the walled in gardens was a set of stables and a hen house. Without a word, he tugged Cordy's hand for her to follow him across the short space. He frowned at the crunch of their boots but there was no help for it. Circling behind the stables, he nodded toward the hen house. Eggs would need to be collected. Perhaps there was a basket inside to add to Cordy's disguise.

They stepped inside, and Marcus shut the door. The smell of chickens, cac, and corn feed made a sneeze well up quickly. He turned his face down, his hand over his nose and mouth to sneeze.

Someone inside the dark hen house gasped.

"All is well," Cordy said, her hand held out to a slight woman who'd straightened from the laying boxes. She held a basket over one arm. "We are good English souls," Cordy assured her.

"He ain't." The maid pointed at the wrap around Marcus's hips that showed a few inches of the furs he wrapped around his legs above his boots.

"I am one of Queen Elizabeth's ladies come to warn her about the French here," Cordy said, leaving Marcus out of it. "They are here, aren't they?"

The maid nodded, her face bobbing like one of the chickens pecking at the scattered feed around their feet. "They forced their way in and brought in those lucky souls who survived the ambush on the way here." Her face was tight, her pouty bottom lip quivering. "We don't rightly know where the queen is or even if she be alive."

Cordy moved closer to the girl. "What is your name? I am

Cordelia."

The maid sniffed. "Amanda, milady."

"Amanda, the queen wasn't even part of the ambush." She reached out and squeezed the lass's hand. "But we think she is headed here unaware that the French are inside."

Relief turned to wide eyes set in Amanda's thin face. "What can we do? The French captain is a cruel man."

"What's he done?" Marcus asked.

The maid looked at him. "He's been making the ladies sit with him and his men and wait upon them."

Cordy's hand went to her throat. "Have they…taken liberties?"

"With their eyes, they have," Amanda said. "And their words make the ladies blush and cry. They be in French, so I don't understand, but the queen's ladies do. That captain keeps his men in line, but I'm afraid to be caught alone with any of them, being just a housemaid."

"I'll ride up with the horses," Marcus said. "And go inside as if I'm still part of their mission. They may be sitting here waiting for the queen and Walsingham to show." He looked at Amanda. "Did any men survive the ambush?"

She nodded, although she still looked like she distrusted him with his northern accent. "Lord Oliver and Master Winslow, but I'm not sure what the French captain did with them. Soon after they arrived, they disappeared. I think they be in the dungeon because Cook makes up a tray to go down once a day upon the captain's orders."

"There were two more guards," Cordy said.

The maid shook her head. "I only saw two with the three ladies."

Cordy exhaled. "At least they are still alive."

Marcus tipped his head to indicate Cordy while watching the kitchen maid. "Can ye hide this queen's lady in the kitchens? Captain Noire and his men have seen her face, but 'tis too cold to keep her hiding out here."

Amanda nodded. "Mistress Wendel can give you a maid's dress, apron, and cap. Milady, you just have to explain what's going on to her. She's most distressed."

"How are Lady and Lord Manners being treated?" Cordy asked.

"They were locked immediately in their bed chambers. One tray of food and drink goes up to them as well." A door slammed outside, making Amanda jump. "I best be getting back before one of the men comes looking for me."

"How many are there?" Marcus asked.

She blinked. "I don't rightly know. About a dozen." Clutching her full basket, Amanda moved to the door, peeking through a crack before stepping out into the twilight.

Marcus caught Cordy's shoulder before she could follow the maid. "Don't let them catch ye, Cordy." He wanted to pull her into him but stopped himself.

"I won't," she said. "They'd know something was wrong if your lute teacher followed you."

That was part of it, but he also didn't want anyone saying or doing anything to bring fear back to her perfectly slanted eyes. His gaze dropped to her lush lips, which were parted as if waiting for a kiss.

"Aye," he said, the word smooth like the stroke of his hand against her cheek. "And I don't want ye harassed. Noire and his men can be as dangerous as those wolves."

"Agreed," she whispered, staring at him for a moment as if she'd say more. But instead she inhaled through her pert nose and turned, following after Amanda. "Keep your wits about you too, Master Blythe." The smile she presented held tension that he saw in the pinch of her brows. And then she hurried after Amanda across the snowy landscape to the back gate.

Marcus scanned the grounds, but no one was about to notice that one maid had turned into two while collecting eggs. He made his way back to Elspeth and Racer, mounted and led Cordy's horse back through the woods to come out along the road a quarter mile back from the manor. From there he trotted, leading the second horse up to the soaring front of Haddon Hall.

As he dismounted, patting Elspeth in a casual manner, Noire stepped outside the double doors. He stared down at Marcus, wheellock pistol in his hand. Noire scratched his longish nose with a finger. The captain used the pistol to point at Racer. "You brought me a gift, oui?"

"I found him along the road. Might be one of the queen's horses that broke free during the ambush. The saddle and tack are rich." Marcus ignored the firearm, but his muscles contracted with energy to leap out of the way if the man's finger twitched. Could he beat a bullet?

Noire snapped his thin fingers at a lad waiting there who hurried forward to take the reins from Marcus. "See they are watered and fed," Marcus instructed, and the lad led them toward the stables.

"No sign of the heretic queen?" Noire asked, his breath puffing out white in the shadow created by the looming castle. He continued to hold the pistol trained on Marcus, deciding between his Scottish contact's life and death. The Frenchman was a venomous serpent ready to strike.

"Nay," Marcus said. "She may have returned to Whitehall." Marcus stood his ground despite the heavy beat of his heart. He supposed talking casually while a pistol was trained on him was one of his special skills. "Bloody lucky woman." He waited and after another long moment, Noire slowly lowered the pistol and turned. Marcus let himself fully exhale and followed Noire inside the keep. The antechamber was decorated with swords and spears as if the English were trying to prove their battle prowess.

In the Great Hall, Noire's men sat at a long table set with tankards and meat pies. The aroma teased Marcus's empty stomach, hollowing it out even more. As if he were one of the group, he sat down and helped himself to a thick slice of turkey pie and a tankard of beer. Hopefully Cordy was getting fed in the kitchens.

Noire murmured something about the Scots being barbarians before taking a seat in the high-backed chair at the head of the table. Marcus ignored him.

"We have been told by the ladies," Noire said, nodding toward the group of Elizabeth's ladies near the flaming hearth, "that the queen was not part of their retinue. That she was accomplishing some task with Sir Francis Walsingham."

"Task?" Marcus asked, setting his tankard down. "What task? Without an army around her? Just Walsingham?" He chuckled. "That sounds like a lie."

"'Twas clandestine," Noire said, shrugging. "But she wouldn't have traveled all the way back to London with only her Spy Master to guard her. Non..." he drew out. "The queen must be coming here before returning."

Marcus crossed his arms and leaned back in the chair. "If she doesn't turn up soon, ye should head back across the channel when the weather opens up."

One of his men snorted but didn't say anything. Marcus grinned, glancing between the soldier and Noire. He tilted his head. "Ye frightened of the de' Medicis?"

"'Twould be foolish not to be," the same man said.

Noire continued ignoring both question and answer. "I believe the English queen will arrive here. Why send her entourage ahead without a plan to join them?" He shook his head, hair staying in place as if he waxed it. "There will be no need to disappoint the Queen Mother."

"By now someone has probably alerted the English queen, and Walsingham has mustered forces to ride her back to London in safety." Marcus narrowed his eyes with irritation. "I suppose ye won't pay me my due then."

"Of course not." Noire cocked his head to the side. "Why have you come to Haddon Hall if you think the English queen has returned to London?"

Marcus leaned forward, meeting the man's weasel-like eyes. "Until ye told me what the queen's ladies said about her not being part of the group, I assumed she was somewhere roaming the countryside, trying to hide. I've been searching since we parted ways in Bradwell Parish. When I couldn't find her trail, I came here, hoping that you'd found her on the way." Marcus crossed his arms.

Noire rested his pistol on the table, the bulbous butt of the weapon making it fall to the side. Noire's hand rested on the handle.

Marcus bit into the piece of pie he held and chewed. When he swallowed, he nodded to the gun. "Ye look like ye want to shoot me, Noire."

"He will if he thinks you're deceiving us," said one of his men in French.

Marcus's brows lowered. "My father changed his heart to favor Mary as the queen of Scotland and England, and I follow his ways. Why would I deceive ye? And why would ye think I am trying to do so? I came here to finish the mission."

Noire stroked the barrel of the pistol like it was a living thing. Lord Morton had warned Marcus that Jacque Noire was as dark as his last name, with a suspicious nature and a penchant for shooting traitors without bothering with questions, an eager executioner.

"And yet you talk of her riding back to Whitehall," Noire said.

Marcus shrugged. "I still have hopes to get paid if she hasn't." He stood, stretching his arms overhead as if daring the captain to shoot him in the chest. "As soon as 'tis light again, we should ride out to see if we can intercept her."

"We are expected soon at port," another of Noire's men said. "This delay will not look good."

"Tais-toi," Noire said. "The snow has made the going slow and treacherous, and we would not endanger the queen."

Just taking Elizabeth across the channel would endanger her. As far as Marcus knew, the Queen of England had never left her country, preferring to keep herself firmly seated on her throne lest someone try to fill it.

"Then we should take up the hunt again," Marcus said. "Like I said."

Another soldier set his cup down, glancing toward the darkening sky beyond the glassed windows. "Not at night when the wolves roam."

"Mon Dieu," another soldier cursed. "The beasts are vicious and hungry."

"Not as vicious and hungry as the de' Medicis," Noire said, finally moving his hand from the firearm. "They are wolves, non?" he asked his men who all nodded in full agreement.

One of the soldiers held a glass decanter upside down to show that the wine had been finished. "Woman," he called in heavily accented English toward the trio of ladies in velvets sitting in a corner near the hearth. "Bring some more of this rich wine." He waved his hand toward the back hall where Marcus knew the kitchens were housed.

One lady with a fierce frown stood. With even strides she neared, her gaze resting momentarily on Marcus and his Scottish costume. She whispered a curse under her breath, which made the Frenchman grin as he handed her the decanter. "She is not fond of the Scottish either," he said.

Without acknowledging the comment, even though Marcus was certain she understood French, the lady pivoted toward the kitchens. Would she see Cordy there? Cordy mentioned that she was not favored at the English court. Would this queen's lady give her away, thinking she was a traitor who was helping the French?

Despite the many disastrous possibilities, Marcus made himself smile with casual ease and lifted his goblet to Noire. "To finding the Queen of England, making yer Queen Mother of France relax, and saving the souls of these heretics."

Noire stared at him as if trying to read past his eyes into his mind, but he finally raised his half-filled glass to the toast. "With God's blessing and hearts loyal to the true religion."

The other men raised their glasses as the two remaining ladies looked on in horror. Playing his part in this farce, Marcus knew that Elizabeth's ladies would never believe he was there to save their queen. He must get to Elizabeth before Noire. And then what? Help her escape to London or drag her across the border to Scotland? Holding in his sigh, he took a big gulp of the rich wine.

CHAPTER ELEVEN

In 1564 Queen Elizabeth asked Sir James Melville, a Scottish nobleman, "How did her hair compare with his queen's? Which of them was the fairest?... When pressed to say more, he pronounced Elizabeth the fairest Queen in England and Mary the fairest Queen in Scotland." Elizabeth wasn't pleased with his noncommittal answer and went on to question him about the younger queen she saw as a rival.
Allison Weir, The Life of Elizabeth I

"YOU CAN FILL the butter crocks and knead the bread for the morning buns," said the brisk cook to Cordelia. Mistress Alice was tall and thin but showed amazing strength as she hefted the stew-filled cauldron off the fire, setting it on the wooden table. Releasing the two handfuls of apron she'd used to hold the hot pot, she pointed at another table where rising dough sat in clay bowls, waiting to be punched down and shaped. "Those wily Frenchmen want flaky pastry rolls, but they will have buns like the rest of England. They can go home if they want pastry rolls."

Cordelia had helped her sister bake occasionally in their house in London after their mother died and Lucy was trying to feed as many hungry orphans as she could. So Cordelia had some experience in preparing breads. She scooped the churned, pale butter into clay jars with the dull knife. The grease made her hold slippery. She should remove all her rings.

"Now onto the buns," Cook Alice yelled out as if barking orders on a battlefield. Cordelia jumped and hurried toward the row of rising dough.

The maid, Amanda, pointed to a bowl next to her. "Cook gets even bossier and louder when she's nervous," she whispered, glancing toward the archway leading to the rest of the castle.

"Seems appropriate," Cordelia said and pushed her sleeves back, sinking her hands into the sticky dough. It was warm from sitting near the hearth to rise.

"Knead the air out and cut them into thirty buns," Cook Alice barked as she hustled around the warm, fragrant room.

What was Marcus doing out in the great hall? Had he made it inside yet? He wouldn't have ridden away, leaving her there to try to find the true queen. Would he?

I will not leave ye to the wolves.

Cordelia drew a full breath and pulled the deflated dough out onto the wooden surface and pushed against it, folding it, and pushing it in again with her knuckles. She cut the dough in half and then again and again, reducing them down to buns.

"They want more wine."

Cordelia turned at the familiar voice, her eyes widening at the sight of Anne Bixby in the doorway of the kitchen. The lady's gaze fell directly onto Cordelia, and she gasped. "What are you doing here?" she whispered, hurrying across the room. "Do you know where the queen and Walsingham are?" Anne stopped before her, grabbing her shoulders as if to shake her.

"No," Cordelia said, abandoning the buns and pulling Anne behind her. Glancing at her over one shoulder, she whispered. "But I think Walsingham will bring her here if he hasn't been told about the French." She tugged Anne toward a small door and entered the cupboard. The room was lined with shelves of jars and clay pots. Cordelia left the door cracked for light.

Anne clasped Cordelia's hands and dropped them, making a pained face at the grease and dough that had transferred to her own hands. She rubbed them briskly to clean them. "If the queen arrives here, they will have her." Panic rode sharply on the backs of Anne's words. "That damn captain won't leave until he has her. Lord Gupton escaped, but if he doesn't find the queen, she'll ride right into this trap." Anne laid a palm over her large forehead. "If our fair queen doesn't die on the journey to France, she will at the hands of the de' Medicis. You know about the horrors of the Saint Bartholomew's Day massacre and the months that followed where they killed thousands of Protestants."

"I know," Cordelia whispered. She'd heard the awful stories of hangings by the hundreds. The brutality and blood that was spilled to punish the Huguenots. Lord Walsingham had seen it too while visiting France and had returned right away with dreadful reports.

"And our queen is the figurehead of Protestantism in Europe." Anne sounded like she might be crying.

Cordelia stroked her arm. "Catherine de' Medici might force her to wed a Frenchman, not kill her."

"Our proud queen will kill herself then," Anne said, her words ending with a sob.

She was right. The proud Elizabeth would not be forced to wed anyone. *I am wed to England.* It was her response to every push, whether it be gentle or forceful. "We must do something," Cordelia whispered.

Anne dabbed at her face with a handkerchief, her breaths coming slower as she regained control. "I have Elizabeth's makeup and clothing."

A prickle of unease slid up Cordelia's back. She waited, the comment sitting between them in the dark.

"If they find you and believe you're the queen, they will leave," Anne said. "Then if the queen arrives, they will be gone."

"They will leave…with me," Cordelia whispered so softly she could hardly hear it in her own ears.

"You will be a patriot," Anne said, her hands clasped before her with the handkerchief sticking up between like a white flag. "And once you reach France, word will come that you are not she. England will pay for your return."

If I'm not already dead. Cordelia closed her eyes and pushed past the lump in her throat. If she tricked them and saved the queen, her family name would surely be cleansed. If she didn't do this thing, Anne would make certain everyone knew that she refused to risk her life for the queen.

"I could have Marcus find me out in the woods and bring me in," Cordelia said, her eyes adjusting to the minimal light. "Has he entered the Great Hall?"

Anne's eyes widened, and she looked toward the door. "The Highlander? The one at whom the French captain pointed a pistol?"

Cordelia's stomach tightened. "Did he shoot Marcus?"

"No," Anne said, studying her, "but it wouldn't matter if he did. The Highlander is in league with the French. He's Catholic and wants Mary Stewart on the throne of England."

Cordelia shook her head. "He's a spy, Anne, working for one of King James's regents. Someone in our trusted circle sent word to France when Walsingham made plans for us to come to Haddon Hall. Marcus was a spy over there and brought word of it on the next crossing to Lord Morton who ordered him to help abduct the queen."

"What if he's double crossing you, Cordelia? You don't know him."

Lord, how she knew him, knew every inch of Marcus Blythe. Cordelia's cheeks heated, and she was thankful for the darkness. "I trust him, Anne. He would have…" She exhaled. "Well he would have simply abandoned me when he found out I wasn't Elizabeth. Gone on his way to find her."

"He really thought you were the queen? When you weren't wearing her makeup?"

"I look like a younger version of her," Cordelia said. "And I have her ring." She held up her hand in the darkness, and her breath caught. She couldn't see, but she didn't need any light to feel the nakedness of her finger. The ring was missing.

Meet at the snow arches just after dawn.

That's what the note had read before Marcus had burned it in the hearth of his room at Haddon Hall. Now he watched the dawn fully light the sky through the spindly trees shooting up from the snow-covered forest. He'd been about to hunt down Cordy when the henhouse maid had handed him the note, telling him she was well and hidden. That he mustn't bother her until meeting her at dawn.

Mustn't bother her? Was that her way of saying she didn't welcome him in her bed anymore? He crossed his arms over his chest and leaned against one of the stone arches of the small roofless chapel. The passion that had flared hot between them had seemed powerful enough to at least lead to another night together. He'd made certain his room was secure and away from the French in hopes that he'd find her. Not that he should be thinking about such things on this crucial mission.

Marcus's breath puffed white in the freezing air. He turned when he heard the crunch of horse hooves breaking through the thin layer of ice that had formed over the snow. His gaze fastened on the white horse walking through the silhouetted trees deeper in the forest.

Riding toward him was an alabaster vision of royal femininity. The queen? Her face was painted white, making her ruby lips stand out. Coal lined her eyes, and her hair was curled and piled high with pearls woven into the brilliant red hue. She wore royal crimson-hued garb under a rough woolen cape to hide it.

He blinked. This vision of the queen was riding Elspeth who blended in with the snowy landscape. Despite the masquerade, this queen possessed the perfectly shaped golden eyes he remembered staring into over the last days. The eyes that had slid over his hot skin as they were coming together at the inn. "Cordy?"

"Only to you, Marcus," she said, her lips in a straight line. "To everyone else, you must take me to Haddon Hall as the queen you found with Walsingham, whom you killed and left for the wolves."

"Good bloody hell," he said, coming up to hold onto his horse's curb strap under her muzzle. Elspeth pressed into his shoulder as if she felt his unease. Marcus stared up at a young portrait of Elizabeth come to life.

Cordy turned away toward the icy woods. "'Tis the only way to get Noire and his men to leave the hall before Elizabeth arrives to a den of bandits. I will go in her place and act the part for as long as I can."

"Ye will cross the channel to Catherine de 'Medici?" he asked, letting his anger out with his words.

The snowy forest was frozen in stillness around them, as if it too held its breath. "Once I am discovered, England will pay my ransom, especially when the queen learns of my sacrifice for her safety."

He moved in front of Elspeth's nose. "Cordy, look at me."

After a few long seconds, she turned her hauntingly smooth, pale face to him. "Cordy, they could kill ye or ye could die in the crossing. 'Tis not an easy voyage in the winter."

"My family's name will be cleansed," she whispered and then cleared her throat. "And with God's help, I will survive to return." She stroked a hand down Elspeth's white neck.

"'Tis too risky."

"Take me in as if you found me arriving and threw me on your horse you had with you. That you killed Walsingham and let the other horses wander off. If Noire can be convinced to leave immediately for the coast with all his men, Elizabeth will be safe. Her ladies will tell her what has happened."

"Ye thought all this up last night?" he asked, rubbing a hand through his hair. *Daingead*. He should have found her last night. To talk this through or…to touch her for the last time.

"Elizabeth's lady, Anne Bixby, helped me. She did my

makeup and hair and helped me dress. She's quite clever."

"Is she also one who condemns ye for being your mother's daughter?" he asked.

"That will be no more once I offer myself up to keep the queen safe."

"Foking hell, Cordy," he cursed. "Ye aren't some sacrifice."

"I must be, Marcus." A bit of the ice that seemed to freeze her white face into apathy thawed. "What else can I do? Hide away while her ladies are threatened, Lord and Lady Manners are held prisoner, and Master Winslow is locked in the dungeon? If Noire leaves, everyone will be released, and the queen will be well when she arrives. You can even convince her to follow you to Canonbie if you must, while I lead the villains away and resurrect the honor of my family."

"Who cares about the bloody honor of your family?" he said with ferocity that surprised even him.

She bent over the horse's neck as if hugging Elspeth, the tight bodice keeping her back as straight as a claymore. Her white face was turned to him. The thickness of the makeup hid her well, but her eyes remained those of Cordy. "I could ask you the same, Marcus Blythe."

"'Tis not the same," he said, grabbing the back of his neck. "My mother and sister are alive and still in Edinburgh. If I fail, they could fall to ruin."

"My sister and I have already fallen," she said, her voice soft. "And this will raise us back up. I will leave England as a hero not a traitor."

He raised his hand to touch her cheek but stopped. "Blast it, Cordy, I can't even touch ye in all that." He gestured to her makeup and gown. The white paste was as untouchable as drying paint preventing entry to a place for which he longed. As if he were cut off from home. Not Edinburgh but something he yearned for more.

She met his gaze, her brown eyes warming. "Where would you touch me, Master Blythe?" she asked, her voice softening.

The thrill of it sent a shot of lust through Marcus.

"Just Marcus," he whispered, the surname sitting like a rock in his chest.

"Marcus," she whispered back. "Where would you touch me?"

He rested his hand on her leg that lay bent over the side of his horse. "I would kiss your soft lips, Cordy lass, and then your long, sensitive neck over to your ear to whisper in it."

Her lips fell open slightly. "What would you whisper?"

A grin turned up one corner of his mouth. "That I would make ye moan with my touch."

Her hand went to her neck, touching it lightly, but she pulled it back so as not to rub off the makeup that ran all the way down and across her chest. "Show me where," she said, her eyes watching him.

There was time to touch her. Thoughts of hunting for the English queen faded. He ran his hand up Cordy's leg, under her petticoat to the warm skin beneath. "Here," he said, massaging her calf before rising higher. "And here."

Cordy's lips parted as she took a larger breath. "I would touch you too, Marcus. To make you moan."

Marcus slid his palm over his jack that had woken fully at her words. It would gladly abandon his mission and honor to press into the warmth of Cordy again. "Aye." He raised her petticoat, exposing her skin. "Ye aren't coated in makeup under here," he said with one brow rising.

Her lush mouth turned up at the corners. "I am not." But then her gaze rose to the woods, and she shook her head. "But there is no time, and…I am made to look like someone else above."

Marcus nodded to the inside of the crumbling church. "I can turn ye to face the wall." He grinned at her so that she could choose to think he was jesting.

She huffed, and a puff of breath came from her in the cold. "If only there was time." With all the makeup on, he couldn't even tell if she blushed. Heat certainly filled him, making his rigid erection ache. But she was right. Elizabeth and Walsingham could arrive any moment if Oliver Gupton hadn't intercepted them on the way. Marcus didn't know what he hoped. That the queen was safe and on her way back to London, or that she was still headed there so Marcus could convince her to meet with Lord Morton.

He nodded, agreeing with her. "Ye're right." He exhaled long. "Cordy, ye have the focus of a warrior."

She leaned forward over the horse to nearly lower her face to his. "If you knew the ache your words have inflicted upon me, you'd call me a rogue."

Marcus couldn't help himself. His hands lifted under her arms, and he lowered her from the horse, pulling her against him so she could feel how much he wanted her. His lips settled on hers carefully so as not to mess her ghost-like skin. Beneath all of it breathed a woman who ached as much as he.

He backed her up against the stone wall, barely noticing the snow drifting down over them. They would stop soon. Just another kiss, another inhale against her sweet mouth, another press of her warm body against his. His hands lifted the edge of her petticoats until he reached the hot skin beneath.

"Bloody foking hell," came a voice behind Marcus. "Get your filthy hands off the queen, Scot!"

※※※※

CORDELIA GASPED AS Marcus dropped her petticoat and turned away from her. Breath flew from between her open lips. She stared at his back, and he pulled his sword while acting as her shield.

"What a randy lech," another man said.

"Your Majesty? We're here to save ye." The voice sounded familiar, and Cordelia peeked out from around Marcus's large form, her bare fingers curling into his short cape.

"Mathew? Luke, John, Henry?" They were the four men from the village. She moved out from behind Marcus. "Did you follow us?"

"Step away from the queen, you bastardly scoundrel," Luke said. He was the roundest of the four, and his dark curls kept falling in his eyes. Mathew was wiry and tall, and Henry the broadest with the most muscle, but Luke held a pistol. The smallest, John, held a vicious looking club.

"She's a virgin queen! Or have you defiled her?" Mathew asked, his fists tightly held before him like he wished to box.

Cordelia held out her hands, palms out. "I am not, in fact, the queen," she said. "And Master Blythe has taken no liberties."

The four stared at her. John knocked Mathew's arm with the club. "I told you she was only a lute teacher."

"Look at her!" Mathew flapped his hand toward Cordelia. "She looks like her and said she was. She even has the queen's ring. The one she turned around in the tavern. Show them." He pointed at her hands.

Cordelia exhaled and almost rubbed her forehead but stopped herself before she could smudge her makeup. It was dry now, but she didn't want to chance ruining Anne's work. So she dropped her hands, and all four villagers' gazes dropped in unison to follow them.

"Unfortunately..." She looked at Marcus. "I've lost the ring."

Marcus took her cold hand, enveloping it in his warm one. "Ye lost the queen's ring?"

She huffed, feeling her face tighten, which had nothing to do with the horridly thick makeup. "I think it fell off in the kitchen. I was churning butter and kneading bread. It had been loose. I was going to take it off, put it in my pocket with the rest, but then...Cook Alice yells a lot."

"Mo chreach," Marcus said, running his hand up through his hair. "We could—"

"I looked through all the dough I was allowed to poke. Cook

had already put some in the oven and stored away the butter I put in crocks."

Mathew looked aghast. "You lost the queen's ring that she never takes off. It has rubies and diamonds fastened in it."

"My ma says there are tiny pictures of her and her mother inside the locket part," Henry said. He was so big and rough that it was hard to imagine him talking with his mother about the queen's ring.

"Daingead," Marcus cursed again.

"Why yes," Cordelia said frowning at him, "I am damned if I cannot return it to Elizabeth, another reason I must risk playing this role for her." She indicated her brilliant, rich ensemble.

Mathew gasped. "Is that why you're dressed this way? Are you trying to lead the French frogs away from the queen?"

"Yes," Cordelia said. "They want to take her to France, so I'm acting in her place."

Mathew slapped John's arm. "See, we are still helping the queen."

"Are you really a lute player?" Luke asked.

Mathew rolled his eyes. "You heard her play. You can't make that up."

"I mean teacher," Luke said. "A lute teacher."

"No," Cordelia said.

Marcus waved his arm impatiently. "The real queen may show up today. We can't let her fall into the hands of Captain Noire and his men."

"How many are there?" Henry asked, crossing his thick arms.

"At last count there are a dozen," Marcus said. "Only a few went into the village so as not to cause alarm. There are more at the coast with the ship."

"We have a pistol," Luke said, brandishing it around.

"They have ten," Marcus said.

"Bloody that," Luke murmured, lowering his weapon.

"They will leave if they have the queen," Cordelia said. "Noire is already behind schedule. Anne says he's anxious to leave." She looked at Marcus. "This is the best plan."

"What plan?" asked Mathew, frowning as much as Marcus. "For you to go in her place? That's a right terrible plan."

"'Tis the only way," Cordelia said sharply, not wanting to explain it again. So far she'd managed to push the fear away, but repeating the scheme and hearing the dreadful outcomes kept inviting it back.

Marcus turned to Mathew. "Can ye watch for the real queen? She would show up with Sir Francis Walsingham on two horses and possibly a couple of guards."

"Her Spy Master?" Henry said. "My ma says he could ferret out the devil himself."

"Maybe if ye do good by the queen, Walsingham will enlist ye into his ring," Marcus said.

Henry stood straighter and began to peer through the forest as if hoping to spot them.

Marcus pulled out his short sword and unlaced his boot, shoving at the heel for it to come off. He peeled away a woolen sock.

"What are you about?" Mathew asked.

With the tip of his sword, Marcus nicked the ball of his foot. "Bloodying my sword to back up my story of killing Walsingham. Unless one of ye wants to volunteer."

"Well no use volunteering now that you've already cut yourself," Mathew said, indicating Marcus's foot. "But I would have if needed to protect the lady." He looked at her. "What's your real name, milady?"

She smiled. "Cordelia. Thank you for coming to my rescue. All of you."

They bowed their heads as if she were actually the queen. It gave Cordelia courage. "And I am sorry that I am not truly your queen."

"No bother," Mathew said. "We are still on a mission to help the queen and..." he frowned, "hopefully save you, Lady Cordelia."

She breathed through her nose that felt much too thin to allow sufficient air flow and offered him a smile despite the flipping of her heart. Cowardice was making her whole body tense, but she couldn't show it. "We should get me to Captain Noire then," she said, looking at Marcus.

He met her next to Elspeth. His firm hands slid around her waist, lifting her up onto the saddle.

"You look just like a queen on that white steed," Mathew said, doffing his hat and grinning at her.

"Aye," Henry agreed. "So majestic."

"Thank you," she said, feeling a true smile touch her mouth despite the trembling in her hands.

Marcus climbed on behind, pulling her into the V of his legs. He looked down at the men. "Patrol the forest, one of ye in each direction. Don't let the French see ye, but if they do, try to take them out. Less for us to deal with later if this all goes awry."

All four of them nodded. Mathew looked at Cordy. "I swear ye look exactly like her."

Cordelia smiled, and Henry pointed. "Don't do that though. The queen has blackened teeth from what me ma says."

"I will take care to frown continuously then," she said.

Marcus pressed into Elspeth's sides, pulling her around to return to Haddon Hall. For a moment, Cordelia leaned back into his arms, feeling the warmth that radiated out from him.

"Marcus."

"Aye?"

"Will you come for me if they take me to France?"

There was a pause before she felt his lips at her ear. She heard him swallow, and his words came with the solemnity of an oath. "I won't let ye leave this isle, Cordy. That ship will sail without ye or not at all."

With a dozen French soldiers with firearms and more on the ship, she knew he couldn't guarantee that, but the words warmed her inside. They gave her hope that this plan would somehow work. *I will not leave ye to the wolves.*

They rode through the forest and then straight out across the meadow. As they neared the front of Haddon Hall, French soldiers gathered, yelling in excitement at the sight of Marcus riding up with the queen.

Cordelia took a full breath and let the mask of the queen settle over her features. *Heart of a lion. Queen of all England and Ireland.* Shoulders back, she rode in amongst the enemy.

Chapter Twelve

"If ever any person had either the gift or the style to win the hearts of the people, it was this Queen. All her faculties were in motion, and every motion seemed a well-guided action; her eye was set upon one, her ear listened to another, her judgement ran upon a third, to a fourth she addressed her speech; her spirit seemed to be everywhere."

Sir John Haywood upon the arrival of Elizabeth, the new Queen of England, 23 November 1558

Cordelia tipped her head higher as she walked evenly through the entry of Haddon Hall, the hem of her crimson and gold gown swishing across the stone floor. Marcus followed behind her with his sword in hand. He'd washed it with snow so that it looked wet. Yet he left a bit of blood dried on the tip, blood from his own foot that was wrapped up tightly once again in his boot.

"Behold the mighty Protestant Queen Elizabeth of England," one of the French soldiers proclaimed as if he'd been the one to find her.

"Queen of England and Ireland," she intoned. "Now someone tell me what is going on and arrest that man behind me. He's slain my dear Sir Francis and will be hanged for it and for touching my royal person." Cordelia threw one long arm out toward Marcus, her fingers adorned with the other rings she'd kept in her pocket with the card from the fair, all the rings except the locket ring, the only one she really cared about.

Marcus walked past her to stop before Noire, who had leapt out of the throne-like chair at the head of the table. Yanking a rag from his belt, Marcus wiped his wet and bloodied short sword before re-sheathing it. "She and Walsingham were riding up through the trees, not along the main road. The lord would not let me pass or persuade her to accompany me, so he had to be slain. I covered his body in snow, but the wolves will feast tonight."

Noire walked past Marcus. "Your Majesty," he said, giving a curt bow of his head.

She snorted as if his gesture was far from sufficient. "Where are my hosts and ladies? Who are you? And do you realize that you will die most painfully for this insult?"

Noire motioned for her to go before the fire to warm herself. He looked to the huddled ladies there who all bowed into deep curtsies before Cordelia. Apparently, they'd been prepared by Anne who'd told them to treat Cordelia like the true queen, for there was no hesitation in their movements.

"Your Majesty," one said.

"God save Your Majesty," another murmured, real tears in her eyes.

Cordelia clasped their hands in a display of comforting them and pivoted around to pierce Noire with a gaze as sharp as an ice pick. "Answer my questions or hang with the Scot."

"Votre Majesté," he said. "I am Captain Noire, sent by the dowager-queen Catherine de' Medici to invite you across the channel to France."

"Dowager-queen," Cordelia scoffed. "She makes everyone call her Queen Mother to show her rule over her young son."

He ignored her correction. "My men and I will escort you. Your hosts are comfortable in their rooms above, and I am preventing my death by...obtaining you." He smiled.

Her gaze snapped to Marcus. "And who is the villain?"

"Marcus Blythe, who works for…the Queen Mother," Noire said.

"Marcus Blythe," Cordelia said, spitting the name out. "I do not know you or your family, although your accent and costume identify you as Scots."

"A Scot who works to see Queen Mary back on her throne to restore the true faith to my country and England," Marcus said, crossing his arms over his chest. His hands curled into tight fists. "Removing ye from this land is the first step."

Her gaze snapped back to Noire. "I will never leave England as long as breath resides in my body."

Noire's lips twitched upward as if he laughed inside. "Then you must prepare to hold your breath, for we leave this place at noon and this country on the morrow at high tide."

Cordelia moved to the chair that Noire had vacated and sat. It was the closest to a throne she saw, and she'd not bothered to ask before claiming it. A colorful tapestry with Lord Manner's heraldry flanked the wooden wall behind her where squares of carved molding set a formal design across it, making the room grand. Light from candles in a silver chandelier along with the flames in the hearth cast a warm glow even though the room was chilled.

Noire sat near her, and every time his gaze roamed across her face and form, a prickle of panic slid under Cordelia's skin. Did he suspect that she was not Elizabeth?

"I will attend the horses," Marcus said. "Ready them for our ride to the coast." Without even a glance her way, he traipsed from the room.

She'd made Marcus promise to leave the hall to help Mathew and his friends stop the real queen as soon as she arrived, but Cordelia's stomach felt hollow as the clap of his boot heels faded.

"For you, Your Majesty," Anne Bixby said as she held a goblet of wine. Anne took a drink first before setting it before the queen to show it was safe. Her sister, Margaret, opened a blanket to lay across Cordelia's lap. If Margaret despised waiting on Cordy, she didn't show it. Perhaps she was a fabulous actress, but Cordelia hoped her act of sacrifice would melt the icy hearts of the court ladies. That they would speak well of her if she never made it back to Whitehall.

All four of the ladies brought chairs nearby, sitting equidistant from each other around the front of Cordy as if creating a barricade between her and her oppressors. Luckily Lady and Lord Manners hadn't yet been released. Would they recognize her as an imposter? The thought made Cordelia's mouth go dry, and she took another sip of the sweet wine.

She cleared her throat. "I understand one of my guards sits in the dungeon. I demand he be released and housed above in a comfortable room," she said with regal, barely checked fury.

Noire motioned to one of his men who stood, walking away. If the French captain thought she was an imposter, surely he wouldn't follow her demands. Had Catherine de' Medici ordered him to treat her as befitting a queen?

"I also insist that you leave my ladies here in good health so that they may travel back to London to explain my capture."

"I will take only you, Your Majesty," Noire said, his gaze slipping to those of her ladies.

Cordelia held her breath. Was this a test? The silence in the room made her heart pound hard.

Then Anne Bixby stood, her eyes cast down. "I will remain by Your Majesty's side. I will see to your comfort whether in England or France."

Margaret stood next, repeating the same, which encouraged the third lady to stand with the others to pledge her loyalty. Cordelia allowed a smile, being sure not to show her white teeth.

"Your loyalty warms my heart," she said. "But I will allow no harm to befall any of my ladies. You must return and tell my council of these treacherous affairs." She looked at Noire, her smile turning downward. "Which will surely lead to war against your country."

He smiled in return. "The Queen Mother wishes only to

introduce you to a man of noble birth so that you may marry."

She snorted loudly. "My advisors won't allow it. Nor I. No man may take the place of King of England while I still breathe."

Noire nodded slowly, a wry grin on his pointy face. "The Queen Mother most likely knows that," he said, his voice soft.

Cordelia's gaze snapped with what she hoped looked like lightning. "War then, captain. This will come to war."

He dismissed her threat with a wave of his hand. "As soon as we eat, we leave for the coast, Your Majesty."

Cordelia turned her face away from Noire. She would do nothing to slow down their departure. Hopefully Marcus would forestall Elizabeth and Walsingham. *Marcus*. If she were to die or never see him again… The thought tightened her chest enough that she couldn't inhale.

I won't let ye leave this isle, Cordy. Marcus's words played through her mind, giving her strength. She sat straight in the high-backed chair, concentrating on breathing inward. Elizabeth would never swoon. The tight stays helped keep her erect.

A cart was rolled into the room from the corridor leading back to the kitchens. A cauldron sat on it with a stack of wooden bowls and a ladle. On another shelf below were baskets of buns and crocks of butter. Even though Elizabeth was known to pick at her food, especially when under duress, Cordelia was planning to eat as much as she could. Who knew how long before she saw a proper meal again? If Marcus wasn't able to help her escape, how long was the channel crossing? She should have listened more to her father when he spoke of touring the continent.

The cook began to ladle out bowls while Amanda set buns and butter crocks along the table for Noire's men. She squeaked when one of the soldiers ran a hand down her backside, the basket nearly colliding with his chin. The men around him laughed heartily, and Amanda scurried off.

"I understand that you speak fluent French, Your Majesty," Noire said in French as he slathered butter on a warm bun.

"I also speak fluent Greek, Italian, and Latin," she said in

French. "And can understand Spanish and Scots when spoken."

His brows rose in surprise. "Most impressive."

She hoped he wouldn't quiz her. Elizabeth was gifted with her ability and discipline around languages, but Cordelia was not. "Is your Queen Mother not educated? It seems she is a fool to invite war from so powerful a kingdom as mine."

"Catherine de' Medici and King Henry wage war on the false religion that plagues your kingdom," Noire said. "They would see a Catholic queen on the throne of England or a king."

"Mary Stewart will never sit on my throne," Cordelia said, her words seething. "And I will never marry a Catholic." Even though she didn't feel like eating, she raised a bun to her red lips.

"Mon Dieu, what poison is this?" one of the soldiers asked from down the table, making everyone stop, hands and spoons part way to their mouths. Several spat out whatever was in their mouths. From the butter crock the one soldier worked his fingers to pluck out something hard.

Cordelia's stomach flipped as he wrapped it in his napkin, wiping the grease from it. He held it up. "'Tis a ring."

Cordelia's stomach clamped down on the swallowed bun as if it were poison itself that must be purged. She sat back in the chair, letting it hold her up while stars sparked in her periphery.

"It has rubies and diamonds," another said, looking over his friend's shoulder.

"I prefer rubies and diamonds to poison," another said with a smile.

Noire's gaze dropped to Cordelia's hands that she'd adorned with the rings she'd hidden in her pocket. But one ring was missing, the one Elizabeth would never remove, the one that Noire's soldier was now holding up in the air.

Noire rose and moved quickly to snatch the ring from the Frenchman.

"This was in your butter?" Noire asked and rubbed at it with his napkin. "'Tis the ring the Queen of England is reputed to wear always. It has the E in diamonds set on a band and circle of rubies.

The Queen Mother told me to look for it."

Cordelia sat still as stone. Her heart pounded, making her blood rush, and she was thankful the chair was holding her up. *I am Queen Elizabeth. Heart of a lion.* She sucked in slow, even ribbons of breath. With Anne's talent, Cordelia knew she looked like the famous, red-haired queen with her porcelain white face, styled hair, and queenly clothes. But she must breathe life into the role to be believed.

With a straight back and annoyed countenance, Cordelia let out a bark of laughter that didn't sound joyful at all. "A forgery." She flipped her hand their way and shrugged, rolling her eyes. "But believe what you wish."

Noire flipped open the locket. "There are portraits in here of you and your mother." He looked to her.

She waved him over with long fingers. "Let me see this thing."

He brought it to her, his hand snatching up her left. "And you are not wearing a copy nor the original."

She pursed her lips and stared at him like he was dull-witted. "This adventure was dangerous enough. I wasn't about to bring my favorite ring with me. 'Tis safely locked up with my jewels at Whitehall." She peered at the tiny portraits. "There's butter on it, and that doesn't look anything like me," she said, holding it up next to her face as if to prove a point that couldn't be proven for so many reasons. For she wasn't the woman in the picture, the artist wasn't exact, and the butter may have altered the ink. Elizabeth would be irate if she knew butter marred her pictures.

"What was it doing in the butter?" he asked her, his words direct.

"How in all of Christendom could I know that?" she retorted. "I just arrived, well after that butter must have been churned." She picked up her little crock and sniffed it, wrinkling her thin nose. "Churned a fortnight ago from the smell of it."

The soldiers along the table sniffed their own butter cups. One made a face, believing her suggestion that it was rank. With a simple suggestion, people could be made to believe so much.

Noire stared at her, but Cordelia didn't even blink. Then he turned on his heel. "I want the cook and kitchen staff brought out here at once."

"Won't that take more time, captain?" one of the soldiers asked. "And we are expected on the coast by nightfall."

Noire shoved the ring onto his smallest finger and wagged it at Cordelia, squinting his eyes. "Something is not right here." Perhaps she'd return the ring to Elizabeth still on Noire's severed finger. Just the thought gave her courage.

"There's a lot not right here, le capitaine," Cordelia called out. "You have detained the Queen of England and Ireland and will be hung, drawn, and quartered as soon as my armies descend upon here."

Noire dropped his hand. "Your armies think you are safe with your ring of intimates behind Whitehall's walls, Your Majesty."

She leaned forward, her hands braced on the arms of her chair. *Heart of a lion.* "Sir Walsingham, before he was murdered by that Scottish swine, sent word of your failed ambush."

"You know nothing of that," Noire said, narrowing his eyes at her.

"One of my guards escaped, sending word back to Lord Walsingham." She leaned back in her seat, letting a dark smile cross her face. "By now my council will have assembled my loyal men and even townspeople along the way as they make their way here. Your best course of action is to flee like the rats you are." She flipped a hand toward the door where Marcus had walked out. "You can leave your Scots pig to take the blame and punishment for murdering my dear Spy Master."

Noire kept his face neutral as he looked from Cordelia to his men. The ladies near her stared with wide eyes, either at her performance or audacity. "Ready the horses," Noire said. "We will head to the coast within the hour."

Marcus saddled Racer and adjusted the bit Cordy had put in Elspeth's mouth. Several French soldiers readied the carriage that Noire had taken in the ambush. The clever captain wouldn't let Cordy ride horseback, knowing it was easier to escape or break her neck trying. Even if Catherine de' Medici wanted Elizabeth in France, she didn't want her dead, at least before trying to manipulate her.

He kept his gaze on the front doors, watching for their departure. He must let them ride away, still believing they had captured Elizabeth. But then what? If he gave himself away as helping the Protestants, he could never return to France as a spy. His role would be over, and he'd be useless to Lord Morton and King James. *Think, man.*

Tightening the straps on the horses' bridles, he listened to the five men around him. They spoke in quiet French as they harnessed horses.

"She is fairer than the Queen Mother said. Younger too." Suspicion laced his words.

"They say her teeth are rotten."

"I didn't see them because she frowned so."

One laughed as he helped another soldier pull the carriage outside. "I would frown too if I'd been caught by my enemy."

"Shouldn't Noire look in her mouth? She didn't have the ring."

"But they found it in the butter."

Marcus's fingers stopped, and he turned. "What did they find in the butter?"

"The queen's locket ring with the rubies and diamonds," said the man, standing proud with the information. "But the crocks were made up weeks ago, and the English queen says it's a forgery."

"I had the butter and it tasted fine and fresh," said the suspicious soldier.

"Well she arrived this morn, so it can't be her ring," Marcus said.

The men continued to talk, but Marcus led his two horses out of the barn. Off in the distance he saw a man waving his arms. "Ballocks," he murmured and raised his arm to Mathew. Luckily the man had sense enough to run back into the forest after Marcus spotted him. The others were around the front of the stable, setting the horses before the carriage.

He tied Racer loosely to a post and mounted Elspeth. With another glance over his shoulder to make sure he wasn't being watched, he pressed Elspeth into a slow run toward another part of the forest behind the great estate. The horse stretched her legs, and they made it to the edge of the trees quickly. Once farther inside so it would be harder to be seen, Marcus made his way toward the stone chapel. Halfway there he met an out-of-breath Mathew.

Mathew smiled at him, waving his arm. "We've got her!" he yelled and then grimaced at his outburst. "The queen," he said in a hushed voice that carried.

Marcus surged ahead, breaking through the web of winter-dead twigs and bramble, riding directly to the chapel. There before the three other Bradwell men stood two cloaked figures. One was a hooded woman in an outfit of white that blended with the snow. The other was a man with a pointy beard, hawkish nose, and felted hat.

"Your Majesty," Marcus said, dismounting to bow. He looked at Walsingham. "Lord Walsingham. The French have captured your retinue and are preparing to abduct the English queen to take to Catherine de' Medici."

The man's long nose was bulbous at the end. His pointed beard made his face look even longer. He held a gun aimed at Marcus's chest. Luke still held his but didn't seem to know where to aim it.

John hit his arm. "Put that thing away before you're charged with treason by accidentally pointing it at the queen."

"And you are?" Walsingham asked Marcus.

"Marcus...Marcus Blythe, sent on secret mission by Lord Morton in the name of King James of Scotland."

Marcus looked at the frowning queen. How could he have mistaken Cordelia for Elizabeth? They each had red hair, and Cordy looked quite pale with the heavy layers on her face, but the age was apparent in the monarch. And her eyes were sharp and wary in a way that made Marcus understand how formidable she must be surrounded by her guards and power.

"Jacque Noire and a group of five other French soldiers are inside Haddon Hall, with seven outdoors," Marcus said to her. "The patrons of the manor are locked in their rooms above. Your ladies are forced to remain in the hall waiting on the men."

"God's teeth," Elizabeth murmured. Some rosiness shone through her white makeup from her ride through the cold, as if trying to break through to show she was human rather than an uncaring statue. "And they wish to abduct me to France?"

"How do they know we're here?" Walsingham asked, no longer looking quite like he wanted to shoot Marcus but still wary.

"One courtier in your inner circle sent word to the de' Medicis as soon as ye invited them to go to Haddon Hall."

"One of my confidants?" Elizabeth asked, her face hardening to the point that Marcus could imagine it cracking. It was said that once wronged, Elizabeth Tudor would never forgive. She demanded loyalty to herself and England in that order.

"They were ambushed on the way here, Oliver Gupton got away, and Geoffrey Winslow is in the dungeon. At least one guard was slayed, perhaps two."

"And my ladies?" the queen asked.

"Cordelia Cranfield?" Walsingham asked at the same time. Where the queen looked concerned, Walsingham looked suspicious.

"Lady Cordelia is playing your role so that Captain Noire will take her to France in your stead."

"And my ladies are playing along with it?"

"Aye, Your Majesty, in hopes of getting the French to leave with Cordelia before ye arrive."

"Poor Lady Cordelia," Elizabeth murmured. "She certainly didn't know this would be part of her mission."

"There were numerous times she could have escaped, but her worry for ye kept her here to warn ye away and get the French to leave," Marcus said.

"Aye," Mathew said, nodding. "She is loyal above all."

"And beautiful," Luke said.

"And she plays the lute like an angel," Henry added.

Elizabeth frowned. "I am very aware of the talents of my fair ladies." She looked back at Marcus. "Lady Cordelia's loyalty seems quite intact."

Hopefully Cordy was right that this act to save the queen would cleanse her family name. *By God.* The things one did for family. It wasn't worth her life. Marcus would have taken Cordy and run her to Scotland if all these other chains didn't shackle them to their individual missions.

"Where do I go now then? 'Tis cold and the nearest settlement is far off," Elizabeth said. "How fast will they leave?"

Too soon and not soon enough, Marcus thought.

"Any time now, Your Majesty," he said instead. "These four brave Englishmen will see ye to Haddon Hall once they depart."

"You will not accompany me?" she asked.

"I will go with Noire and play my role as spy. My country depends on me," he said. *So does Cordy.* And he wouldn't let anything happen to her.

Chapter Thirteen

"As but one sun lights the East, so I shall have but one queen in England."

Queen Elizabeth to Lettice Knollys when she came to court in 1579, after wedding the queen's favorite, dressed magnificently and leading a contingent of servants. Lettice did not return to court for years after Elizabeth's public rage.

Cordelia stood regally despite her insides twisting like hair plaits. Where was Marcus? Was he riding the woods with Mathew and his friends, to stop the queen from showing up before they left? Would he catch up to them on the way to the coast?

"Your Majesty, we kept the carriage so you may ride with me in luxury," Noire said.

"I prefer to ride astride in the fresh air," she said, hoping to at least have Racer with her.

Noire *tsk*ed. "And have you ride away from me." He shook his head. "Non, Your Majesty, you could fall and break that fragile neck." His thin lips turned up in a smile as if the thought was not averse to him. "And the Queen Mother has forbade your death on this mission."

Cordelia sniffed, a wry smile touching her brightly reddened lips. "Catherine de' Medici forbade my death so she can do it herself." She had already sent perfumed gloves to Elizabeth on more than one occasion. Luckily the queen's garment inspector had discovered the white powder inside them before Elizabeth had put them on.

"Non, Your Majesty. The Queen Mother would never sully her hands with another queen's blood. She may treat you like you have treated your own cousin, the Queen Mother's once daughter-by-marriage, Mary Stewart."

What had Mary written to her first husband's powerful mother? That she'd been left in drafty castles with barely any food or provisions? The Scottish queen was known to exaggerate her descriptions to match her moods.

The group of Frenchmen surrounded Cordelia as she walked with Noire to the entryway. The queen's ladies behind her made a show of weeping. They were decent actors if one didn't look too closely for real tears.

They walked across the wide-planked floors, their boots clipping. Cordelia felt like an observer of some great opera, the orchestra made up of weeping women, clipping boots, and the swish of her petticoats. She could almost hear a melancholy drumbeat marking her steps toward a scaffold in the well-choreographed drama.

Where the bloody hell was Marcus?

Halfway to the entry chamber, the outer doors swung inward, and Cordelia heard a man traipse inside. Her stomach flipped with hope.

Her steps hastened as if seeing him would rid her of the weariness that came with worry and frantic scheming. But then she stopped at the voice, a voice that seemed familiar but out of place.

"I've spent yesterday and this morn hunting for Elizabeth and Walsingham but could not find them, Noire," the man said, throwing off a cape. "There were blasted wolves about. I had to outrun one pack that was in the distance." He stopped, staring at Cordelia surrounded by French soldiers. "How, how!" he said. "Who do we have here?"

Holy Hell. It was Lord Oliver Gupton, the courtier that had thrown her on his horse during the ambush, the horse that was missing nails in his hooves. She glanced between his shocked handsome face and that of Captain Noire's. Gupton was working with the French? Racer was his horse and had not been properly shod. Had he planned to have the queen thrown when it lost a shoe on its frantic flight? A second plan in case she tried to flee the ambush?

"As you can see, Gupton, we have found the Protestant queen," Noire said.

Oliver Gupton squinted at Cordy, and she felt her knees weaken. "I see that you've found a woman, Noire, but this woman is not Queen Elizabeth of England and Ireland."

※※※※※

"There cannot be that many Frenchmen in there," Elizabeth said, swatting her hand in the direction of the Great Hall. "Go in there and slash them to bits."

Marcus glanced at Walsingham and then at the regal queen where they stood near the stone chapel in the ankle-deep snow. "Your Majesty, there are but two of us with swords—"

"And one pistol," she said, nodding to the wheellock firearm at Walsingham's side.

"Two," called Luke.

"And I can pummel some frogs," Henry said, punching a fist into his palm.

"There are a dozen French soldiers on the grounds, most with pistols and swords where several of your ladies could be shot."

"They would gladly lose their lives for me," Elizabeth intoned, looking down her nose at him while still being shorter than he. It was a talent that she must have been taught as a child. She'd certainly perfected it over the years of her reign. "Although I prefer that not to happen."

"As would I, Your Majesty," Marcus said. "For if they are killed and we are killed, ye will be left out here alone without protection, and they will carry you off to France."

The queen's lips pinched tight as if she'd eaten something bitter and wished to spit it out. "I didn't survive the Tower and my sister and the pox to be killed by a crusty, perfumed, French Catholic dowager-queen." She sniffed.

Walsingham nodded. "'Tis best to let them leave and then enter for warmth."

Mathew kicked his boot at a holly branch lying in the snow, its bright red berries contrasting against the background. "So they didn't suspect that Lady Cordelia could be someone other than the queen?"

"Did they look at her tee—?" Henry broke off before insulting the queen by reminding everyone that her teeth were decayed, while Cordy's were pretty white pearls.

"They seemed to accept her," Marcus said, turning toward Haddon Hall that he could barely make out in the distance between the stark trees.

Elizabeth gathered the blanket that Walsingham laid upon her shoulders in front of her. "She has my ring. That alone would make anyone accept her as authentic since I never remove it."

Marcus didn't look at her. Instead his gaze followed some men rushing out past the carriage to the barn. He took several steps away from the group toward the forest's edge, trying to see. "Yer ring was found earlier in the butter," Marcus said. "Lady Cordelia had to say it was a forgery."

Elizabeth's eyes grew wide. "My locket ring? Was in *butter*?"

"A necessary hiding place that unfortunately was found."

Ire built in her words "I told her to guard it with her *life*."

"Cordy..." he started and turned back to the queen before continuing. "Cordelia struggled with worry over the ring, but Captain Noire was closing in and she had to hide it. She didn't want him to take that away from ye. Now she is guarding *ye*, Your Majesty, with her life. Out there." He indicated the direction of Haddon Hall. "Willing to be dragged to France where she will no doubt be discovered and tortured or executed."

Elizabeth's face snapped to Walsingham. "That will not do. We will pay a ransom for her."

"Or *you*," Walsingham said, pointing at Marcus, "will prevent her from being taken onboard a ship and save us the pain of negotiation."

That was his plan. Saving Cordy. But at what price for his mother and sister if he couldn't finish his mission?

"Yer Majesty," Marcus said, rubbing his jaw and feeling the prickle of nearly a week's worth of growth. "I would ask of ye to meet with Lord Morton at a tower house northwest of here on the Scottish border. He waits there with troops from King James to make certain that ye are not taken to France. Like I said, I was sent to infiltrate the French group and protect ye."

"An army?" Elizabeth said. "And he sent only you?"

"Sending a Scottish army onto English land could be viewed as an act of war, Yer Majesty," Marcus said.

Walsingham stroked his beard in thought. "True." He pierced Marcus with a narrowed gaze. "Ride for them now? You have England's permission to bring Morton's troops here to surround Noire and his men."

"That's over a hundred miles from here," Elizabeth said at the same time. "And I have no intention of riding out of England."

"Noire will have taken Cordelia, or ye, Your Majesty, out of England before I could even reach them to request King James' forces," Marcus said.

"Will Lord Morton have information about who in my circle is a traitor?" Elizabeth asked.

Lying to a queen would be considered treason, but she wasn't *his* queen. "Aye, by now his own spies would have obtained the information." Marcus looked to Walsingham. "Once I accompany Noire and Lady Cordelia away from Haddon Hall, I would have ye take Her Majesty north to Canonbie where Lord Morton will meet ye at Gilnockie Tower."

"We can help guard you, Your Majesty, on your journey," Mathew said. He stuck one leg out and bowed low over it as if he wore hose and short, velvet breeches. In contrast, his muddy work trousers would have made the genuflection look like a farce if not for the serious tone and face of the man. He would surely give his life for his queen.

"I plan to follow Lady Cordelia," Henry said. "Help the Scot save her."

"She ain't going to…teach you the lute when she's got *him*," John said, pointing at Marcus.

"He might not be…taking lute lessons from the girl," Henry shot back.

John looked Marcus up and down, his brows rising high. "Oh, I'd say she is."

"God's teeth," Elizabeth swore. "Why are they arguing about music lessons?" She looked to Walsingham. "Or is this some code for something carnal? Some dalliance?"

"I believe the second, Your Majesty," Walsingham said.

Marcus took several steps away from the group to look more carefully through the trees, partly to retreat from the queen's assessing gaze but also to catch a glimpse of Cordy. The soldiers were assembling quickly on the side of the manor but then dispersing as if they were searching for something.

"What is going on?" he murmured, hands fisting at his sides.

Mathew stopped beside him, mimicking his stance. "They are looking for something or someone. Could Lady Cordelia have escaped?"

"While surrounded by armed French soldiers?" Marcus said. He shook his head. "I need to find out what's going on. I'll ride back and join the group."

"If you're leaving, I'm coming too," Henry said from behind.

Marcus didn't even turn to look at him. "Too suspicious. If ye want to join, wait until we reach a town and follow on." But he wasn't thinking about the English brute joining on the expedition. Something didn't look right up at the manor. Arms moved about, men pointed, several jogging around the corner.

"Keep the queen safe here," Marcus said. "Wait until we leave the area before escorting her up to the manor for the comfort she can find from her released patrons."

He barely looked at the queen before mounting Elspeth. "Yer Majesty." He spun the horse around and, dodging trees, pressed through the woods, reaching the open moorland. Marcus rode across the snow, making more tracks that crisscrossed the snowy landscape. If anyone with tracking sense studied them, they'd easily follow the trail to the stone chapel.

As he neared the scene, he saw a man he didn't recognize walking around Racer. He had dark hair and a short beard and mustache. Tall and erect with muscle, his clothes hung well about him. They were richly made, and he walked with confidence. Marcus slowed Elspeth, his gaze fastened on him as he picked up Racer's foot, running his thumb over the horseshoe that had been missing hoof nails. He walked to the next and next, checking each one.

"I found that horse south of the ambush sight," Marcus said, dismounting. His gaze swept the French soldiers who continued to round the manor.

"'Tis my horse," the man said in an obvious English accent. This was no Frenchman. "I put the queen on Lancelot when Noire ambushed us," he said. He looked much too clean to be the guard that had been housed in the dungeon.

"I found your steed wandering on his own. I found the queen on foot the next day. She must have been unseated."

The Englishman snorted and turned his full attention on Marcus. "The queen? Whom you found?"

"Aye," Marcus said, his brows lowering.

"You've been deceived, Scot. That is no queen in there." The man indicated the hall with a brisk tilt of his head.

Marcus didn't have to curb his surprise. "Bloody hell. What?"

"That is one of her ladies dressed and made up as her." He shook his head. "But Cordelia Cranfield is no queen. Her mother kept the true faith, but the daughters were led to heresy with the current queen." He shook his head.

Shite, shite, shite! "Who are ye?" Marcus asked.

The Englishman smiled and leaned in. "Your contact."

Marcus's mouth unhinged slightly as he stared at the aristocratic man. *Contact?* Marcus worked alone. Morton knew that. There was never a contact.

"Ye are the informant from Whitehall," Marcus said. "Gupton, is it?"

"Yes. Lord Gupton, Baron of Beaumont Hill in Rutland." He narrowed his eyes. "I wasn't expecting a Scot, but that makes sense. Mary Stewart is your queen, and George Douglas of Lochleven is paying."

Lochleven? George Douglas had tried to whisk Queen Mary away from her captors on more than one occasion. He always managed to escape being caught but had never been successful. Occasionally, because Marcus's family was thought to sympathize with Mary's plight, the Catholic Douglases searched him out for a paid mission. This last time, he'd said no. They must have hired Oliver Gupton to take Elizabeth to the Douglas brothers, William and George, who were far from their cousin, Lord James Douglas of Morton, the king's regent. Had they told Gupton that Marcus was part of their mission?

What a tangle this had become, and all he could think about was how Cordy would receive it. Had Gupton revealed him to Cordy? Lord, he should have told her who he truly was. Was it too late?

Marcus glanced at the castle and then back at the Englishman. Was Gupton also working for Noire and the de' Medicis? A spy who worked for both factions? Some could accuse Marcus of doing the same. *But I said no to the Douglases.* He would do nothing to lose his trusted position with Lord Morton.

Gupton considered Marcus as he unbuckled the harness around his horse's head. "Noire says you are Marcus Ruthven, son of William Ruthven, who worked for Lord Darnley and helped kill Mary Stewart's secretary under Darnley's orders."

Marcus stepped closer to the man, both of them on the far side of the horse. "I prefer to keep my name quiet."

Gupton shrugged. "I'm surprised George Douglas has put his faith in you. Ruthvens are slippery creatures, twisting to whatever side they must to move ahead. Your father went against Mary, but then it is said she bespelled him to her side when he visited her, and that now he plots against King James."

Marcus frowned, feeling his secrets knocking around inside his chest. "My father and I do not see eye to eye on political and religious matters. He has no influence at court anymore."

Gupton grinned, one brow rising. "You are Catholic?"

"Aye."

Gupton considered him. "I wonder where your loyalties actually lay. With Mary and perhaps your father, or with the Protestant regents and young King James."

The man hit too close to the mark, but Marcus had learned to lie through a life of straddling the line between religions and political parties. He looked him right in the eyes. "I would not risk my life to see Queen Mary back on the throne of Scotland unless I was of the true religion."

The man snorted, turning back to his horse. "When we liberate Queen Mary, she will sit upon the English throne. Her son has control of Scotland, and despite the de' Medicis' desire to control Scotland, Catherine de' Medici must agree that having England under her wing will be more advantageous than a rebellious country of crags and warring clans."

He turned back to his horse that Cordy had named Racer, but who was in fact Lancelot, and lengthened the stirrups that Marcus had shortened for Cordy.

Could Lord Morton have tasked Oliver Gupton to play the traitor just like Marcus? He'd originally said Marcus was his contact. "I saw ye in the ambush," Marcus said.

Gupton nodded and unbuckled the girth strap holding the saddle in place. "I was to help Noire capture the queen and yet she got away somehow. And then Cordelia Cranfield shows up here and pretends to be the queen. 'Tis a tangle that is not making Noire very well-mannered."

Ballocks. Marcus looked to the hall. His hand curled around the post beside Racer, keeping him rooted there. *Daingead.* Cordy had been discovered. "What is Noire doing?"

"First I had to convince him that she wasn't the queen after her conspiratorial ladies had all acted like she was Elizabeth. And he'd already sent word to the coast to inform the captain that they were coming with the queen, so he was certainly not pleased."

"What has he done with the ladies? All of them?"

"Locked the lot of them up in one of the bed chambers, except for Lady Cordelia. He keeps questioning her about how she'd come and who had brought her. Something about Walsingham being killed." Gupton shook his head and looked to Marcus. "Noire said the Scot killed Walsingham. I assume that's you?"

Without hesitation, the lie rolled off Marcus's tongue. "There was a man with her. She called him Walsingham, but I've never seen Elizabeth nor her Spy Master." He shrugged and made himself lean back against the wall of the barn, crossing his arms as if he weren't struggling to stay in place. "I can't believe I was tricked."

"Well, you might still have a chance. Noire is convinced the real queen is hiding somewhere around Haddon Hall, because someone found her ring in the butter."

Marcus's browed lowered. "Butter? How ridiculous."

"Yes, but he thinks she must have been here if the ring is authentic."

"And he thinks it is?"

"I suppose, although I would never have thought Elizabeth would part with it. Some say she plans to use it to signify who she wants to be her heir. She will say it before her last breath and the ring will be taken off her bony finger." He glanced over his shoulder at the soldiers trotting about the exterior of Haddon Hall. "He's sent half his men to search the entire manor and surrounding woods. Haddon Hall has rather an extensive acreage." He cocked his thumb at two men riding across the moorland over which Marcus had returned. With any luck, Mathew's crew would take the two men out, reducing the number of French soldiers that Marcus would have to kill. Aye, kill, because he wouldn't let them take Cordy, especially if she didn't have a crown protecting her.

"So we aren't leaving to meet Noire's ship now?"

"Without the real queen?" Gupton laughed darkly. "Noire would have lost his head if he'd brought Cordelia Cranfield back to France instead of Elizabeth Tudor."

"How would Catherine de' Medici know? They have not met, and the lady I brought in looks so much like the queen."

"When no alarm was sounded here, she would know," Gupton said. "And there are those at the French court who *have* met the English queen. Cordelia is too young and lovely to be mistaken for that Protestant witch."

Oliver Gupton was a traitor down to his core. He hid it well to be considered one of the English queen's inner circle. A slimy, slithering traitor who must be clever indeed to fool Walsingham and Elizabeth.

Marcus pushed off the side of the barn while Gupton removed his horse's tack. Considering how he'd sacrificed the beast, sabotaging his footing that could have ruined him, Gupton seemed to treat him well. Marcus began to walk across the courtyard.

"Where did you say you dumped Walsingham?" Gupton called after him.

Marcus turned still walking away backwards. "A ravine two miles to the west. Covered him with snow and made it look undisturbed, so he won't be found until spring unless the wolves get him." Would Gupton go to look for him to prove Marcus's story false? "He might already be torn to bits. I heard the pack howling last night."

Without waiting, Marcus trudged onward to the front of the house while several muttering Frenchmen dodged around him, looking under anything that might hide a queen. They apparently didn't know much about the proud Elizabeth Tudor, for the woman he'd spoken with at the stone chapel would never stoop to hiding under a wheelbarrow.

Marcus stepped briskly up the front steps and into the entryway.

"Where is the queen?" Noire said in loud French, his patience as thin as the skim on scorched milk.

Cordelia had been set in a small high-backed chair that looked quite uncomfortable. Her hands were tied behind it, probably in an attempt to intimidate her rather than detain her since there were four armed guards also in the room.

She looked directly to Marcus when he entered but then looked away immediately, probably because Noire studied her every expression. Any relief at Marcus's presence would shatter the cover Marcus operated under. Aye, she was a talented actress. If Gupton hadn't shown, she'd have convinced them to ride, and somehow Marcus would have gotten her safely away before they sailed.

"What is this?" Marcus asked, accusation in his voice. "She is not the English queen? The man with her who I killed was not the English Spy Master, Walsingham?"

"Oliver Gupton arrived and verified that she's an imposter, a Lady Cordelia Cranfield." Half of Cordy's white makeup was rubbed away, but there was still enough on, and her hair was tucked up so well that Noire hadn't realized that she was the woman from Bradwell who had sung and played on the stage in the tavern.

Marcus stomped up to Cordy and placed his hands on the arms of her chair. He came mere inches from her face. "Where is the Queen of England, lass?"

The twinge of relief he saw in her golden-brown eyes disappeared in a blink, and she narrowed her gaze as she stared defiantly back. "On her way back to London. In fact, she is likely already there, safe, sound, and healthy behind the walls of Whitehall Palace."

"Ye were a decoy?"

"Of course." Cordy tilted her pert nose upward and looked toward the painted ceiling above. She showed nothing but contempt. *Clever, brave lass.*

"But her ring is here in the hall," Noire said, holding the piece up.

Marcus took it from him, looking at it from all sides. "We are certain 'tis not a forgery?"

"The gems are real, and it looks exactly like the ring from what Gupton says. He also said she would never take it from her finger," Noire said. "It means that much to her."

"So…" Marcus began by drawing out the word, "the queen somehow let her precious ring slide from her finger to land in the churned butter here? I don't see the queen even entering the kitchens, let alone losing her beloved ring to a crock of butter."

"Sacrebleu," Noire cursed. He walked up to Cordy. "Where is the queen?" he yelled in heavily accented English, his chin-length hair brushing into his face. It was the most unraveled Marcus had ever seen the captain.

"Nowhere you can enter without being captured, hung, and ripped apart," Cordy said.

Noire pulled his arm back as if winding up to slap her or worse. Marcus caught his hand that had begun to fist. "Ye do not strike the lass. I am the one who was fooled and brought ye the wrong woman. Send her away or up with her ladies while we hunt for the true queen."

After long seconds, Noire's arm relaxed, and Marcus released the man's tight fist. "If Elizabeth is not in this area, ye must let your mistress know that she never came this way. 'Twas a false report. Gupton will take the fall. He won't be able to return to France nor England nor Scotland once I tell the king about his fanatical Catholicism."

"You think 'tis so easily solved," Noire shook his head, running his hand through his usually immaculate hair. "You do not know the de' Medicis," he murmured, and Marcus caught a glimpse of fear in this stoic man. The emotion caused hairs at Marcus's nape to rise. An enemy was dangerous, aye, but an enemy with fear for his life was unpredictable and lethal like a cornered beast.

Noire looked at Cordy. "The Queen Mother will require blood to be spilled for this false report, someone to blame. And it will not be mine."

Marcus stepped between Cordy and Noire, blocking her with his body. "What do ye mean?"

"La fille will die," he said. "And you will retrieve the body of the man masquerading as Walsingham. If you do not, then your body will do. But either way, I will bring an Elizabeth to my mistress. And probably that incompetent Englishman, Gupton, who spread the false report. Perhaps a pile of court ladies and that guard in the dungeon will also help appease her anger."

He spoke as if the dowager-queen of France was some great monster that required blood to appease her appetite for dead Protestants. Perhaps a woman descended from Grendel, the bloodthirsty creature that Beowulf defeated in legend.

Marcus's hand slid along the hilt of his sword. "First of all, the body has probably been torn apart by wolves overnight. I doubt any of it is left except for blood in the snow. Secondly, killing innocent women is a sign of a lunatic. And thirdly..." He slid his sword from its scabbard, holding it slightly raised and ready. "Lady Cordelia Cranfield will remain whole and healthy. And if ye insist on murder..." Marcus held his sword ready, very aware that the four remaining French guards had moved in with three swords and a cocked pistol, "ye won't be so lucky."

Marcus's heart slammed in his chest as he watched the French soldiers surround the two of them. One could easily skewer Cordy while he battled the others.

Noire smiled and rubbed at the corner of his mouth as if wiping away a crumb. He turned to the table next to him and pulled a card from the surface, holding it up between his fingers. He tipped his head as if considering him, and then his brows rose. "I didn't recognize her with all the paste on her skin, but once Monsieur Gupton revealed the lie, I had Lady Cordelia's pocket searched." He held the card up so Marcus could see it contained skaters on a pond. "Bradwell Village" was printed below the scene.

Noire looked at Cordy, and his face screwed up with a dark, macabre type of mischief. "Do you by chance play the lute, mademoiselle?"

Cordy didn't answer, and Noire looked back to Marcus. "So you see, Highlander, your duplicity is exposed." He shook his head like he addressed an errant schoolboy who'd been caught with falsifying grades. "You did not find the queen, killing her Spy Master. Instead you sent this poor woman in here to her death while you attempt to find the true Queen Elizabeth."

Marcus's mind scanned the room, trying to latch onto a viable plan that would get Cordy safely out of there. Without the pistol, he'd have a chance against four soldiers, but he couldn't outrun a bullet. Or could he?

Noire exhaled and shrugged. "'Tis a shame. Such talent, but the Queen Mother must see the truth of what was presented to me by Marcus Blythe, who I'm certain now is a spy." He shook his head at Marcus. "I will add your body to make up for Walsingham whom the wolves have torn apart." He snorted.

Marcus backed up to stand directly before Cordy, using his body to block her from the bullet about to be fired. He eyed the man with the pistol. The frowning soldier was young, probably new to killing. Could he be led astray? All Marcus needed was a distraction. And once the firearm was discharged, without hitting him, he could easily take it from the lad. Marcus focused on Noire. "Ye will return to France and be killed, Noire."

"I will return to France and be honored," Noire countered.

Behind him, Marcus heard Cordy scooting the chair as she struggled to free her hands.

"Shoot him," Noire said, and the lad pointed the deadly end of the pistol at his chest.

"No!" Cordy yelled. She grunted as if she'd broken free and grabbed ahold of the back of his tunic.

"Un…deux…" Marcus called out, and twisted, throwing himself against Cordy as he yelled, "trois."

Bang!

Marcus felt the burn of the bullet hitting his shoulder as he fell on Cordy, covering her completely on the floor, the chair tumbled over beside them.

"Marcus!" she screamed. He met her wide eyes, her mouth open in terror. Following her gaze, he saw the blood begin to leach through his white shirt, spreading across his shoulder.

Chapter Fourteen

"She is able, by her great wit and sugared eloquence, to win even such as before they shall come to her company shall have a great misliking."
William Cecil speaking of the dangers of Mary Queen of Scots

C ORDELIA'S HEART POUNDED about in her chest like a panicked horse tethered in a stall, trying to kick its way out of her.

"Now kill the girl," Noire ordered in French. The cool, unemotional order, said in a language that had always sounded so fluent and passionate, caused a chill in Cordelia that added a shiver to her already trembling hands. She must do something, but Marcus's heavy body had pinned her under him. How was it that when they'd lain together his weight had not seemed so much? *Dead weight.* The thought pushed a sob from her, and she shoved at the shoulder that wasn't bloody. "Marcus!"

The chair she'd been sitting in lay shattered in pieces beside them. Cordelia grabbed frantically for one of the legs to use as a club. But as her fingers touched the curved surface, Marcus rolled off her suddenly. "I'm well, lass," he said as he lifted onto his feet, but she saw him grimace.

The French soldier fumbled with his pistol, trying to reload it with shaking fingers. The other three soldiers lifted their swords.

"Bloody frogs!" boomed a voice, and Cordelia watched Henry charge across the room like an enraged bull. He used his shoulder to slam into the pistol, throwing the young man through the air along with the firearm. The man didn't move where he laid crumpled against the table legs, and the pistol slid across the wooden floor.

Marcus slashed against all three swordsmen who advanced on him together, although hesitantly so as not to skewer each other. Henry didn't bother with the gun, instead turning back to charge once again. This time he knocked two of the soldiers to the floor, their swords skidding away.

Cordelia pushed upward, running toward the pistol where it had halted under the table. Noire had the same idea and dove under the heavy wooden furniture.

"No, no, no," Cordelia said, scrambling to reach it first, but her huge royal petticoats nearly tripped her. She fell forward onto her stomach, knocking the breath from her. The golden and scarlet petticoats flew out around her in a way that made them seem to swell.

Noire cursed in rapid French. "Get out of the way, woman."

But Cordelia swung her legs, kicking at the man as her petticoats filled the space under the table, covering the pistol. His hands grasped her wildly kicking legs as if to rip her from the spot, but still her arms flew out along the floor searching until one of her hands bumped into the heavy metal.

Her fingers wrapped around it. Had the soldier managed to reload it? Otherwise, it would be useless. But as long as Noire couldn't use it, they had a chance.

She let him shove against her and hid the pistol in the folds of her gown. The floor was dirty with melted slush and hard as she used her elbows and impotent slippers to roll and crawl out from the table in a tumble of silk, lace, and gold embroidery.

Where were the other soldiers? Even with the gun shot, no one else had run inside the hall to see what was going on. Marcus must have noticed this too. He held a napkin to the top of his shoulder as Henry stood after holding one soldier around the neck long enough for the man to fall unconscious to the floor.

"Where are the rest?" Marcus asked.

"Chasing Mathew," Henry said, breathing hard. He wiped his arm over his sweaty forehead. "They think he's the queen."

"What?" Cordy asked from where she stood, breathing in gulps of air, the gun at her side. Noire was still under the table searching for a firearm that was no longer there. He continued to curse loudly.

"He's wearing the queen's dress and wig. Riding west while that Walsingham fellow rides the true queen east."

"Bald and naked?" Marcus asked.

"Wrapped in a cloak," Henry said, nodding. "Luke is picking off the frogs with his pistol, and John's throwing rocks at them." He shrugged. "I came for our lute player." He smiled at Cordelia, but then his grin changed to a yell of warning. "Watch out!"

Cordelia spun around, the gun right before her, lodged against her middle. Noire held a short sword. He lunged for her.

"Nay!" Marcus yelled, running to intercept the fatal slice.

Cordelia's finger moved, lighting the flint with a spark. *Boom!*

She yelped as the pistol discharged, the force of it thrusting her hand upward and under her breastbone. As the small cloud of smoke dissipated and Marcus reached her, her breath caught at the look of surprise on Noire's face. Marcus spun her around as if blocking the thrust of Noire's sword, again shielding her with his body. But Cordelia knew the thrust wouldn't come. She squeezed her eyes shut and heard the thud of Noire hitting the floor.

"Good shot," Henry said, and Cordelia turned her face to see Jacque Noire laying on the floor in a growing pool of blood.

Smoke from the gun hovered in the air. Cordelia sought to even out her jagged breaths and looked up into Marcus's eyes. "You're shot."

"Not as much as Noire," he answered, a grin growing on his face.

She turned to his shoulder, stepping out of his arms to look at his ripped tunic where the shot had torn through it. The blood swelled from a grazing across the top of his shoulder. "He was aiming right for your middle," Cordelia said. "How...?"

"Un, deux, trois," he said.

"You counted to three?" she asked, looking closer at the wound. It might need a stitch or two and generous cleaning, but it had only sliced the skin instead of shooting him through.

"We are taught early on to count to three before doing something. With the stress of the moment, and the youth of the soldier, I gave him something familiar, and I dove at the count of two to beat the bullet."

Her anxious brow relaxed, and she grinned up at him. "You certainly are clever, Marcus Blythe."

Henry was pushing the unconscious soldiers over and binding their hands. He didn't bother with the dead one or Noire. "Eventually they're going to realize that Elizabeth isn't the one they're chasing out there."

Cordelia made to dash away, but Marcus caught her arm. His humor was gone. "Cordy, there's something I need to tell ye. About me."

"The ring," Cordelia said, rushing toward the prone body of Noire. The blasted ring that she must return to the queen. She avoided the man's open eyes and grabbed his hand. It was still warm but would cool soon. She tugged on the queen's ring, pulling it from his little finger and placing it back on hers. Relief flooded her, adding to the emotions rolling like boulders down a slope through her. Being captured, tethered and threatened, and then seeing Noire's man shoot at Marcus, the red spreading across his shirt. If she could keep moving, perhaps she wouldn't be crushed.

She turned toward the stairs. "The ladies!" She looked to Marcus. "I'll release them and Lord and Lady Manners. You get Master Winslow from below."

Without waiting, Cordelia raised her petticoats and ran to the stairs that led to the bed chambers. "Lady Anne!" she called. "Lady and Lord Manners!" Her slippers pounded up the stairs. She needed to get them out before the remaining soldiers stormed back inside to find their captain dead and their captives freed.

Down the long corridor most of the doors were shut, but the third one on the right was gaping open. Cordelia ran up to it. "Ladies?" She stopped, her hand catching the doorframe to stop herself from falling into the room.

Oliver Gupton stood with Anne Bixby before him, a knife at her throat.

>>><<<

MARCUS POINTED AT the entryway. "Bar the door," he said to Henry. "And then free the soldier in the dungeon and anyone else that Noire may have locked down there. I'm helping Cordy." Something didn't feel right. During the scrabble for the gun and fighting the French soldiers someone had entered the hall, but Marcus barely had time to notice. A man. Had he run back out or to the kitchens? *Or above?*

Marcus ran up the stairs two steps at a time. "Cordy!" he yelled at the top and saw the light from windows of a bedroom spilling into the corridor. As he ran up to it, the door slammed shut. The sound of a key turning in the lock made Marcus react, and he threw his shoulder against the door while pressing the latch. The door flew inward, and several screams and gasps accompanied his barreling entrance.

The room had a large bed with a canopy of scarlet matching the curtains flanking two glassed windows. Three well-dressed women clung to one another on the far side of the bed, and Cordy stood right before him, the key in hand. To the right Oliver Gupton held one of the ladies, a blade against her jugular.

"Cordy," Marcus said.

"He said he'd slice her through if I didn't lock the door," she answered his unasked question.

"Gupton, drop the dagger," Marcus ordered, his voice rough with threat.

"Have you flipped to the Protestant side then, Ruthven?" Oliver Gupton asked. The man had wild eyes, and the dagger grazed against the lady's neck.

Cordy's gaze snapped between Gupton and Marcus. "Ruthven?"

"Let the woman go, Gupton," Marcus said.

Cordy turned back to the English traitor, her lips pursed. She pried the queen's ring off her finger. "How much do you think Elizabeth will give you for its return? Your head perhaps. Your freedom?"

Gupton's eyes fastened on the precious, easily-recognized ring. Most of England would look to the owner of it as Elizabeth's heir for it was a signal to follow and support the wearer. What havoc could Mary Queen of Scots do with that ring?

"Release Anne, and the ring is yours," Cordy said. Anne's eyes widened, but she didn't say anything. She couldn't. With the blade against her skin, she was as helpless as a newborn bairn left in the snow.

Gupton's mouth pinched and moved side to side in a look that was nearly comical. It gave him the dangerous look of a madman who was backed into a corner. "Or I give this lady up, and Ruthven tries to run me through before I can tell all his secrets." His words, spoken with such confidence, entered and spread through Marcus's body like a poison. He held his sword higher, ready to follow through on the man's bloody prediction. It would be easier that way. He could deny all and there'd be no one who knew everything. *Except me.*

"The secret that I'm a spy against France and the Catholics who wish to put Mary on the Scottish throne," Marcus said, knowing his time as a spy against the French was over. "That I play the Catholic to keep in aristocratic circles in France."

Gupton smiled wryly. He tipped his head to the side, his gaze glancing toward Cordy. "Does she know that you also work for William and George Douglas on the other side of the political coin?" Gupton said.

Marcus felt heat rise in his neck. "'Tis a deep cover, Gupton, nothing of truth in it."

Gupton huffed through his nose. "A fabulous liar as ever. Just like your good old father who switched sides from King James to Queen Mary and back again when the wind blew in favor of the Protestants."

One of the ladies from behind the bed looked at Marcus. "George Douglas tried to help Mary Stewart escape Loch Levan Castle with six-thousand men before Mary crossed into England in retreat. They say he's in love with her still and works to free her."

"And he pays Marcus Ruthven to help him," Gupton said and laughed. "And Lord Morton pays you too. I have to applaud you, Ruthven, being paid by both parties to push political figures around until one of them ultimately wins. Then you can be the hero, saying you're the spy against the loser."

"Marcus…Ruthven?" Cordy asked. "Does he speak the truth?"

"Now is not the time," Marcus said, hating the audience for the airing of his secrets. "We will talk when all is secure."

"Secure?" Cordy asked, backing away from him closer to the bed. "From whom? Noire's men or whomever you are working with?" She glanced toward the window. "Marcus, are you really trying to capture Queen Elizabeth to take to Mary's supporters? Is Lord Morton and his army really waiting for her at the border? Or are the Douglases waiting there?"

"Lord Morton," Marcus said. "I swear it, Cordy."

"Is he lying then?" Cordy asked.

Marcus opened his mouth to deny Gupton's revelation, but the words wouldn't come. Because the bastard spoke the truth.

―――※―――

CORDELIA FELT HER chest hollow as if the middle of her had rotted out. Marcus had been lying about his name from the moment she met him. What hurt more was how he'd kept the lie going even after they'd been together. The world she was living in was completely counterfeit. She wasn't the queen. Marcus wasn't a simple, skillful man working for the Scottish regent to keep Elizabeth safe. Did he have feelings for her at all? Was it all a huge illusion in which he could hide?

"Marcus?" *Ruthven, not Blythe.* "Is Oliver Gupton lying?"

Marcus kept his gaze on Oliver. "Right now, Gupton needs to release this lady and be happy if he gets to keep his life."

"I have no life now," Gupton said, pulling Anne back with him until the bedchamber wall stopped him. "Not in England with that Protestant witch on the throne."

The ladies gasped at his vehement words. The usually polished courtier had become a wild-eyed madman before their eyes. *Like my mother,* Cordelia thought.

Oh how Cordelia remembered that crazed look when her mother attacked the queen. That wretched, dagger-wielding gaze popped up in Cordelia's nightmares.

"You're the one who sent information about this journey to Catherine de' Medici," Cordelia said to Gupton. "And when attacked, you gave the queen your horse, your horse that you meant to sacrifice with barely tacked shoes." If Marcus had refused Oliver's claims, she'd have believed him, for the English courtier lived with lies. But it looked as if Marcus did too.

The foundation that she'd built over the last days with him, working to save Queen Elizabeth, crumbled beneath Cordelia. Her knees felt weak, and her head swam. *Trust me that I will never let harm come to ye.* He'd asked her to trust him even as he lied about his name and family.

But the look in his eyes, the feel of his touch…Could any man be that good a liar? Probably, but would that liar, with no feelings for a woman, throw himself over her to stop a lethal bullet?

Cordelia looked away from Marcus to focus on Oliver Gupton. His normally waxed and combed hair stuck out at odd angles, and his lips pulled back exposing clenched teeth. "Lord Oliver," she said, her voice mild. "I believe you. About the Scot being a spy without loyalties and about you being passionate in your beliefs."

"Cordy," Marcus said, but she held a palm out to him without looking his way. She kept her eyes focused on Oliver's jerking gaze as it moved frantically about the room. He was nearly beyond reasoning.

"And I know that you don't want to spill Anne's blood only to find yourself facing God's judgement when whoever this Scot is runs you through. So release her and be on your way. Probably to France if you wish to keep your head."

"Not with him there ready to strike," Oliver said. "Make way, Ruthven, and Lady Anne and I will be on our way."

A small sob came from the lady who had always been a thorn in Cordelia's side, but silly thorns didn't matter with the woman's life in the balance.

Cordelia looked to Marcus. "Put the sword down, Master Ruthven, and slide it across the room."

He frowned fiercely, and she thought he'd shake his head. But slowly he lowered his sword to the floor.

"Let him leave the room if he doesn't have Anne," she continued. They all waited until Marcus gave one nod and backed aside from the door.

Cordelia looked back to Oliver. "If you don't release her, Marcus won't let you leave. 'Tis that clear, Lord Gupton."

His gaze flicked back and forth from her to Marcus, and he edged his way around the perimeter of the room, Anne still before him.

"Let her go," Cordelia demanded, but he still held tightly to his captive. "Take me instead." Anne's eyes widened, meeting Cordelia's gaze, but Oliver continued to inch his way to the open door. His hold never lessened, and a thin line of red appeared on Anne's pale neck.

Holy Mother Mary! She needed to do something. Who knew

what would happen to Anne if he dragged her with him. She frowned and complained and whispered rumors about Cordelia's family, but she didn't deserve to be terrorized, tortured, and killed for her loyalty to the queen.

"Lord Gupton," Cordelia said, holding the precious ring high. His gaze stopped on it as if it were a beacon. Even without the significance behind it, the gems themselves were valuable and could bring him riches. And riches had been the downfall of many a man and woman. "Catch!" Cordelia called and tossed the ring toward him. And just like the soldier below had reacted to a cue in Marcus's counting, Oliver Gupton loosened his hold on Anne in an attempt to catch the precious ring.

It clacked on the floorboards in the open doorway, and Cordelia lunged for Anne's arm to pull her away. At the same time, Marcus's fist swung upward, catching Oliver's jaw as the man dropped to reach the ring. The resounding crack of knuckle against bone made the ladies gasp, and Oliver Gupton flew backwards with the force. He landed on his back, his head slamming on the wooden floor. Marcus stood over him, both fists ready to fly, but Oliver didn't move.

"Good Lord, Anne," her sister, Margaret, cried out as she pulled her from Cordelia's arms. Both ladies clustered around her, Margaret dabbing a handkerchief along Anne's neck.

Cordelia snatched the ring off the floor and hurried over to Anne. "I would entrust this with you," Cordelia said. "Keep it safe for the queen."

Anne met her gaze. "Thank you," she said, the words breathless, trembling.

Cordelia's mouth relaxed, but Marcus's lie felt heavy inside her, making the smile barely there. "We aren't safe yet," she said, purposely ignoring Marcus as she ran to the window to stare out over the snowy landscape. "There are still Frenchmen racing around out there."

She felt him step up next to her. All Cordelia wanted to do was throw her arms around him, but she couldn't, not without the truth.

"Elizabeth is out there," Marcus said.

Cordelia's face snapped to him. "The real Elizabeth?"

"She showed up with Walsingham after ye'd entered to play your part. When Gupton revealed ye, and Noire found the ring, Noire was certain the real queen was somewhere on the property."

Cordelia turned away from the window, hurrying out of the room. She wanted to put distance between her and Marcus so she could think. "I must help her." She held the rail as she ran down the narrow wooden staircase into the Great Hall. She heard Marcus right behind her.

A ragged looking Geoffrey Winslow sat at the table chewing and washing the food down with ale. Henry stood beside him, arms crossed. He scowled. "The man had only been fed broth these past days since they locked him in there."

"He's too weak to help then," Marcus said.

"I will fight to save Her Majesty until my last breath," Winslow said but remained seated. "I hear Gupton was the traitor."

"He's upstairs unconscious," Marcus said. "Being tied up by the ladies."

Footsteps on the stairs heralded Lord Manners, the owner of Haddon Hall. "God's teeth," he said, his words exploding as he took in the dead bodies in his Great Hall. "What can I do?"

Cordelia met Marcus's gaze. His brows were low, his eyes troubled as if he wished he could explain about his duplicity. But there was no time, and she wondered if there was anything he could say to make things right between them again. *He saved me.*

She cleared her throat but spoke softly. "I trust you, Marcus Ruthven, to keep me safe. But can I trust you to save Queen Elizabeth from her enemies?"

Chapter Fifteen

"Grief never ends, but it changes. It is a passage, not a place to stay. Grief is not a sign of weakness nor a lack of faith: it is the price of love."
Queen Elizabeth I of England and Ireland

Pressure built in Marcus's head and chest to the point he wanted to yell and swing his sword against foes, real and imagined. But his sword would do nothing against this wall that Cordy had erected between them in the space of heartbeats, each of Gupton's words being another stone, and each of his own silences being the mortar. Would she even listen to his explanations?

"What other choice do ye have, Cordy?" he asked. "Those soldiers will return eventually whether they capture the queen or not."

Her soft lips were clamped tight for a moment. "Very well, Master Ruthven, what do we do?"

Daingead. Her use of his formal name was not a sign of softening.

Her gaze dropped to his injured shoulder, and her hands followed. "You need a tighter binding, or you'll bleed to death."

"Here," Henry said, tossing her a long napkin from the table.

"It grazed me, is all," Marcus said and grimaced as she tied it tightly. The brush of her fingers along his arm made the pain more than bearable.

Marcus nodded to Henry. "Has anyone tried to come in the barred door?"

"Nay. They must all be chasing Mathew."

"You said he's dressed like the queen?" Cordy asked behind him as he strode through the entryway to the barred window near the door.

"Aye, to lead the frogs on a merry chase," Henry answered.

Looking through a small, barred security window, Marcus saw a couple of French soldiers trotting about the yard, but another four could be seen riding in the distance. He threw off the bar, and it clattered to the floor as he swung one of the double doors open. Cordy stepped out next to him ready to work together. He'd always worked alone but having her next to him felt right. Her hair was a tangle of pins, pearls, and red-gold curls around her shoulders, and she'd taken a rag to wipe off a good portion of smeared white makeup.

Henry stopped on Marcus's other side to stare into the side yard where a wildly flying horse and rider ran toward them. "Bloody devil," he said, a smile in his voice, and he shook his head at the preposterous sight.

"O me, my God," Cordy murmured.

"That's Mathew?" Marcus said, but no one need answer him, because the counterfeit queen was racing toward them.

Mathew was dressed in a wildly flapping white gown. A red wig of half-unpinned curls was held on top of his head by one hand as he bent low over his horse's neck. His eyes were wide, but he wore a grin as he flew past them. Half a dozen soldiers followed in a gallop.

"Where did he get the clothes and wig?" Cordy asked, almost afraid to hear the likely answer.

"Walsingham wrapped the queen up in her cape and rode her in the opposite direction," Henry said with approval.

"God's teeth," Lord Manners said, shaking his head. "Her Majesty is out there somewhere naked."

Henry slapped the man on the back, making Lord Manners

almost fall over. "Aye! Our queen is bold and brave."

"They'll kill him if they catch him," Cordy said about Mathew.

"I think he knows that, lass," Henry said, his face going grim. "He'll ride them back toward John and Luke, and they have two pistols now that Walsingham loaned them a second. He's a rather straightforward man for a court dandy." Henry's tone held respect for Elizabeth's security chief. "And quite brave with the queen. I'd never be able to order her to strip her gown off."

Lord Manners pointed a sword that he'd probably pulled down from those adorning the entryway walls. "I sent a kitchen maid running to the village to alert the constable to round up help."

Marcus turned to the three with him on the stoop. "The soldiers don't know Noire is dead or that he discovered I was a spy. I'll throw them off Mathew's trail before riding to find the real queen. Henry, take Cordy with ye now to find her. Sneak her and Walsingham back here. I'll join ye when I can." He turned. "Lord Manners, I'm depending on ye to guard the hall until we return with the queen. Gather the ladies and help them find firearms and load them."

"The ladies?" Manners asked, wide-eyed.

"Unless ye plan to take on seven Frenchmen with pistols on your own," Marcus said, striding toward the barn where Elspeth was still dressed to ride.

"I had Racer ready for ye," Marcus said to Cordy as she ran up with Henry. "But Gupton unsaddled him. Also, his name is Lancelot." He nodded to the bay.

"Lancelot?" Cordy said, leading the horse out of the stall. Only Racer and a shaggy pony were left inside the barn. "Racer is a more noble name. The legendary Lancelot was a seducer of women and a loyalty breaker." She glanced at Marcus. "Perhaps a good name for you to use on your next mission."

"Cordy," Marcus said, shaking his head. He glanced at Henry but knew that Cordy and he would probably never have a moment alone. He couldn't think straight with this pain and anger hanging between them. So he walked right up to her. "Cordy, look at me."

She turned to frown up into his face. Even with the smeared makeup, she was beautiful, and he had to stop himself from pulling her against him. Instead, he rested his hands over her straight shoulders.

"The only lie I told ye was my name. Everything else was true." He leaned in so that they were mere inches apart. "Everything," he said slowly with emphasis. Would she understand what he was saying?

She stared into his eyes as if taking the measure of his words, of his heart. "You are asking me to put my faith in you after I found out you've been lying to me. Not only about your name." She shook her head. "Lies of omission are as bad."

"Uh, I'm…" Henry pointed to himself and then the door of the stables. He'd thrown a hastily fastened saddle over the shaggy, mid-sized horse. "I'll trot on out to the west and see if I can find them."

Cordy still stared at Marcus, waiting for his defense. But he had none. He released a long breath. "I am a spy for both Lord Morton and the Douglas Clan. They are on opposite sides of this whole political, religious mess between France, Scotland, and England. 'Tis purely a job for me. I go into situations and listen and report."

"That's not what you were doing while helping to abduct the queen," she retorted. "Riding me down is not listening and reporting."

"When asked, I interfere if I agree with the request. In this mission, I intended to save the Queen of England and carry her to Scotland, where she could be thankful that Lord Morton had sent someone to save her."

"And what would the Douglases have thought of that?" she asked.

"I doubt they would hear of my involvement. Lord Morton

would give all the credit to King James and himself for rescuing her."

"So you do all this for money, like a mercenary."

Marcus slid his hands from her shoulders. "My father has been ostracized since his involvement with the Riccio murder. He was nearly imprisoned when the Douglas Clan said that he'd been bespelled by Queen Mary after he arrested her. So I am the one who brings money in for my family, for my mother and sister. They depend on me."

He scratched a hand through his hair as if trying to rub away a thought that wouldn't leave him alone. "Both sides contacted me for hire once Gupton sent Catherine de' Medici the information about this secret journey, and I returned across the channel. George Douglas wanted me to bring Elizabeth to him so Mary could take the throne, and Lord Morton ordered me to bring Elizabeth to him so he could put her safely back on the English throne in the name of King James. 'Tis a political tangle."

Cordy stared up at him. In the dim light of the barn her golden-brown eyes looked dark. Anger seemed to war with some softer emotion. Hope?

Without breaking the gaze, Cordy asked a simple question. "Where does your heart lie, Marcus?"

He dropped his hands to his sides, the words that would expose him to immense pain right on his tongue. She wanted truth about his politics, but none of that mattered. He raised one finger slowly and touched the tip to Cordy's chest. "Right here. My heart rests right here."

Did she remember their night together at the inn when she'd touched him the same way? The slight softening of her face gave him hope that she did.

"That doesn't answer my question," she said, her words still sharp.

"I told Douglas I was already engaged. That I couldn't take on his assignment."

Boom!

A gunshot in the distance made Cordy jump, her eyes widening. "The queen!"

Marcus shook his head, grabbing her hand. "Catherine de' Medici wants her alive." But they would easily shoot Walsingham or Mathew once they realized he wasn't the queen.

Elspeth was already saddled, and he lifted Cordy up, mostly with his good arm, to seat her, and mounted behind her. "Hold on," he said near her ear as he guided the horse out of the stable doors, his one arm wrapping around her. As soon as they were clear, they lunged forward toward the western side of the meadow. They must find the queen, but even more important, he must prove to Cordy that he wasn't…a spy? A mercenary? A liar? He was all of it. He didn't deserve Cordelia Cranfield. He pushed the tight fist of self-loathing down inside.

The woman before him was warm and soft. He breathed in her light scent, washed away quickly with the winter breeze as they raced over the snowy field. But he tried to hold onto the smell, a detail that he'd be able to remember when she was gone.

Another gunshot echoed through the trees, and he pulled Elspeth back to a trot. She threw her head up and down, wanting to surge forward. "I would leave ye here out of gunfire," Marcus said against Cordy's ear.

She shook her head, glancing back at him, her face determined. "I have to prove my loyalty as much as you need to complete your mission, Marcus. Firearms or not." She pointed forward. "Go!"

They wove through the trees toward a group of soldiers in blue and three men holding pistols aimed out from them as they stood with their backs against a large oak tree with low limbs.

"My God!" Cordy said, and Marcus looked up to see a figure in a tree above them, a wool and white cloak trimmed with ermine wrapped around a slender figure. It was the queen, treed like a cat with wolves barking up at her.

"Make way!"

Marcus turned in time to see Henry, riding the shaggy pony

straight toward the group. The large man on the smaller horse was comical, but he brandished a pistol.

Boom! He shot at the Frenchmen, and they scattered. One fell to the snow, hit.

From the far side, Mathew entered the chaos, the wig dangling from his saddle. He aimed his horse toward the running soldiers as if seeking to trample them. Two more shots echoed as John and Luke fired their pistols. Only Walsingham kept his ready while they reloaded.

"Your Majesty!" Cordy yelled up. "Are you well?"

"Well?" Elizabeth yelled back. "Walsingham shoved me up in a tree, unwigged and unclothed. What do you think, Lady Cordelia?"

"Are you whole then?" Cordy asked.

"Yes, at present," Elizabeth said. "Man, hand me my wig." The command came as if delivered on the edge of a honed sword.

Mathew shook the red wig out, but several small twigs were tangled in the frizzed locks. He handed it up to the long fingers reaching down.

"Look away," Cordy ordered the men.

"Where have the soldiers gone?" Elizabeth yelled down.

"To alert the rest of them where ye are, Yer Majesty," Marcus said, pulling Elspeth around. "I've lost track of the current number."

More gunfire erupted from near the manor house, and they all looked that way. Henry was the first to speak. "You think Lord Manners is holding them off by himself?"

"He's dead then," Walsingham said. "Come, Your Majesty. We must ride you away from here."

"Take my hand, Your Majesty," Mathew said since he was higher on the horse. She did, and then Walsingham lifted her down to the ground, stepping away immediately.

The woman stood wrapped in fur and wool, her face haggard from the ordeal and her wig sticking out this way and that from Mathew's abusive ride with it. But Elizabeth Tudor's chin remained even, her dark eyes sharp, and her shoulders straight. She was a queen through and through even if her queenly trappings were askew or missing.

Cordy shifted to dismount, and Marcus leaned back to avoid her swinging leg. She jumped down, air under her petticoat making the red and gold fabric billow out like a bell as she hit the ground. Grabbing the voluminous satin, she hurried to Elizabeth, stopping short and curtseying. "Your Majesty," she said. "Anne Bixby has your ring. 'Tis safe."

"From the butter?" Elizabeth asked, her lips tight.

Cordy hesitated. "Uh…Yes, 'tis safe from everything," she said. "I am sure the ladies will hide it in the manor if the French have overrun the place."

Elizabeth nodded and sighed heavily. "You've done well then. Keeping yourself alive too." She looked Cordy up and down. "Although your makeup is askew."

And the queen was completely askew, but no one was foolish enough to mention it.

"We must ride, Your Majesty," Walsingham said, adding his own cape around the queen's shoulders.

Marcus moved his horse closer as Elizabeth's man lifted her onto the horse Mathew had been riding. "Skirt the edge of the meadow until ye are north of the manor."

He stopped at the sound of hooves riding their way. Marcus brought Elspeth around until she blocked whoever was racing toward them. It was Geoffrey Winslow, the guard from the dungeon.

"The English militia from yonder village has arrived," he yelled before stopping. His eyes widened at the look of Elizabeth, wrapped in a blanket and furs and completely mussed. "Your Majesty," he said, bowing his head. "Haddon Hall is secure." He grinned. "The day is saved."

Relief should have fallen over Marcus with the news, but he glanced at Cordy who didn't look at him. Nay. The day was not saved. He'd failed in his mission, and the soft spark in Cordy's eyes when she looked at him had been extinguished.

The guard's grin faded as he looked at Marcus. "And you, Marcus Ruthven, are under arrest for colluding with the French to abduct our great queen."

Marcus sat there, a numb feeling spreading in him. He looked to Cordy, but she kept her gaze on the queen as if she held tight to Elizabeth to stay afloat in an angry sea.

Marcus exhaled, and felt the fight drain out of him.

⇉⇉⇉⇇⇇⇇

CORDELIA'S EYES OPENED to a burgundy canopy above her face and tried to remember where she was. Warm, soft sheets wrapped around her, and a soft pillow cradled her head. Surrounded by comfort, she still felt the heaviness of dread weighing her down, like a gray shadow that couldn't be banished by the sunlight brightening outside her window.

She rolled to the side, blinking. *Haddon hall. The queen's mission. Marcus.* Cordelia pushed up onto her elbow. Where was he? Had Walsingham thrown him in the dungeon? Had he escaped to run off in the night? Had Henry helped him get away after Lord Manners called him a traitor when they returned to Haddon Hall and Cordelia was ushered upstairs with the ladies? The rough Bradwell men had argued immediately for Marcus.

Cordelia pushed herself up to sit in the bed, her heart jumping into a rapid beat. "I do not care," she whispered to the empty room. "He's a traitor. I will have nothing more to do with him." She couldn't. Not if she wanted to finally be free of the suspicious looks and mean-hearted whispers from the people at court and to save the Cranfield estate for Lucy and herself. Why then did it feel like she, in fact, cared *very* much? As if Marcus's innocence was the most important thing in the world? More so than her own.

She slid out from the warm blankets, pulling one to wrap around herself as she hurried to the hearth to blow on the half-extinguished coals, adding a block of peat to them. She straightened, standing still in the room, watching her breath puff out, and listened. The house was silent even though dawn had broken. It was as if the new day was still exhausted from the last. Had the queen already departed? Elizabeth would never go to Scotland to meet Lord Morton after the misadventure of yesterday. She might already be on her way back to the safety of Whitehall.

"God's teeth," Cordelia murmured, hastening to tie her petticoats over her smock. Could Walsingham have ordered something dreadful? Like an execution in his haste to placate his queen? She glanced out her frosty window, her heart pounding, but there was no quickly erected scaffold. She should have stayed below last eve, adding her defense along with Henry.

Marcus had thrown himself before a bullet for her. He'd carefully stitched her head after her fall and hadn't abandoned Cordelia when he discovered her own lie. The need to see Marcus swelled within Cordelia.

Where does your heart lie? She'd asked him in the barn about his loyalties.

Right here. And he'd touched her chest.

His simple words and touch had nearly pushed her into his arms, but there was too much between them, too many unanswered questions. And if Marcus Ruthven was snatched away from her, she'd never learn the full truth.

Rap. Rap.

Cordelia spun toward the door. She was only half-dressed, her bodice still unlaced over her petticoats. But she hurried to the door, snatching it open.

Her heart dropped, and she felt the pressure of tears behind her eyes. "Anne?" she said.

Anne Bixby stepped forward, and Cordelia backed up to let her inside. Without a word, Anne looked her up and down. She took up the ribbons of the bodice and began to lace them for Cordelia.

"'Tis so quiet," Cordelia whispered. "Do you…? Has the

queen left for London?" She really wanted to know about Marcus but fear of Anne's censure or a possibly horrible answer caught her tongue. *I'm a bloody coward.*

"No, she hasn't left yet," Anne said, finishing the bow and stepping back. Her gaze raised to Cordelia's, and there was a softening in her eyes. "I wanted to tell you…" She wet her lips. "I am…most grateful for your help yesterday." Her fingers lifted to the thin line that had scabbed over across her throat. "No matter what the queen or Lord Walsingham say about your association with Marcus Ruthven…" She swallowed. "I believe you are noble and a trustworthy woman, Cordelia Cranfield. And Margaret and Mary, who witnessed your bravery yesterday, agree." She nodded.

Cordelia blinked back the tears that threatened, and a sad smile curved her lips. "I am happy for that."

"Here," Anne said, thrusting a small, hard object into Cordelia's hand. It was Elizabeth's locket ring. "Be the one to return her ring to her. Perhaps it will soften her to you."

Cordelia wrapped the precious token in her palm and nodded. "Thank you."

"I'll help you with your hair," Anne said. "'Tis rather atrocious."

After the insanity of yesterday, Cordelia hadn't had time to tame the curls, and they must be sticking out like the coat of a shaggy sheep. But Anne yanked and smoothed her curls, letting most hang down her back.

Cordelia had washed the white makeup from her face and neck last night and shook her head when Anne offered it to her. "I am dressed as a country woman," Cordelia said, giving her a smile. "I might never be allowed back at court. I have no need for makeup."

Anne squeezed her hand. "Give her the ring and stare her right in the eyes so she can see the truth inside you."

Cordelia nodded her thanks and the two of them headed out the door. The corridor was dark, and they walked down the staircase without a word. Anne brought her to the archway that led to the Great Hall. "I'll tell them back in London how brave you were," Anne whispered and then turned away as if she'd done her duty in getting Cordelia dressed and down there, but then she hurried back up the stairs, leaving her alone.

"Come before me, Lady Cordelia." Queen Elizabeth's voice broke the silence. She'd been waiting for her. Cordelia inhaled fully, clasping the ring in her palm, and stepped forward to meet her fate.

Chapter Sixteen

"Her temper was notorious; she was not above boxing the Secretary's ears, throwing her slipper at Walsingham's face, or punching others who displeased her…"
Allison Weir, *The Life of Elizabeth I*

Marcus stood between Geoffrey Winslow and Lord Walsingham. Cordelia released the breath she'd been holding when she saw his hands were free, although his sword was missing. Marcus looked fresh with a bleached tunic and clean plaid as if he'd been allowed to bathe and change. The thickness of a bandage lay under his sleeve around his upper arm.

Lord Manners stood beside his beautifully coiffed wife whose brows were raised over wide eyes as if watching a theatrical scene. They remained at the long table that had been righted. The entire hall had been cleaned of bodies, blood, and debris from the day before. The smell of wet wool and lye warred with beeswax and smoke from the fire. Tension swelled in the quiet room where serious faces turned toward Cordelia.

"Your Majesty," Cordelia said, curtseying low before the queen who sat in the same throne-like chair she had used when playing her part.

"Rise," Elizabeth intoned. She wore a rich blue velvet ensemble with gold embroidery. Her hair and makeup were perfectly done. Jewels were displayed from her ears, neck, wrists, and fingers as if she wished to weigh herself down once more with queenly trappings and forget about the stripping she'd endured the day before.

Cordelia wanted to hold up the locket ring, but she didn't dare speak first, feeling the thin ice beneath her. Elizabeth stared in her eyes, and Cordelia fought not to look away. *Let her see the truth.*

Cordelia noticed that Marcus took a step forward out of the corner of her eyes. "Lady Cordelia Cranfield had nothing to do with Lord Morton's plan nor Captain Noire's—"

"We've heard from you," Walsingham interrupted Marcus. "Now 'tis Lady Cordelia's turn."

"Yes," Elizabeth said. "Tell us your part in this ludicrous tale that I doubt even Master Shakespeare could have dreamt up."

Cordelia took a full breath. "Your Majesty. Master Ruthven followed me as I rode away from the ambush. When I fell from the horse, he rescued me." She touched the back of her head where the stitches still itched from healing. "He sewed my wound closed and nursed me back to wellness, thinking that I was you. We were caught in the snowstorm that delayed your departure from Chatsworth House. Once he discovered that I was not you, he agreed that we should ride to Haddon Hall to intercept you before Captain Noire could capture and force you to France to be married off or controlled by Catherine de' Medici."

Elizabeth snorted. "Never." She flapped a hand at Cordelia. "Continue."

Cordelia kept her gaze fastened to the queen's sharp, brown eyes. "Master Ruthven and I worked to trick the French commander into believing I was you so he would leave Haddon Hall before you arrived, but the traitor, Oliver Gupton, gave me away and the search resumed for Your Majesty."

"Gupton is in the dungeon," Lord Manners said. "I have hired some men from the village to help transport him to London for trial."

Elizabeth nodded and flicked her fingers at Cordelia to continue.

"The four men from Bradwell Village followed Lord Ruthven and myself, first thinking I was Your Majesty and then helping you when you arrived." Cordelia blinked. "And by the grace of God, you are once again safe."

Walsingham rapped his knuckles on the table. "And what was Master Ruthven's mission involving Her Majesty? Why was he even here working with Captain Noire and his men for the dowager-queen of France?"

"I...I know now that Master Ruthven is a spy for King James of Scotland and was working to prevent Her Majesty from being taken away to France," Cordelia said.

Walsingham's voice rose as if he were coming to his conclusion. "His plan all along was to take Her Majesty out of her realm to Scotland to meet with Lord Morton."

Cordelia turned her gaze to Walsingham but felt Marcus's eyes on her. Would he hate her for giving away his secrets? He had to know that his head balanced on her abilities to persuade the queen to his cause. "Only because he was ordered to do so by Lord Morton, acting as King James, who would then ensure that Her Majesty be returned with protective troops to London."

"And what of George Douglas?" Walsingham asked, his words snapping out like pistol shots.

Cordelia kept the flipping of her stomach hidden, turning completely back to the queen. *See the truth in my eyes. Hear the truth in my words.* "Master Ruthven did not plot with any sympathizer of Mary Stewart to take Her Majesty away so that the Queen of the Scots could be placed on any throne, English nor Scottish. I have staked my life and family reputation on this fact." Cordelia held the ring out for the queen and stepped forward to place it in her open palm. "We do what we must to see the right win the day, Your Majesty." Cordelia backed up but nodded to the ring. "I have done my duty for you, Your Majesty, as Master Ruthven has done for his king. We are both faithful servants of our realms."

Cordelia folded her hands before her and bowed her head slightly before meeting the queen's gaze again.

The queen looked back shrewdly, weighing her words. "Lady Anne Bixby came to me today to plead your innocence in all this."

Cordelia blinked. "That is appreciated but…unexpected," she said.

The queen's lips twitched in amusement. "Yes. She was never a supporter of you nor your sister, but you apparently saved her life and possibly those of my other ladies. You also tried to protect me by playing the part of queen so they would carry you away to France instead of me, something that would surely have seen you dead."

She tapped a finger to her lip. "And you're not the one who shoved me up in a tree." Her gaze sliced over to Walsingham.

Walsingham bowed his head and held his tongue.

Elizabeth stood, walking forward. She placed the ring back on her own finger and rested her hands on Cordelia's shoulders. "And you returned my portrait ring, fairly unharmed."

Her thumb touched Cordelia's cheek in an affectionate swipe. "You've done your duty, Lady Cordelia, and are rewarded with fifty pounds and my well wishes as you travel away from court. Your estate will remain in the Cranfield family." She turned away, walking back to sit once more.

Cordelia's heart leapt inside her as the weight of worry slid away. "Your Majesty," she murmured and curtseyed low. "My gratitude is beyond measure."

Elizabeth flapped her hand as if pushing her aside, and Cordelia stepped over. "Master Ruthven," the queen called out, waving him forward. Walsingham walked beside him as if ready to throw himself between the queen and an armed assassin.

"Stand down, Sir Francis," she said, glancing at her Spy Master before meeting Marcus's eyes. "'Tis my understanding that your father, Sir William Ruthven is unable to make a wage to support your mother and sister in the fineness of which they are accustomed. And therefore you must act for Lord Morton to bring comfort to your family."

Cordelia's eyes widened. Had Lord Walsingham found this out overnight or did he already know about all the players surrounding the ill-fated queen of the Scots?

"Aye, Yer Majesty," he said.

"It also seems as if you truly were working to save me," she continued. Her gaze shifted to Walsingham. "Without stripping me naked and shoving me up in a tree."

The security advisor released a long, tired breath. "'Twas the best way to keep you from being carried off, Your Majesty."

"My memory suffers with it," she murmured. "And that memory is etched now. Right up here," she tapped the side of her head and gave Walsingham another frown.

Elizabeth sniffed and looked back to Marcus. "'Tis my hope that a courageous, brawny Highlander will be of use to us in the future."

God's teeth! Was she going to ask Marcus to spy for her?

"Your Majesty," Cordelia started out.

"Shush," the queen said without even glancing her way. "One of those uses right now is to carry this lady safely up into your country to be with her sister, Lady Lucy Cranfield Buchanan."

"Yer Majesty," Marcus said, bowing his head. "With great gratitude I accept my freedom and yer understanding. However, to travel to Scotland, having failed my mission and possibly having been labeled a traitor, Lady Cordelia may not be safe with my escort."

Cordelia's stomach felt like it was folding in half, making her want to curl downward into a ball. Where would Marcus go? What would become of his family?

Elizabeth huffed. "The mission to keep me alive is not enough?"

"I was also to bring ye to Lord Morton where he waits in Canonbie at the western border."

"Canonbie?" Elizabeth said, tapping her finger on her lip as her gaze slid from Marcus to Cordelia.

"Your Majesty is absolutely not journeying to Canonbie," Walsingham said, shaking his head.

"Hmmm…" Elizabeth intoned, nodding slowly.

<hr>

MARCUS RODE ON Elspeth before the small contingent of men and one woman. Just behind him sat Sir Francis Walsingham on his charger. Beside Queen Elizabeth's Spy Master was an exquisite vision of royal grandness riding a bay that had been brushed until he gleamed in the lowering of the sun. Behind them, in regal silence, rode the four men from Bradwell parish: Henry, Mathew, John, and Luke. Every time Marcus turned to glance at them, Henry was tugging his waistcoat down over his protruding gut and John was sliding his hand along his pistol that he'd demanded to keep as it had been his father's.

Bringing up the rear of the contingent sat forty Englishmen conscripted and paid for by Lord Manners to guard the queen on this last step of her journey. They rode toward a gathered army of Scots. The royal Scottish flag, held by a young page, fluttered over them in the breeze of the late afternoon. Lord Morton sat his horse at the head of his men.

Despite the Scotsmen before him and the Englishmen behind him, all Marcus could do was think about the only woman present. He'd argued vehemently against this plan, but the queen and Cordy had won out. And now Cordy rode in royal grandeur wrapped up in a precious ermine-lined cape of crimson to stand out against the snow. No one could miss the queenly target.

Marcus raised his hand, and their small party halted, bridles jingling in the crisp air. "Her Majesty, Elizabeth, Queen of England and Ireland, may I present James Douglas, Fourth Earl of Morton and regent to King James VI of Scotland."

Lord Morton had a full red beard and long, pale face. He

wore courtly hose and knee-britches instead of the customary Scottish wrap. The regent dismounted and bowed low over one extended leg. "Greetings, Your Highness."

Cordy sat straight, her cold brown eyes dipping to view him. She wore the white makeup that Elizabeth favored in public, along with pearls stuck in her pinned curls. In the lowering light, there was nothing that hinted that she was not the one and only queen of England. Walsingham's presence added to the convincing portrayal.

Walsingham dismounted. "I am Sir Francis Walsingham," he said, introducing himself for he had never met Lord Morton before. "Security Advisor for her Royal Highness." Before Morton could continue, Walsingham kept going. "We are not happy with the forced attendance upon you outside the English realm. We have been through a treacherous time avoiding French capture with pistols being shot too close to Her Majesty."

Cordy's voice rang out with crisp authority. "I would not be sitting here without the efforts of your man, Marcus Ruthven," she said. "He, with the help of Sir Walsingham, and these good Englishmen behind me, saved me from being transported to the de' Medici dungeons, or worse, the wedding altar."

Cordy worked a pearl and ruby ring off her finger, not the locket ring, which Elizabeth had kept as she waited across the border inside England, but another ring from her vast collection of jewelry. She handed it to Walsingham and flicked her fingers toward Morton.

Marcus dismounted, taking the ring from the English advisor, and carrying it to Lord Morton while Cordy spoke. "I gift you with this token of my thanks to your young King James."

Marcus held it out to Morton, who took it right away, placing it on his smallest finger. He stared at it for a moment and then looked to Marcus. "Ye have done a service for yer king too, Master Ruthven."

"And you will see he is rewarded, he and his family," Cordy said with confidence that her dictate would be carried out.

"Of course," Morton said.

"Whatever sins the parent has committed should not reflect upon the child," she continued. She could very well be talking about King Henry and his rough wooing of the Scottish people decades before, but Marcus knew Cordy spoke of her own mother.

Marcus stepped aside as if he played a scripted role in a pageant, and Morton stepped up to Elizabeth's bay horse. Walsingham hovered near them, not allowing the man to get too close to her.

"With great appreciation, I will carry this to my king," Morton said with a formal bow.

"Very well," Cordy replied with the lofty tones and even chin of a great queen.

"Allow me to send my army to escort ye safely back to London," Morton said.

Cordy sniffed, offering a small, closed-mouth smile to the man. "As you should. You may escort us to your border, but once in England, my own men will bring me safely home to Whitehall." She tipped her head, still meeting Morton's gaze. "I would not want my countrymen to rally in defense against an army of Scots marching across my kingdom. I would have no way to ensure your safety home, Lord Morton, and will not start a war with your king over your deaths."

Lord Morton bowed again. "As you wish, Your Majesty. At our border, I will return to my king's side to surround and continue to ensure his safety so that he may grow strong and well-guided in matters of state and kingly duties."

Cordy laughed lightly. "I have no doubt that you will prepare him well for *my* duties."

Morton, his face tinged with a red hue, continued to push his purpose. "King James will be ready if and when you and your councilors decide to—"

Cordy waved her hand, interrupting him. "I will not declare my successor until a time when 'tis necessary, Lord Morton. To do so now, will only bring the dissenters to my rule out of the shadows." She shook her head. "I will not do it." Her words were a defensive volley of determination.

He opened his mouth again, but she held up a finger to stall him.

"However," she said, "I do consider King James as a potential heir. You must be satisfied with that at this time."

Lord Morton's firm mouth relaxed into something close to a smile. "I am that, Your Majesty," he said, bowing again. He backed away.

Relief uncoiled inside Marcus. Lord Morton looked convinced that Elizabeth was considering King James in a good light.

Cordy looked down at Walsingham. "Take me home, Sir Francis," she said and steered her horse around in a tight circle. Both Walsingham and Marcus remounted and followed Cordy on Racer out through the small army that had parted to allow them to leave. Having been told Cordy was indeed the real queen, they all bowed their heads as she paused in their midst.

"My good men of England," she said. "Your efforts to protect your queen are most appreciated and show your honor." With a flourish of her hand, Queen Cordy rode on into the snowy woods, her contingent, followed by the Scottish army, moved through the trees at the pace she set.

As expected, Lord Morton and a couple high-ranking guards trotted around the Englishmen to catch up with the queen. Marcus followed.

"I would have my Security Advisor beside me as well as the resilient Highlander," Cordy said. Marcus kept his smile hidden behind a mask of indifference as Morton made room for him. Although, Marcus knew this arrangement had little to do with Cordy wanting him next to her. She must keep Morton away from her youthful face, white teeth, and real hair.

Marcus still hadn't had a chance to speak with Cordy alone since he'd been released from Haddon Hall's dank dungeon. The need to do so ate at him. Would they reach the border where she would leave, heading south while he must return to Edinburgh? *Daingead.* Elspeth twitched her ears as if feeling the tension coiling inside him in the way he held her reins. Well if he couldn't speak with her alone, he'd do it before everyone.

"Lord Morton," Marcus said. "I would speak with ye about my position with the Scottish government."

"'Tis not the time nor place, Lord Ruthven of Gowrie," Lord Morton said. His use of the title was to remind Marcus that Morton could give his father, and therefore Marcus, back his Earldom.

"I wish to alert ye to my absence," Marcus said, keeping his eyes forward but watching Cordy in the periphery. "I will not be returning to the Scottish court nor France."

Chapter Seventeen

"I do not choose that my grave should be dug while I am still alive."

Queen Elizabeth I explaining why she will not choose an heir

Cordelia's inhale felt like it turned to rock, unable to move in or out. Absence? Where was Marcus going? She surely couldn't look his way or give any indication that she cared about his whereabouts moving forward. She was Queen Elizabeth of England and Ireland, not some foolish girl in love.

Love? Was that what this ache was that swelled inside her chest, twisting between sorrow and fury when she'd learned of Marcus's double spy life? Could the nausea and pain behind her eyes at not knowing if they would ever speak again be love unfulfilled?

Luckily Racer, who Cordy had claimed as her own with Oliver Gupton's arrest, walked without her guidance between the riders on either side. Because Cordelia was lost inside herself. She knew she couldn't go back to the English court. Elizabeth and Walsingham didn't want her there in case she spoke about this disaster and how close Elizabeth had been to dying or being forcibly taken to France.

"You're not returning to Edinburgh?" Morton asked, looking sideways at him.

"Nay. And my true leanings have probably been exposed to the French if any of those escaping soldiers make it back across the channel to Catherine de' Medici."

Cordelia wet her dry lips but kept her face forward. "The man has certainly earned a respite after this past week of horrors," she said, with regal apathy she didn't feel at all. She'd rather force Marcus to stop and explain everything to her. He'd said that his heart resided in her heart, whatever that meant. To her it meant love, but to a man used to persuading people to believe him for his own ends, it could have meant something else. A lie then? What type of man lied about love? Well, Johnathan Whitt had lied to her back at court, telling her he loved her so she would sleep with him. But she'd already slept with Marcus. Oh Lord help her, she wanted to—

"Do you agree, Your Majesty?" Lord Walsingham asked, breaking into her swirling thoughts. She had no idea what he'd asked, or even if they were still on the topic of Marcus leaving Edinburgh.

She snorted with indignation. "I agree that 'tis blasted cold out here, and that all discussion should happen before a hearty fire so my mind can thaw enough to agree or disagree to anything." Her reprimand had the desired effect, and all men faced front in silence.

But she wanted to know what they'd been talking about. She flapped her hand about. She'd pulled gloves on after passing the ring over to Lord Morton, even though the real Elizabeth rarely wore gloves. "Continue to talk, my lords. Just don't expect me to answer."

Marcus cleared his throat. "I was saying that no assassins or villains working against King James or yerself, Yer Majesty, would trust me after the mantle of my work for Lord Morton has been snatched away. I am useless to His Majesty and Lord Morton in that capacity."

Cordelia knew that wasn't exactly the case since George Douglas could recruit Marcus to pass him information about Lord Morton and King James. Is that what Marcus meant by saying he was leaving Edinburgh?

The questions built upon one another, this way and that, from personal to political intrigue. Cordelia tried desperately to keep her gaze forward over Racer's twitching ears. Could the horse feel her turmoil? He shifted, sniffing the frozen air. With this huge group of men, there was no fear of wolves.

Unable to stop herself, she glanced towards Marcus. Although his face remained forward, he looked sideways at her. It was an awkward angle, but he was definitely trying to reach her gaze too as if he wanted to communicate something.

"Tell me, Master Ruthven," she said, so he could look at her. His brown eyes were warm and full of questions and answers that he wished to speak but couldn't. "Where shall you go if not back to Edinburgh? Didn't you say that you have family there?"

"My hope, Your Majesty, is that my father is reinstated at King James's court, because I have plans to journey on to…Culross across the Firth of Forth."

Cordelia looked forward again, swaying to the right in time not to be hit by a tree with a bend in it on level with the riders. It was hard to breathe. "Culross?" she asked, the word coming out a bit too high in pitch. Culross was where Lucy lived with her husband, Greer Buchanan. They'd moved out farther from Edinburgh and brought Greer's aging mother with them to live in a small cottage next door to the larger manor house they'd bought. Had she mentioned Culross to Marcus?

"What do you plan to do in Culross?" she asked.

"Oh…" he drew out. "I think I would like to have a few goats, a gaggle of chickens, and maybe a dog."

Cordelia couldn't catch her breath for several heartbeats. *He remembers.* She cleared her throat. "'Tis…a flock of chickens," she whispered. "Not a gaggle."

He looked at her, and their eyes met. "Ye are quite right, Yer Majesty. I would have a right happy flock of chickens."

"You want…chickens?" Lord Morton asked, disbelief in his strained voice.

"Aye," Marcus continued, but Cordelia trained her eyes straight ahead again. "I heard that some lasses actually knit jackets for bairns born to goats to keep them warm up north," he said, his words sounding without care. "I'd like to see that." He made a prancing motion with his fingers. "See the little goat bairns hopping around in woolen jackets."

Cordelia cleared her throat that ached with emotion. "They are properly called kids, young goats."

"Aye, Yer Majesty has such a large vocabulary."

Lord Morton shook his head. "You would give up a life at court to…prance around with goat bairns in jackets?"

"Kids," Marcus corrected. He breathed in deeply. "I think…a life like that…well I believe I'm in love with it."

Cordelia's body tightened, gripping her in an embrace as her heart struggled inside her. "In love?" popped out of her mouth before she could clamp her lips shut.

Marcus turned to meet her gaze, and she saw emotion and a question there. Was he jesting? No, he wasn't that cruel, and she didn't see any sign of playfulness in the deep brown depths that searched hers. Instead there was a bit of worry and the intensity of hope as if he were holding onto a rope dangling him over a ravine.

Walsingham grumbled something under his breath about goats in woolens and clicked to his horse. "Come along, Your Majesty," he said, hurrying Cordelia along so that the tether between her and Marcus was cut. Which was a good thing considering the confused look that Lord Morton now wore and the moisture in her own eyes. "Wolves roam about at night," Walsingham said.

They rode through the trees like water shooting through pebbles along the shore, infiltrating the forest with a hundred men on horses, English and Scottish. Cordelia dared not ask any more questions since she obviously couldn't play the part of disinterested queen when Marcus answered them with her heart's desire.

Dash it all! She wanted to grab him to her and demand he answer her question, the one that mattered most. Did he love her?

⇶⇇

"You will come to Edinburgh Castle to receive your payment, Ruthven," Lord Morton said.

"Aye, after I see Queen Elizabeth safely to the edge of London," Marcus answered. They stood beside their mounts at an inn just over the English border.

Morton grabbed Marcus's shoulder and narrowed his eyes. "Were you serious about…" He waved his hand behind him. "Chickens and goats with woolen jackets?" Morton studied Marcus as if looking for signs of madness.

Marcus grinned. "There's a lass tied to those animals."

"A lass up in Culross?"

Marcus nodded, and Morton looked relieved. "And she knits woolens for sheep."

"Goats." Marcus smiled, although he'd yet to have heard or seen Cordy since they'd arrived. The queen had been hurried into the inn by Walsingham to private chambers. Henry, Mathew, Luke, and John stood guard with pistols before the tavern doors.

Morton shook his head. "Trading spy work and royal intrigue for farming… 'Tis not something I would expect from you." He crossed his arms, giving him a shrewd look. "And something the king may not allow."

Marcus kept his smile, but his gaze hardened. He'd anticipated some royal obstinance. He looked over to Sir Francis Walsingham who was talking to the head of the men who'd gathered under Lord Manners' authority.

Walsingham caught his eye, nodding, and broke off what he was saying to the man. He walked with a confident stride, pulling a letter from his jacket pocket.

"Lord Morton," Walsingham said, handing the letter to him.

Morton frowned, taking it.

After Marcus had explained his plans with the true Queen Elizabeth at Haddon Hall before they parted ways, the queen, who seemed to honestly want happiness for her brave lady, had written in her own hand.

"Her Majesty, Queen Elizabeth, asked me to give you this if requested by Sir Marcus," Walsingham said. He pointed to the folded parchment with the impression of a resplendent Queen Elizabeth pressed into the wax sealing it.

Morton looked back and forth between Walsingham and Marcus as if they were plotting against him. Which, Marcus supposed, they were. Lord Morton's little eyes, pointed beard, and rapid glancing gave Marcus the impression of a badger on the lookout for danger.

"She did?" Morton asked.

"Aye," Marcus answered.

Morton broke the wax seal with a thumb, holding it before him in the darkness and read it in the glow of the lantern behind him.

To King James VI of Scotland and Lord Morton his loyal regent.

Marcus Ruthven has done me and our kingdoms a great service by preventing my abduction to France and thereby the release of my cousin, Mary Stewart. I, the great sovereign queen of England and Ireland support Sir Marcus Ruthven in his bid to leave your spying service if he so desires. Even though he refuses to divulge any secrets of your court, I have offered him a position with my own spy network. He has declined. However, if he is not rewarded with his freedom from your service and a pension for his family, I will take that as a direct act against me and my realm. I may not go to war for Sir Marcus, but I will take your actions into consideration when deciding the person who will inherit my kingdom in the far-off future when I go to be with God.

I send gratitude to King James for sending such a talented, courageous, and clever man to protect me and the kingdom of England.

Elizabeth R

"Bloody hell," Morton grumbled, glancing at Marcus and then back down at the letter where he read it a second time through. He looked up at the windows of the inn where Cordy was sitting until she knew the Scottish contingent had left to return to their side of the border. "So you had already told Queen Elizabeth about your plans to raise chickens and sheep."

"Goats," Marcus said, feeling the hairs on his nape raise. Cordy, acting as Elizabeth, had been surprised by his revelation before. "I explained that I wished to leave the intrigue of spy work behind when I declined working for England. She was unaware of the farm animals."

Morton rubbed his jaw through his too-long beard. He made a rude noise through his clenched teeth and looked at Walsingham. "You can guarantee that this is from the queen?"

"'Tis her own handwriting and seal," Walsingham said, his lips tight in the small space allowed by his mustache and beard. "And I watched her write it."

"Very well," Morton said and turned a scowl on Marcus. "You are free to find your woman in Culross and help her wrangle goat bairns into bloody woolen jackets."

"And my family in Edinburgh?"

Morton's brow pinched. "I will invite your father back to court and provide him with an appropriate salary, but if he acts contrary to King James in any fashion he will be dealt with harshly."

Marcus stood taller with a lightness that hadn't been within him for ages. "I am most appreciative," Marcus said.

One of Morton's men walked closer, out of the gloom. "Lord Morton."

"Yes," Morton turned to him.

"The village does not have sufficient provisions for all our men for the night. I recommend we head back to Canonbie where food and pallets are available at Gilnockie Tower as ye arranged before."

Morton nodded. "Ready the men. We can ride quicker without matching the queen's stride." The moon was full and bright, giving light to the snowy woods.

"I'd stay together though," Marcus said. "Wolves roam."

Morton snorted. "I live with wolves much fiercer than the four-legged beasts in these woods. I'll see you at Edinburgh Castle for your payment before you disappear into the countryside." Morton tipped his head slightly and beckoned Marcus. "Walk with me to my mount."

Marcus nodded to Walsingham and strode with his old employer. Morton stopped at the horse, reaching up to mount. He glanced back toward the inn and then at Marcus, his hands on the saddle. His words were low. "Lord Walsingham is known to me." He tapped his jacket pocket where he'd put Elizabeth's letter. "As is the English queen's seal and signature." A wry grin hitched the corner of Morton's mouth. "And when Elizabeth first arrested Mary Stewart, I rode with Lord Moray down to London to make certain she knew we supported Mary's detention on English soil. Lord Walsingham was in France at the time, viewing the horrors befalling the French Huguenots. I remained in the background, letting Moray lead the meeting. I doubt Queen Elizabeth even knew I was there."

Marcus swallowed against the tightness in his throat as Morton narrowed his eyes. "And the woman I met today, although eloquent and courageous as a queen, was much younger and more beautiful than Elizabeth Tudor."

Marcus began, "Lord Morton—"

"Tut," the regent said, cutting him off as he pushed up into his saddle. He looked down at Marcus. "I will not go back on my word before Walsingham." He patted the letter in his pocket and kissed the ring on his finger before lifting the reins to turn his horse. Morton gave Marcus one last knowing look.

Walsingham walked up to stand beside Marcus. They watched Lord Morton ride to the front of his Scottish army, leading them into the forest.

"I am surprised that farce worked," Walsingham said.

Marcus inhaled through his nose. "I never doubted it," he murmured over the deep thuds of his heart. Feeling a prickle of awareness, he looked to the lit window of the two-story inn. Cordy stood there, devoid of the white makeup and jewels. Her hair was uncoiled to fall around her shoulders. She let the curtain fall back into place, disappearing from his view.

He wanted nothing more than to stride inside and up the stairs, but Walsingham was still talking.

"Come help me with this rabble," the Englishman said, and Marcus followed him to the stables where the militiamen were bunking down with their horses. They would return to Haddon Hall the next day. The real Elizabeth waited at a tower house nearby with her ladies and a contingent of guards and distraught advisors who'd been recalled from London to escort her back to Whitehall once Walsingham joined them.

The night air was full of jostling horses and men talking with excitement over guarding the Queen of England and meeting the Scottish regent. They'd been sworn to secrecy about Elizabeth's journey to Haddon Hall and the tangle there, but in their hearts they would keep the memory, never realizing that part was untrue.

Marcus made certain that Elspeth and Racer were taken care of and stepped out of the stables. The sound of music filtered out the door of the inn, and Marcus turned toward the cheery glow. Clear, melodic words ribboned out through a rapt silence. The song was accompanied by the lute, and he turned toward the siren, his heart beating faster.

"'Tis a silver moon high above
That lights the world in the blackest night,
The shine it coats my love, my dove,
In the brightest, crystal white."

Cordy's voice tinkled like spring water on a summer's day, and it made Marcus thirst like he'd never before. He stopped inside the door, and Cordy's gaze raised to him. A smile touched her moving lips, making the song take on a happier feel as she continued.

"The dove doth flutter o're the field
High above the world that stings
Until she hears her true love's song
And lands within his wings."

Her words trailed away, but the melody continued with Cordy's lithe fingers plucking and strumming across the strings. The patrons stared in awe, and Henry, Mathew, Luke, and John sat right in front at a table. When the last pluck of the lute ebbed, Henry stood, clapping loudly.

"Makes me tear up," he said.

Mathew rose too, not to be outdone, and clapped. He turned to the others in the room and jerked a thumb at Henry. "His mum used to sing it to him as a wee lad."

Cordy set the lute next to the stool. She stepped off the barely raised stage, striding toward Marcus. She stopped, looking up into his face as she curled her fingers into both sides of his short cape, clutching it as if he might try to turn away.

"You want chickens and goats?" she asked. The question came out like a demand, as if he were tied to a chair by inquisitors threatening him with the rack.

He grinned and slowly tipped his head up and down. "As long as ye are there along with me, Cordy lass."

Cordy stepped closer, pulling his face down to hers at the same time. Her kiss was pure and full of happiness. She held nothing back, and he wrapped her up in his arms. Behind them, the friends they'd made along the way cheered, making the other patrons do as well.

"To the Highlander and his lass!" one called.

"To the lady and her Scot!"

"To many lute lessons!" Mathew called, and their laughter erupted.

But Marcus continued to kiss Cordy until they both came up for air. He touched her cheek with his thumb, brushing some of her silky, red hair back. "I love ye, Cordelia Cranfield."

Tears swelled out of her eyes as she smiled, and he caught one as it curved down over her cheek. "I love you too, Marcus Ruthven."

He brushed a kiss over her lips again, and they leaned their foreheads together. "Are we really free?" Cordy asked. "Both of us?"

His forehead rubbed against hers as he nodded. "Blessed by your queen and begrudgingly agreed upon by the Scottish Regent, Lord Morton."

"We can go to my sister in Culross?" she asked.

"Aye, and then we will find our own place."

"Where I can raise chickens and knit woolens for wee little kids."

He caught her chin, feeling the light in her eyes brighten his entire self. "If it will make ye smile like this."

She hugged him tight, and Marcus knew that he'd found the freedom of which he'd always dreamt.

Epilogue

Culross, Scotland
Cottage overlooking the Firth of Forth
11 April 1574

"You, Cordelia, are exquisite," Lucy Buchanan said as she finished tying the last white ribbon in her red curls.

"I think I will go by Cordy now."

Lucy held her mouth open in mock surprise. "You never liked being called Cordy."

"We aren't at court anymore."

"Thank goodness," Lucy said, smiling broadly.

Cordy smiled back at her in the polished glass. "Thank you for making me exquisite." She glanced behind her at her friend, Maggie Darby, Countess of Huntley. "And you."

Maggie came forward, her gently rounded belly before her. She was due later that summer with her second child. Her husband, Kerr Gordon, had inherited his father's earldom in Huntley the previous year, and the young family had moved into Auchindoun Castle much farther north from Culross. Even so, Maggie had insisted they travel down to attend this important celebration.

"I think the gold thread on blue works perfectly with your coloring," Maggie said, smiling broadly.

"Such a rich gift from the queen," Cordy said. "And from you." She indicated the other new gown that Maggie had brought as part of Cordy's marriage chest along with linens and silver to start her home."

Maggie laughed. "I know you are more than happy with your soft woolen gowns that we wear to stay warm up here in the north, but every woman should have something a bit more refined for special occasions."

Cordy stepped into the middle of her bedchamber and twirled, making the silk petticoat flare outward. "Just like at Whitehall."

Lucy groaned. "I hope not. Here there are no sideways looks, poisoned gloves, and treasonous plots."

Maggie laughed. "Absolutely!"

Cordy smiled brightly at her happy friend. "Scotland has made you joyful and content."

"Kerr has made her joyful and content," Lucy replied. "And plump," she said eyeing her belly.

"Well, moving into a drafty, stone castle surely didn't make me joyful," Maggie said, but she kept her smile. "Although I'm making much needed improvements. I'm even having piped water brought in like the queen has down at Whitehall."

"I've asked Greer to add that to our manor house since Marcus said he's planning to add it here." Lucy indicated the newly restored seaside cottage around them. Marcus had been working on it nonstop since he'd brought Cordy north. In order to maintain her honor, Cordy had lived with Lucy and Greer for the last two months while Marcus slept and worked in the cottage. But now it was done, and it was charming.

Rap. Rap. "Maggie?"

"Coming," she said, hurrying over to open the door for her husband. Kerr was as tall and broad as Marcus. In fact, all three of their husbands looked cut from the same rugged Highland mountain range.

Kerr glanced up at the high lintel above the door that Marcus had built to fit his own height. "I think I'm going to raise some of the doorframes at Auchindoun. I'm forever forgetting to duck."

He looked into the room at the three of them and allowed a rare smile. "Almost ready?"

"Yes," Maggie answered.

Kerr nodded to Cordy. "Lady Cordelia, ye look bonny."

She smiled fully. "I feel bonny. Thank you."

"And there's a crate that's been delivered below. Reverend Wimberly brought it with him. 'Tis from London. Whitehall actually."

Maggie and Lucy both looked at her. "From the queen?" Lucy asked.

"Walsingham said he'd ask Lady Anne to pack up my personal things and ship them up here," Cordy said.

Maggie brought Cordy's warm woolen shawl, and the three descended the newly erected staircase. The cottage still smelled of freshly hewn wood. A warm fire crackled in the hearth that Marcus had moved to the outer wall, building a sturdy chimney so the smoke didn't accumulate inside. 'Twas quite modern. The money he'd earned from his last mission had paid for all the building supplies, including glass for the windows that looked out at the calm water of the estuary.

Greer, Lucy's husband, stood beside the crate that looked big enough to hold a body. "I wouldn't let Marcus in here. He's waiting outside with his parents. His sister, Trinity, is watching wee Garrett toddle around," Greer said about Kerr and Maggie's youngster. "She won't let him fall over the ridge into the sea."

Maggie's eyes grew round, and she tapped her open palm on Kerr's arm.

"I'll go check," Kerr said, turning to stride outside.

Greer used an iron rod to wedge under the lid of the crate. It creaked as he pried it open. On top of several bolts of colorful silk sat another box. "It says Marcus Ruthven," Maggie said, picking it up.

"I'll take it out to him," Greer said, leaving the ladies to pull layers of silk, trims, cotton smocks, and stockings from the box.

"These aren't all mine," Cordy said.

"The queen must be very grateful to you for that whole incident we can't talk about," Maggie said. "She's sending more than just your wedding costume for your dowry, I think."

"I'd say she's very grateful," Lucy said, pulling a necklace of fine pearls up from a velvet pouch.

Maggie passed Cordy a square card. In Elizabeth's fine script it read simply:

In appreciation, Lady Cranfield. You and your sister can be proud of your Cranfield name once more.

Cordy blinked as warm relief flowed down through her. Reading over her shoulder, Lucy snorted. "I'm not changing my name back to Cranfield." She had taken Greer's surname when they wed.

Cordy sniffed back the happy tears. "Perhaps I'll keep it."

"'Tis up to you," Maggie whispered. "More ladies are starting to take their husband's surname now, but 'tis not normally done."

"Unless your mother is a traitor," Lucy added.

Cordy took a deep breath. "We are not our mother."

Kerr, holding a squirming child in a white gown, poked his head into the door. "They are waiting, Cordelia."

Cordy waved her hand at her friends who followed Kerr and Garrett out of the cottage. She hastened toward the door, grabbing up the small bouquet of purple primroses and fresh dill that was tied with white ribbons to match those woven amongst her red-gold curls cascading over her shoulders. With one last pinch of her cheeks, Cordy stepped out into the late morning sunshine, so rare in the early spring.

A lute began to play a slow song to accompany her toward the front of the small gathering. Cordy nodded at Mathew who plucked the strings of the one song he'd learned to play to surprise her. The four Englishmen had risked their very lives to journey up into hostile Scotland to visit for the wedding. Which was how they described the journey.

Cordy walked through the grass, the sea breeze catching at

her ribbons, making them dance with her curls around her face. But she held the gaze of the one person who kept her moving forward, not just today but forever through life.

Beside the cleric from the small town of Culross, Marcus stood, a smile full of exuberance on his face. The smile was catching and made her laugh, his joy overflowing to her. Her sister and Greer stood up as official witnesses, although there were plenty present, including Marcus's parents and sister from Edinburgh.

Cordy reached Reverend Wimberly, nodded to him, and turned to Marcus. He wore a crisp white tunic that she'd embroidered with green thread around the neck and cuffs, little leaves. His plaid matched the green and was woven with blue in the fine woolen wrap he wore, and his boots shone with wax.

The cleric began and they listened through the most important questions while Marcus held her hand.

"I do," Marcus responded, "with all my heart, body, and soul."

Cordy sniffed, and he handed her a handkerchief for the tear that escaped. "I do too," she said, "with all my heart, body, and soul."

"Do ye have a token?" the pastor asked.

Marcus drew out the gold ring carved with vines they'd decided she would wear and slid it on her finger. "I have something else," he said. "A gift from a mutual…ally."

From his sporran, he pulled the small box from Whitehall and lifted the lid. On a square of black velvet sat a ring. It was made of gold and had rubies around the base with diamonds that formed the letter C.

Cordy gasped, looking at Marcus. He nodded to her, and she lifted it from the box. The C was on the lid of a small locket that opened. The one picture spot was vacant but the other had a tiny portrait of Queen Elizabeth.

Marcus slid it on her fourth finger on her right hand. "The note said that ye can put a portrait of me in the open side, but that ye'd probably always want to keep a picture of your one and only queen in the other."

Cordy released a small huff of laughter to join Marcus's. He pulled her into his arms, looking down into her eyes. "I love ye, Cordy. And I cannot wait to start living our lives together here."

Cordy's heart was so full that she thought it might actually burst with joy. It pushed the tears from her eyes as she smiled. "I love you too, Marcus."

He bent down to kiss her, and she heard the reverend declare them husband and wife.

THE END

Legend of Queen Elizabeth's death, 24 March 1603.

When Elizabeth released her last breath before the ladies of her bedchamber, Lady Scrope removed a sapphire ring and dropped it out the window to her brother, Robert Carey. He had his horse already saddled and rode for three days to reach Edinburgh, Scotland moments after King James VI of Scotland had gone to bed. The king was roused, and Carey, dusty and exhausted, knelt to present him Elizabeth's ring. King James was then the new king of England.

Although some media portrays this ring as the locket ring, it was not since the ring sent was studded with sapphires. But the locket ring was one of Elizabeth's most treasured possessions. There has been debate about the portraits inside, but experts do believe that one is of Elizabeth while the other is of her mother, Anne Boleyn.

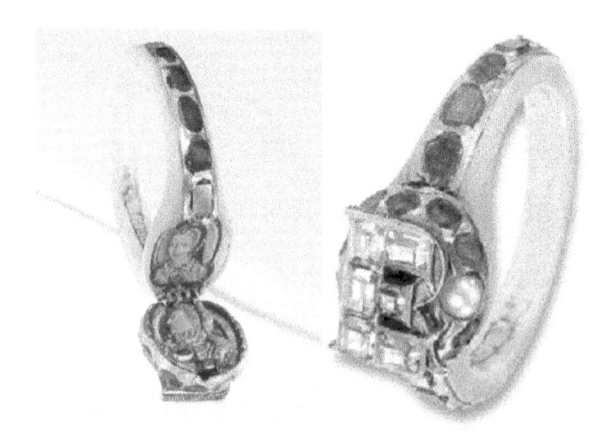

Thank you so much for reading *The Highlander and the Counterfeit Queen*! For more Scottish Historical Romances by Heather McCollum, check out her website and subscribe to her monthly e-mail list at www.HeatherMcCollum.com.

Acknowledgments

Thank you so much for following Cordelia and Marcus on their missions to save their family names! I've been having so much fun with this series, and I'm honored to be able to write the great Queen Elizabeth I. When asked what historical figure I would like to meet, she is always my answer, although I'm sure she would find fault with me.

Thank you to Kathryn Le Veque for inviting me to the Dragonblade Clan and to Amelia Hester, my wonderful editor. We make a wonderful team!

And of course, my heart goes to my very own Highlander, Braden, once again rescued me and this manuscript when my whole writing folder suddenly disappeared last month. Technology tries to run and hide from me!

Also…

At the end of each of my books, I ask that you, my awesome readers, please remind yourselves of the whispered symptoms of ovarian cancer. I am now a ten-year survivor, one of the lucky ones. Please don't rely on luck. If you experience any of these symptoms consistently for three weeks or more, go see your GYN.

- Bloating
- Eating less and feeling full faster
- Abdominal pain
- Trouble with your bladder

Other symptoms may include: indigestion, back pain, pain with intercourse, constipation, fatigue, and menstrual irregularities.

About the Author

Heather McCollum is an award-winning, Scottish historical romance writer. With over twenty books published, she is an Amazon Best Selling author in Highlander Romance. Her favorite heroes are brawny and broody with golden hearts, and the feistier the heroine the better!

When she is not dreaming up adventures and conflict for rugged Highlanders and clever heroines, she spends her time educating women about the symptoms of Ovarian Cancer. She is a survivor and lists the subtle symptoms in the backs of all her books. She loves dragonflies, chai lattes, and baking things she sees on the Great British Baking Show. Heather resides with her very own Highland hero and three spirited children in the wilds of suburbia on the mid-Atlantic coast.

Twitter: @HMcCollumAuthor
FB: HeatherMcCollumAuthor
Pinterest: hmccollumauthor
Instagram: heathermccollumauthor
Goodreads:
goodreads.com/author/show/4185696.Heather_McCollum
BookBub: bookbub.com/authors/heather-mccollum
Amazon: amazon.com/Heather-McCollum/e/B004FREFHI

Ingram Content Group UK Ltd.
Milton Keynes UK
UKHW020650150523
421757UK00015B/705